The Golden Times
A Historical Novel

by

Theodore Iliff

PITTSBURGH, PENNSYLVANIA 15222

ISBN: 978-1-4349-9456-2
Printed in the United States of America

First Printing

For more information or to order additional books, please contact:
RoseDog Books
701 Smithfield Street
Pittsburgh, Pennsylvania 15222
U.S.A.
1-800-834-1803
www.rosedogbookstore.com

To my parents, Ted and Ruth Iliff,
for giving me a good life and a story to tell

GOLDEN TIMES I

Monica sat at the upstairs bedroom window, her favorite perch for as long as she could remember. It was dark outside, and yet it wasn't. The night sky was speckled with flares guiding bombers toward their targets. On the horizon, flashes and rumbles signaled the impending arrival of the Americans, if they were lucky, or the French, if they were not.

It was April 1945. Monica wasn't even sure of the date anymore. Everything in her world was disintegrating, so the day and date were insignificant. On the radio, a familiar high-pitched voice ranted one more time about a future no ordinary German believed in anymore.

"Even now," bleated Josef Goebbels, Hitler's warped propaganda minister, "as the enemy advances, the Fuehrer stays at his post, commanding the resilient armies of the Fatherland that will soon turn back the Red tide with an arsenal of glorious wonder weapons. Stand firm, Germany, for the golden times stand before us."

A hand reached to switch off the radio with such a violent twist it almost fell to the floor.

"Leave it on, father," Monica said with some irritation. "That's the only way we have to find out what's happening to us now."

"We won't learn anything from that idiot," Max snapped, as he watched the approaching spectacle out the small attic window with his 20-year-old daughter. "From now on, we are all on our own. We have to find a way to survive, and that fool and his pack of hyenas won't be around to do anything for us. They're finished."

Monica couldn't ignore the irony in her father's final dismissal of those "hyenas." This from a man who had joined the party in 1937 to keep his job as rector of Forstberg elementary school. He's the one who crossed the Rhine to Strasbourg three years later to "Germanize" the schools after the blitzkrieg put France under German occupation.

Her wry gaze at her father's furrowed face was suddenly diverted by a shower of light in the distant sky. It was a so-called "Christmas tree", a cascade of fire used by the Royal Air Force Lancasters to mark their bombing targets at night. It also inflicted ghastly burns, often fatal, on anyone caught under one as it drifted to earth.

The little airfield down the road was about to be hit again. The first bombs fell far in the distance. Although they were no cause for concern, Max had seen the effects of "bomb creep" before, and he watched with growing anxiety as the blasts, first of high-explosive 500-pounders, then of the smaller phosphorous firebombs, marched steadily from the far edge of the airfield, through the tower and hangars and toward his neighborhood as bombardiers prematurely dumped their "sticks" during frantic runs through the iron clouds of flak.

The approaching conflagration seemed to halt a few hundred yards from the house. Just as he was ready to relax, Max heard a muffled blast accompanied by a blinding white flash. Then came the scream for help from the back of the house. Max ran down the stairs, through the kitchen and into his wife's precious vegetable garden, where his son Axel was frantically throwing sand with the only hand he had into the bright flames from a stray firebomb. Max grabbed nearby buckets of sand that had been collected for such an emergency and tossed one after another into the fire, killing it before it could reach the house.

Axel, exhausted and almost in tears, stuck a cigarette in the stainless steel claw of his artificial right hand and lit it with his shaking left hand that had been spared by the Red Army shell in a Ukrainian wheat field two years earlier.

"My God, I'm worthless," Axel whispered almost to himself, staring at his ersatz arm that would prevent him from, among many things, resuming his career as a musician and journalist.

"Shut up,," Max snapped, tired of hearing what he considered his mangled son's self-indulgent whining. "You're lucky. What about your comrades....the dead ones, the ones rotting in some Russian prison camp? At least you're alive. You'd better start thinking instead about what you'll do when the war's over."

In the darkness, Max couldn't see the resentful daggers in Axel's eyes. But he could feel them, and he didn't care. There were more immediate problems to resolve.

Like what to do with Monica. A neighbor checking to see if the fire was out said he had heard a rumor that the French would be the first invaders to arrive. They would be an ugly, angry bunch when they rolled through..

Max fought to suppress his grotesquely realistic imagination, trying not to think about what they would try to do to his petite, attractive daughter with a porcelain complexion and long, wavy, strawberry blonde hair. She had to leave. She would go to Gmuend, where the rest of the family was waiting out the end of the war. She'd be safe there. If she could traverse the 70 miles eastward, through the bombing and strafing, without any organized transport available, she could reach the family home of the Bauers, the in-laws of her older sister Ingrid. There she could wait in the isolation of their rural village.

Monica didn't think much of the idea, and said so.

"You and Axel are here," she pleaded. "I'll be safer here. I can cook for both of you (where they would find food was another matter) and keep the house in order. How can I get to Gmuend with the trains not running, American fighters strafing everything that moves and the Allies heading east almost fast than I could."

In less turbulent times, Max actually enjoyed the feisty defiance he would occasionally face from his youngest child. This was not one of those times, though, and he cut her off with the time-tested debate killer in any family—I'm your father and you'll do what you're told.

She had made the trip on bicycle as a child, he said, so she could do it again

Conceding that further argument would be futile, even though the circumstances were beyond comparison to those weekend outings before the war, she set about collecting a few valuables that might have barter value, loaded them in a sturdy woven basket that fit on the rack over the bike's rear wheel, and covered them with a red sweater that might help ward off an evening chill.

After a short sleep that was more like a nap, Monica checked her belongings, pumped the tires full of air, and with stiff hugs from her father and brother, set out at dawn for the ride of her life.

Monica had not seen her hometown since arriving from Vienna the previous week. She had spent the time at home recovering from that odyssey by train, truck and foot after being abandoned by the Wehrmacht officer commanding his female flak unit.

Now Monica was on another perilous journey, and its first phase took her through the ruins of what had once been a lovely Baroque town at the northern gateway to the Black Forest. Two years of intermittent bombing had pounded it into a dusty debris field, with century-old landmarks—the castle, the mint, the city hall, the railway station, the main shopping boulevard—destroyed or mangled beyond recognition.

With the German army long gone and invaders approaching almost unchallenged, residents who refused to flee were showing a curious schizophrenia in the way they festooned the pathetic hulks they had patched together for shelter. Some were still defiantly showing the Nazi swastika flag. Others already were displaying white sheets of capitulation.

Monica tried to focus on the littered streets as she pedaled her way through the heart of town, but her concentration was repeatedly shaken by the sights of a city about to suffer defeat and occupation. Women with children pulled wobbly little wagons piled high with whatever possessions would fit. Unarmed soldiers walked aimlessly through the streets, smoking cigarettes, drinking stolen schnapps and talking to no one, except, in some cases, themselves. Priceless antiques adorned a second-floor living room exposed to the elements because two walls were missing. Unshaven old men and unwashed women with hollow eyes and bad teeth stood in a listless line to get bread being handed out from the back of a battered truck.

No traffic. No streetcars. No fountains. No sidewalk cafes. No beer gardens. No spring sales at the department stores. No phones. No working toilets. No hope. And, seemingly, no future.

Monica had witnessed such scenes in other places, but now she could hardly believe she was in her hometown. She wanted to stop and contemplate the significance of all she saw, but she knew she didn't have time. Head down, she walked her bicycle through the rubble until the street clutter eased, and then pedaled away as quickly as conditions and her legs would let her.

East of town, the scene gradually evolved from one of devastation to an almost eerie normalcy. The wooded hills that marked the Black Forest's northern tip were unscarred, other than ruts and gaps left by SS and Wehrmacht units in their glory days when the war was headed west.

Isolated towns and rural villages appeared untouched by war's ravages, although during one brief rest and refreshment stop she noticed how she had not seen one man under the age of 40 since she had left the city.

When she tried to buy a ham and cheese broetchen and some watered-down raspberry juice from an elderly roadside vendor offering a few home-grown items arrayed on a decrepit wooden table, she learned for the first time how different simple transactions would be. Her Reichsmarks were rejected, but a bar of chocolate from the basket on the back of her bicycle was quickly, if not graciously, accepted.

On she rode, finding the going easier as the terrain flattened out and the back roads she remembered from earlier, far more enjoyable outings proved to be passable. The day was thankfully mild and cloudy, keeping the air fresh and the skies clear of warplanes. Near Pforzheim, she entered an extended patch of sunless, damp forest and despite the exertion of the ride, she soon felt a chill.

She stopped, reached into the basket for the sweater, put it on and then pedaled on down the road.

After a brisk 10-mile ride through wooded countryside, she approached Stuttgart's rural edge encouraged by the rapid pace of her trip. Suddenly, the sun broke through the clouds just as Monica emerged from the woods into a meadow occupied by several scrawny cows munching what little grass they could find. A thousand yards ahead, a farmer was plowing a patch of land for late spring planting.

The first sign of trouble was the farmer's odd behavior. He had jumped from behind his plow horse and was waving frantically in Monica's direction. How nice, she thought, although she wondered why he would be greeting her with such enthusiasm.

She self-consciously looked down at her dress, and her red sweater, and then she heard it. The high-pitched scream of a P-38 Lightning, ever louder, coming from behind her. It roared into sight before she could react.

She had heard the Americans were strafing anything that moved – so-called "targets of opportunity" – regardless of their military significance. For them, that included anyone who could help sustain an army in the field. Like a farmer.

At that moment, the rumors were brutally confirmed. Just as the twin-hulled silver fighter roared over her head from behind, it started firing its 50-caliber machine guns at the friendly farmer, still frantically waving by his plow. The four-inch bullets dug their own furrows in front of the farmer before ripping into him and his horse. Monica could see the blood spraying from both as they lurched back from the impact and then crumpled in instant death.

She had never felt that such a searing wave of rage before. She screamed, cried, raised her clenched fists and yelled a long, plaintive WHY?! Then her throat dried up, her hands froze and she nearly choked on her own voice as the fighter wheeled majestically in the far sky and roared back toward the dead farmer, back toward the partially plowed field, back toward the angry young woman standing out in an open field wearing a bright red sweater.

So scared she could barely keep her balance, Monica pedaled furiously back toward the shelter of the woods 50 yards away.

She reached the trees just as the P-38 screamed over the tops without firing. The pilot waggled his wings in greeting, as the warplane droned off the west. She was in no frame of mind to realize she had just been the object of flirting from 500 feet.

Monica knew she didn't have time to think about what had just happened. Before she could force herself to stop crying and shaking, she was back on the bicycle, leaving the protective woods (along with the dangerous red sweater) behind and setting a deliberate pace toward Stuttgart and, beyond that, the sanctuary of Gmuend.

By late afternoon, she was cycling through Stuttgart, or at least trying to. The state capital's devastation was even worse than Karlsruhe's. As a rail junction and industrial center, it had been a favorite target of the American Eighth Air Force's daylight bombing as well as the nighttime carpet bombing of the British.

The city's center was an urban desert—dusty, barren, lifeless, and mostly uninhabited. Guided by policemen and civilians stationed or stuck in the city, Monica found a way through town and out into the rolling farmland to the east. Evening was approaching, but daylight was keeping later hours that time of year, so she knew she could make it without seeking shelter for the night.

Except for one more brief, frightening episode. As she cycled toward an antiaircraft unit camouflaged in a bushy field near Weinstadt, the guns suddenly opened up at a line of contrails high above – Lancasters on their way to some unfortunate target still attracting the attention of allied air marshals.

Monica had been trained in antiaircraft tactics with her Labor Corps unit, and she wondered why the ack-ack unit would waste precious shells on planes out of range and headed elsewhere. As she rode up to the position, she saw why. The crew was entirely young boys, some barely in their teens.

"What are you doing?" Monica yelled to one of the boys as the others blasted away, almost giddy with the percussive, ear-piercing power at their command. "Who's in charge here?"

"He ran away," the boy said with a shy grin, shrugging his uniformed shoulders and pushing his wire-rimmed glasses up on his nose. "But we know what to do. This is our first chance, and we're not going to waste it."

Monica felt a surge of superiority in both age and tactics and was about to lecture them when a clang to her right prompted her to instinctively dive under the cement ledge of the guns' platform. She found an unused helmet and put it on just as a shower of flak shrapnel peppered the ground around the emplacement. She had learned even as a young girl walking through Karlsruhe during air raids that flak could be as dangerous for friendly pedestrians as for enemy flight crews. A few of the boys learned that lesson a second too late, suffering vicious wounds on their arms and backs they ran to shelter in the unexpected metal hailstorm they had unwittingly spawned.

When Monica saw the wounds were not serious and the boys could care for themselves, she looked to the sky and started off again, almost oblivious to the helmet still on her head. She had other concerns—she was starting to think she wouldn't reach Gmuend that night.

The sun dipped below the dull gray horizon as Monica finally reached the outskirts of Gmuend, a typical German rural town with a quaint central square and not much else. She still had the helmet, and along the way she had found a plastic sheet to ward off the evening chill and a light shower that had greeted her in Gmuend.

Through the increasingly muddy streets she pedaled, gliding past the houses and other buildings she had learned to know after her sister had married Fritz Bauer in his hometown.

It was dark when she approached the cluster of buildings that comprised the Bauer family home, farm and small silverplating business. A few townspeople had offered her shelter for the night as she pedaled past them, but Monica knew the way to shelter, and just before midnight, the door of the Bauer home came alive with the incessant pounding of its always-polished sterling silver knocker.

Emma was the closest to the door, and when she cautiously opened it, there in the faded light, wrapped in plastic, topped by a helmet, trembling, hungry and pale, stood her younger daughter.

"Hallo Mama."

"Ach Gott Monica!"

Tears flowed as they embraced, knocking Monica's helmet to the ground. It had been six months since they had seen each other during Monica's holiday leave. Both were thinner, and Emma had aged beyond her 51 years while ushering her older daughter and infant granddaughter to Gmuend three months earlier through the chaos of collapse.

Mother and daughter were quickly joined by Fritz's mother, father and two sisters, all lining up for a chance to greet the latest refugee to seek shelter with them. Father Bauer, mindful of warnings about thieves and marauding deserters, quickly hid the bicycle in the cellar. He carried the treasure-laden woven basket into the kitchen and carefully stashed away the jars of homemade jellies, bottles of schnapps and cognac, chocolate bars and other commodities that war and defeat were converting from everyday treats to coin of the realm.

Oma Bauer led Monica to a small upstairs room furnished with a bed, table and candle. That was all she needed. After a quick goodnight hug for her mother, Monica collapsed into the bed and fell asleep almost before her head hit the pillow.

Monica woke up to the aroma of coffee and bacon—key ingredients of a countryside breakfast she had dreamed of during the bizarre days of her last Labor Service duties in Vienna.

As she stretched under the down comforter and stared at the beamed ceiling of her simple bedroom in Haus Bauer, she thought again of that final day when the Russians were coming and her unit of young women had been handed revolvers by the bookish Wehrmacht lieutenant.

"Aim that way and shoot when you see something," he yelled over the din of nearby artillery fire as he pointed in the general direction of the coming Red onslaught.

The girls stared at their cold, heavy pistols, then at each other in disbelief, and then turned toward the lieutenant to protest. But he was gone. Not a trace of their fearless warrior leader, so they almost in unison said "I'm going home," and headed west.

As dusk settled, Monica jumped aboard a train of refugees and, she suspected, deserters, that was rolling in the general direction away from the fighting. That's all she cared about; the exact destination didn't matter. Luckily, it was heading west along the Danube. The rainy night spared the train from air attack, and it got as far as eastern Bavaria before dawn. Another night train got as far as Stuttgart, and Monica had walked and hitchhiked the rest of the way to Karlsruhe.

Now, after her harrowing dash to Gmuend, she was safe, surrounded by family in a rural town that had hardly seen any warfare, except for the occasional errant bombs or downed planes.

And yet, as she sat at the kitchen table playing with her eight-month-old niece Elisabeth, she knew even the sheltered tranquility of Gmuend was about to end. Rumors were thick that the Americans were not far away. The main question was whether they would arrive before or after the war was over. Everyone agreed it could only be a matter of days, one way or the other.

Then, on a rainy morning a week later, they came. Everyone heard it before they saw it—the squeaky rumble of an armored column approaching the defenseless town. German forces had long ago pulled out of the area, and white flags and sheets were draped from windows and rooftops in hopes of sparing the town from attack.

They worked. Without firing a shot, a detachment of the U.S. Seventh Army rolled through the narrow streets into the town square, quickly deployed troops at key posts and occupied the city hall, then the post office and a bank.

The war was over in Gmuend.

And the mayor was ready. Two days earlier, he had scoured his home and office for any vestige of Nazism and dumped the flags, plaques, letterheads, publications, Hitler portrait and other potentially damning artifacts into a makeshift incinerator. It wasn't much of a fire, but it did the job.

Certain that he had sufficiently exorcized the Nazi icons from his life, he confidently but with proper deference greeted the gum-chewing American major in charge of the occupying unit. The mayor was not sure whether to salute, shake hands or just stand there. So he nodded slightly before speaking in heavily accented English.

"Welcome to the American army," he said. "I am the mayor. What may I do for you?"

"We want your offices, a layout of all the town's vital installations, and the location of any remaining German forces," the major said in a matter-of-fact monotone as he looked around the square, refusing to make eye contact with the mayor. "Effective immediately, there's a dusk-to-dawn curfew. No exceptions.

"We also want the names of all your Nazis," he abruptly added, turning to gaze directly at the mayor. "You're probably one of them. You speak English, so you stick with us. No phone calls, no telegrams, no messages to anyone. You understand?"

The mayor, suddenly feeling extremely vulnerable, nodded a quick yes.

As it turned out, the GIs had nothing to fear in Gmuend. The populace was totally unarmed and thoroughly petrified by the occupiers. Everyone stayed indoors, peeking through curtained windows once in awhile, just to see what the Americans looked like and what they were up to. Most in Gmuend had never been outside Germany, much less to the U.S. So they only knew what they had seen in films and heard from Nazi propaganda. The latter had painted a frightening picture, but the disciplined actions of the experienced GIs soon started to dissipate those fears.

As the occupiers settled in, one private stationed himself in front of a small post office directly across the street from the Bauer house. Armed only with a rifle, he found a chair, carefully studied his surroundings, and then sat down, took off his helmet, propped his M-1 against the wall, unbuttoned his shirt for some relief from the warm spring evening, and lit a cigarette.

Monica's mother watched all this from through a second floor bedroom window. And she was mortified.

As Monica joined her to spy through the curtains, Emma could hardly conceal her contempt for the undisciplined sloppiness of the conquering American.

"Look at him," Emma said, almost hissing with disdain. "How did we ever lose a war to soldiers like that?"

Just then two children appeared from a house adjacent to the post office. Then another, and another. Timid, silent, all in bare feet and ragged shirts and shorts, they stood for a few minutes, staring at the soldier.

He stared back, then motioned for the children to come closer. They froze at first, but his gentle insistence eventually persuaded them to take a chance. With short, hesitant steps, they approached the American in wide-eyed silence.

They froze again when he slowly leaned over and reached into a zippered pouch at his feet. He pulled out two Hershey bars, broke each in half and without a word handed the rare delicacy to each child. After a chorus of "Danke schoens", the children raced back home to show off their first bounty of occupation.

Monica turned to her mother and nodded toward the first American she had ever seen.

"That's how we lost."

Four weeks later, the war was formally over. Hitler and his gang were either dead or imprisoned, surrender documents had been signed, and for the second time in less than three decades, Germany confronted peace in defeat.

But this loss was like no other in modern warfare. Never had a sovereign nation suffered such total destruction. Even the 1918 disaster with the harsh terms of Versailles had left Germany mostly intact.

Germany had brought upon itself nothing short of national annihilation. Under four-power occupation, the government and political institutions were erased. The economic infrastructure was in shambles. Reichsmarks had little buying power; cigarettes were currency of defeat. Schools were closed. A medical system once the envy of the world no longer could cope with the staggering burden of war casualties, military and civilian. Water, power, sewers and other utilities in most cities were just a memory. Public transport was crippled. Up to 20 million were homeless or sheltered in temporary quarters, with millions more surviving in the fractured remains of damaged dwellings. And more than 11 million German men languished as POWs, sharing with their families the daily agony of wondering who, if anyone, had survived.

One estimate had one of every two Germans on the move—to or from home, to or from rural sanctuary, to or from internment or imprisonment, or just wandering aimlessly with no home, no family, no future, no hope.

In Gmuend, uncertainty gnawed at Monica and her extended family. Ingrid had not heard from Fritz since he had been home on leave the previous September to see Elisabeth for the first and only time.

Over and over, as the topic would come up around the kitchen table or in the garden or in the bread line or at the church, Ingrid would recite her mantra: Fritz has to be alive. He was only the leader of a military band. He wasn't in combat. He never hurt anyone. Surely he survived.

Naturally, everyone said they agreed with her. But that didn't stop the constant churning in her stomach as she wondered "what if".

While sharing those concerns with her daughter, Emma's thoughts more often turned to Karlsruhe. Without saying anything to the others, she feared for the safety of her husband and disabled son. Other than one brief letter delivered by a visitor just before the capitulation, she had heard nothing but rumors.

And they were ugly. The Americans, according to the stories, had rolled through without even stopping, leaving occupation to French units spoiling to avenge their 1940 humiliation and four subsequent years of German oppression.

Max could have verified the worst of the rumors, but he chose not to. As the allies approached, he had made a pact with his son to spare the women in Gmuend from any details that might have alarmed them.

As events unfolded, the details were gruesome. The French were merciless, ransacking homes, shops and offices while carrying out summary executions of desperate civilians caught plundering abandoned stores and houses.

The occupation rules were clearly stated in leaflets posted all over the city. Nobody was allowed on the streets before 9am and after noon. All weapons were to be surrendered at city hall.

Banks, restaurants and other businesses were closed indefinitely. Assembly of more than five people was forbidden, except for families. No photography was allowed.

The worst was at night. For nearly a week, Max and Axel anxiously maintained near total silence during the dark hours, hearing the screams of defenseless women being raped by house-to-house marauders. One night in a home down the street, drunk infantrymen took turns at three generations of women—grandmother, mother and daughter. Max recognized each screaming voice and, wracked by frustrated rage, cried for the first time in his adult life.

The next morning, Max and Axel learned new appreciation for the German phrase "luck from bad luck." A trio of French officers walked through the gate as Max was heading out the front door to check on his neighbors.

Captain Gerard Sortain, a short but stocky 30-year-old career officer with a weathered face, suspicious stare and gruff disposition from years of front line combat, barely grunted good morning to Max before leading the two young lieutenants through the front door and into the foyer. One went upstairs and the other checked the cellar while the captain cased the main floor. Axel, emerging from the second floor bathroom, was so startled by the sudden presence of the French officer that he could only stand still and silent as the inspection continued.

After the three huddled for a few moments in the driveway where Max could not hear their conversation, the captain sent the others off on an errand of some kind and then led Max back into the house.

"Do you speak French?" were Sortain's first words to Max, neither friendly nor hostile but militarily assertive. Max had noticed a hint of an Alsatian accent, meaning this man's home could be just across the Rhine. Axel had hobbled down the stairs to hear their exchange.

"Yes, I am very comfortable with French," Max said. "I taught it in my school, and I worked for awhile in Strasbourg."

"What is your name?"

"Max Baumann."

"Occupation?"

"Teacher. I am a school rector."

"So you were a party member?"

It was Max's first encounter with an issue that would shape, and in some ways stain, the rest of his life.

"Yes, it was required."

"Anyone else in the house with you?"

"My son Axel," Max said, pointing. "He was wounded in the Ukraine."

Sortain stared at Axel for a few seconds, mumbled something sounding like sympathy and then continued what had become an interrogation.

"You said Strasbourg. What did you do there?"

Max sensed he was entering a perilous topic but knew that the officer could quickly find out if he was lying.

"I was sent there to adjust the local curriculum after we re-entered the Rhineland."

Sortain answered Max's choice of words ("adjust")with a menacing smirk, but it almost instantly dissolved into a look of vague recognition without malice.

"I think I heard something about that," Sortain said. "I'm from near Strasbourg. Not far from here, actually. But we can talk about that later. I'm moving into this house, along with the two lieutenants."

The unheralded announcement stunned Max and Axel. Max waved off a protest forming on his son's lips while trying to comprehend the consequences of what he had just been told.

"Where will I go? What about my son? This house is all we have. We have no place to go."

Sortain shrugged.

"That's not my concern. Be gone by noon."

As Alex slumped onto the stairs and stared at nothing, Max tried to think of some way to forestall their eviction. He tried to subdue competing thoughts of the French systematically carting off all the small treasures and keepsakes the Baumanns had collected over the years. The crystal. The silver. The ceramics. His books. Emma's jewelry.

He forced himself to concentrate instead on conjuring a strategy to prevent this calamity. He blurted out his first idea almost before it had finished forming.

"I could be your butler," he said, thinking how ludicrous the words sounded. Me, a rector. Serving French officers in my home. But it was all he could think as frantic slid toward panic.

"I know this house and what's in it. You officers could use someone to handle routine chores. I could do most of the work, and my son could help too."

Sortain was listening, so Max kept spewing his ideas as they took shape.

"I know how to cook, and Axel does cleaning and some repair work when we need it. We would sleep in the cellar, and you would have total privacy."

The captain was as impressed with Max's resourcefulness as he was with his French. He had heard of fellow officers requisitioning homes and making similar deals with the occupants, and he knew there was nothing in the regulations to prevent it.

Almost on cue, the two lieutenants arrived pulling a cart loaded with their belongings (and, Max suspected, some loot). Sortain again took the two other officers aside in the driveway to explain the German's offer, and they both agreed to give it a try. Not only did they like the convenience of the arrangement, but the idea of a proud German, a veteran of the earlier war, lowering himself to servant status gave them no small degree of gratification.

"OK," Sortain said as turned toward Max, who was leaning in the doorway, trying to seem nonchalant while beads of betraying sweat rolled off his forehead.

"You and your son work for us. You do what we ask and stay in the cellar. Any trouble, and you're out, or worse."

Max, with some help from Axel, quickly collected clothing and other basics and relocated to the cellar, with its two thin mattresses that had served as beds in the war's last days.

The French occupation of the Baumann family home for the most part turned into a godsend. The officers treated Max and Alex with tolerant deference, first empathizing with the younger man struggling with his grievous war wounds, and later in grudging admiration for Max's willingness to swallow his pride to serve them cordially and effficiently.

Max's Strasbourg work never came up, and Max was always careful not to let any conversation with the French officers drift that way. The episode had already caused too much pain, and he had a premonition it could cause more trouble later.

The relative tranquility in the Baumann house did not escape the notice, and muted resentment, of neighbors. They understood why he tolerated French occupiers in his home, but some compared Max's relative security with their own insecurity and could not resist the temptation to imagine motives and motivations that ranged from silly to slanderous.

Later, a particularly vicious theory would emerge, haunting Max as much as the cries of his helpless neighbors in those first nights of defeat.

A month later, Americans arrived to take over the occupation of Karlsruhe. A few French marauders were still active, but the Americans soon stopped the worst atrocities.

The morning after the Americans offcially took charge, Captain Sortain and the lieutenants packed up and, after a brief and perfunctory farewell, loaded up a waiting truck and drove away, never again to have any contact with the Baumann family.

As the truck turned the corner at the end of the street, Max rushed inside and conducted a frantic inventory. He couldn't believe his good fortune when he confirmed that almost nothing was missing. The only real item of value that left with the French officers was a book of medieval music manuscripts. A small price, Max thought, compared to what might have been.

The Americans seized some houses in the area, but they inexplicably ignored the Baumann house. For a few weeks, Max grew nervous whenever an American military vehicle drove toward the house. But none ever stopped.

GOLDEN TIMES II

By the middle of summer 1945, the brutal shock of defeat was giving way to the depressing reality of occupation.

With the June 5th "Berlin Declaration," the victorious powers had divided Germany into occupation zones, with Gmuend and Karlsruhe falling under the American military government based in the former IG Farben headquarters in Frankfurt. But just barely. The French controlled sections of Germany north and south of Karlsruhe, and unlike the other Western allies, Paris had no intention of allowing a rapid German recovery. It wanted reparations and, for lack of a better word, revenge.

All this was, for the moment, of little interest to Max. The security situation in Karlsruhe was improving, and he wanted his family back together again. He had decided the best opportunities for a decent life would be in Karlsruhe, not the rural isolation of Gmuend.

Axel was also becoming a problem. He was drinking heavily, although Max had no idea where or how he was finding the stuff. Max needed the entire family's help in dealing with his damaged son, and he thought their presence might help Axel.

So in early July, a hand-carried letter arrived in Gmuend calling the family home. Emma and Monica were to escort Ingrid and infant Elisabeth through 70 miles of occupied, and still somewhat treacherous, territory. The baby would slow them down, making the trip a two-day journey, but Ingrid was sure someone would take them in for the night.

Fritz's parents made sure the band of wanderers was properly provisioned for the trip, and on a bright summer morning the four females set off for home. Ingrid pushed the baby carriage conveying Elisabeth. Emma marched alongside, and Monica followed, alternately walking with or riding on the bicycle that had carried her on the grueling journey from Karlsruhe.

They made good time on the first day, keeping a steady pace along the main roads full of military vehicles and civilian refugees under the sometimes indifferent direction of homesick American MPs. Elisabeth seemed amused by the adventure and stayed in good spirits, although her mood was helped by copious amounts of milk and treats stashed in the back of her pram.

As dusk approached, the trip's tenor changed. They had intentionally skirted Stuttgart, thinking the city might not offer acceptable haven for the night. But west of the city, they approached several farm houses and homes in villages and were repeatedly refused shelter for the night. In every case, the curt response was "no room" or "we only have enough for ourselves" or some other abrupt excuse followed by a slammed door. Even the presence of a baby could not evoke compassion.

As the tired women with a thankfully sleeping baby approached a crossroad, they were startled four French soldiers acting like sentries. They were from Algeria, which meant they hated the country they were serving almost as much as the country they were occupying.

The sight of a baby made no impression on them. It was Monica's bicycle that caught their fancy.

"I need this," one of the soldiers said in broken German. He grabbed for the bicycle, but Monica held firm as Emma and Ingrid pulled Elisabeth's pram back into the shadows.

"This is very important for us," she said, drawing on the French that all German children had learned in school. "Please leave us alone."

Two of the soldiers stood by, treating the confrontation as nothing more than free entertainment. But the fourth decided the German fraulein needed to be taught a lesson in respect for the victors. He walked up behind her while his compatriot argued, and without a word he jerked the bicycle from Monica's grip, cutting both hands.

Monica screamed in pain and froze in fear all at once, not sure exactly what had happened and definitely not sure what was about to happen.

In the confusion, nobody had noticed U.S. Army truck, lights not yet on, rumbling toward the intersection. It was there before the French allies could react.

Out from the cab jumped a GI, rifle in hand, followed by two others from the back. with rifles slung over their shoulders. The Algerians had left their weapons lying by the road, but they were still defiant as the Americans approached.

"Which way to Mannheim?" the lieutenant asked. Then, as he waited for the answer, he studied the curious scene before him, and his eyes narrowed.

"What the hell is going on here?" he asked, shifting his glance back and forth between the Algerians and the women.

Monica startled herself by responding in schoolgirl English she hadn't used in years.

"They are trying to take my vehicle," she said.

"Bicycle, ma'am," the lieutenant said.

"Yes, bicycle."

"This is not your business," said one of the Algerians, in stiff but surprisingly good English.

"You're in the American zone, buddy. Just what are you supposed to be doing here?"

"We are on our way to our unit in Baden-Baden. We wanted the bicycle so one of us could go ahead and find us a ride."

"Well, these women need that bike more than you do. So leave them alone."

"You have no right to give us orders," the Algerian said. "We are soldiers of the French army."

Three M-1s clicked in unison but stayed pointed to the sky.

"I don't give a shit who you are. Leave these women alone and get going. Now."

The Algerians picked up their weapons, being sure not to make any menacing moves. They separately agreed the bicycle was not worth dying for.

The Americans stood by their truck as they made sure their allies were gone for good. Monica by then had seen a fourth GI in the shadows, standing near the back of the truck, just watching or occasionally jotting something in a notebook. She resented his aloof indifference, but before she could think of something to say, the officer barked his order.

"Load up," he growled, gesturing toward the distant silhouette. "You too, Mike. There's no story here."

As they hopped back in, he repeated his question.

"Do you know the way to Mannheim, ma'am?"

"Follow this road," Monica said, pointing to the northwest, "and after 50 kilometers you will say the main road."

"See the main road, ma'am."

"Ach yes, see," Monica said, annoyed that she had translated "sehen" into the sound-alike English word.

As the driver fired up the truck in the growing darkness, Monica wanted to know how late it was.

"Do you have the time," she asked with a shy smile.

"O baby," the grinning driver said, "I wish to hell I did. You work on that English of yours, and maybe you can ask me that again some day."

It would be years before Monica realized the double meaning of her simple question. Her first direct encounter with Americans left her confused and mildly curious about these gallant conquerors she had heard so many bad things about.

The crossroads confrontation signaled a turn of fortune for the small band of women.

The next farmhouse they approached was well lit, indicating the occupants were still up.

They let Ingrid do the talking as she stood behind the buggy sheltering a still sleeping Elisabeth.

"Would it be possible for us to spend the night here?" Ingrid asked as pleasantly as her tired voice could muster. "I have a baby, and my mother and sister are with me too."

The old farmer didn't hesitate.

"Of course you can."

He introduced himself and his wife, poured them generous portions of apple juice and mineral water, placed a sumptuous selection of cold meats, cheese and bread before them and asked if there was anything else they wanted. After they had devoured his offerings, he led them to a large upstairs room with two beds. Ingrid shared one with Elisabeth, while Emma and Monica shared the other.

At daybreak, the women awoke to the smell of coffee. They washed up as best they could and then dove into a breakfast of rolls, butter and homemade jams plus more cold cuts and cheese. The farmer packed additional portions for them as they prepared to leave.

As the women wheeled a chirpy Elisabeth out of the house to start the last leg of their journey, Monica could not leave without asking.

"We tried many places last night," she said to the farmer. "Everyone turned us away. Why were you so nice to us?"

An embarrassed and angry Emma moved toward her impertinent daughter, but the farmer held up his hand to absolve her and smiled.

"I have a daughter with two children," he said. "Her husband is a prisoner of war somewhere in Siberia. She is on her way from Berlin, as far as we know. I just hope someone helps her the way I could help you."

Monica shook his hand, repeated her thanks, and the three women with a baby started the final stretch of their trek home.

As the day wore on, the landmarks started to appear. The huge radio tower on a Black Forest mountaintop east of Karlsruhe. The parapet of an ancient fortress high above the Rhine valley. Off in the distance, the Rhine itself, dotted with river traffic signaling the first stirrings of Germany's postwar economy.

The roads grew ever more congested as the women neared the city, and they again skirted the center to avoid debris-clogged streets. But as the sun dropped toward the horizon, they started wondering whether they had again misjudged the time and would not reach home before dark.

They made it through the forest bordering their neighborhood while it was still light, but the last stretch of highway was strangely deserted. They saw the worried expressions on each other's faces but said nothing as they kept walking, hoping Elisabeth would stay quiet just a little longer.

Then, in the distance, the silhouettes of five men rose from the road's horizon. The images grew larger as they walked on the highway directly toward them.

"Who could that be?" Ingrid asked as if someone new had moved into the neighborhood. But as the men approached in the twilight, it soon became clear they were not locals.

"O my God," Monica whisptered as she realized what was approaching. "They're wearing prisoner of war uniforms."

By then, there was no place to run or hide. Within minutes, the five Russian POWs, stinking and unshaven, were glowering at the women on the deserted highway. They had tired of waiting for repatriation and left their internment camp to make their own long march home.

The three German women tried to control their shaking but could not shake the prejudicial specters crafted by years of Nazi propaganda, even though the Russians merely stood in front of them without saying anything.

Then, out of the pram, came the unintelligible babble of a baby making sounds for itself.

Ingrid froze, ready to do anything to shield her child. Monica and Emma also tightened defensively, and Monica almost made a move when one of the Russians leaned over to see the source of the curious sounds.

He reached into the carriage as Ingrid gasped. He merely raised his hand as if to pacify her, then reached in again and lifted the now quiet Elisabeth out of her rolling sanctuary.

For the rest of their lives, the women would marvel at what came next, sharing the story over and over again to convince themselves that it really did happen.

The Russians carefully passed Elisabeth around, smiling at her, babbling at her in their language, oblivious to the adult females in their presence.

One Russian, after handing off Elisabeth to a comrade, smiled at Ingrid and stammered in broken German, "I also have children. We all have children. Russians love children."

Elisabeth, however, had had enough, and she started a pitiful wail that is the universal cry for mother. The Russian holding Elisabeth put her back in her mother's hands, took some good-natured ribbing from his comrades about his parenting skills, and then led them off down the road toward their distant home.

The women stared open-mouthed as the Russians left. The encounter had run contrary to everything they had ever heard about Russians.

After collecting themselves, they continued down the highway, turned left at the school house onto the side street, and then the final half mile, past the stucco-clad, two-story cubes that were the functional fashion of the day when built a decade earlier. Most were dark; a few were obviously abandoned. One was a burned-out hulk.

It was almost dark when they opened the driveway gate. Max was out first, thinking the noise was intruders. He knew his women were on their way, but he didn't know when they'd arrive. So the sight of wife, daughters and granddaughter was a joyous shock. He struggled to maintain his paternal stoicism as the weeping women hugged him in the driveway, leaving Elisabeth and her carriage on the sidewalk until Ingrid came to her senses.

Another round of hugs, although slightly more awkward, was shared with Axel, who counted on the darkness to conceal the tears rolling down his cheeks.

Once inside, Max found a bottle of Mueller-Thurgau wine, his favorite, that he had been saving for a special occasion—in this case, the reunion of his family for the first time since the war ended.

He allowed himself to overlook one technicality: Fritz was still missing. But he was probably on his way home, and he wasn't flesh and blood. Ingrid, always intimidated by her father, did not contradict him. Emma let it slide, but Monica couldn't.

"What about Fritz," she said as the glasses were filled.

Max, briefly flustered by the challenge, decided to let it pass for the sake of celebration.

"Right you are, daughter," he said. "We'll drink to our reunion and to the day Fritz lets us celebrate again."

That was good enough, and Max's family let him celebrate. They could worry about Fritz again tomorrow.

For the next several weeks, all the family's efforts were devoted to one goal—survival.

When Max had decided in 1934 to buy the plot of land on the edge of town, in what Americans would later call a suburb, Emma had been livid.

"There are no shops," she had argued, arms flailing. "We have no friends there. It's so far from everything. That's just no way to live."

Max had other ideas, and even Emma knew that his would be the only ones that counted. The land was cheap, so he could afford to build a house big enough for the family now and for sharing, perhaps with one of the children after they married and started their own families. The plot had plenty of room for a garden, which could produce a bountiful selection of fruits and vegetables. The city was growing, and services would reach the neighborhood soon enough. And it was close to the school where Max served as rector. He could walk or ride a bicycle to work every day, and he could come home for his midday meal.

So, as usual, it was done Max's way. And it saved the family. The area was spared the devastation of the city center, where the train station and several factories had attracted allied bombers as early as 1942. Many of the friends and shops Emma had wanted to stay near were now gone, but their house outside of town still stood, as did most of the surrounding dwellings, except for a few that had been the unfortunate victims of stray firebombs or invading forces suspicious of what might be inside.

They had shelter and a garden to augment the meager 1,500 calories a day called for under occupation rationing, although the real figure was closer to 1,000. Max had plenty of savings to draw on, and Axel's war wounds brought a bit more compensation. But Reichsmarks weren't in high demand, and there wasn't much to buy anyway.

So Ingrid and Monica were regularly dispatched to Gmuend for what had become something of a national pastime—bartering. German agriculture had mostly survived the war intact and was producing some foodstuffs, but nothing close to the volume needed to feed the population. The Bauers could spare a few basics from their farm, but the Karlsruhe household needed more. So the young women would take silver serving pieces, a carpet, some jewelry or whatever might be valuable in a swap with other farmers willing to take family treasures in return for a few potatoes, apples or ears of corn.

Emma died a small death each time one of her lifelong treasures walked out the door, but there was no acceptable alternative. They had heard of townspeople trying looting, burglary or some other illegal means to survive, but occupation forces had little pity or patience for such scoundrels. In the weekly crime columns of the newly reconstituted local newspaper, shootings often outnumbered arrests.

Even though Ingrid had Elisabeth to take care of, she was always more eager than Monica to make the journey to Gmuend. The train was running again, making the trip tolerable. But Ingrid had another motive. Her last letter to Fritz had been from Gmuend, and she was guessing he might head for his hometown first when freed from internment. It was only a hope, but it was about all she had.

So one Saturday in early August, Ingrid grabbed four crystal goblets from her mother's china cabinet, wrapped them carefully in one of Elisabeth's blankets, and put the bundle in one of two suitcases that she hoped she would fill with Schwaebish delights to keep the family going.

The two-hour train ride ended at Gmuend's little brick station. She had walked the two miles to the Bauer farmhouse so often that she had become a passing acquaintance for scores of townspeople along the way. They would usually nod, maybe say "Good day, Frau Bauer," and then be on their way.

This day, however, was different. People who normally would give her little more than a nod of recognition were now addressing her as a friend or neighbor, even as they adhered to the formal "Sie.".

"I'm so happy for you," one woman said.

"You must be so relieved," a butcher standing outside his shop said to her, with a sympathetic smile.

"Congratulations, Frau Bauer," an elderly woman said as she swept the pathway in front of her house. "It appears your war is officially over today."

Ingrid was increasingly perplexed by each of these comments, until the postman who usually delivered the Bauers' mail smiled at her and said, "He hasn't changed a bit."

Her face flashed hot and then drained cold. She could hardly catch her breath, but that didn't stop her from dropping the suitcases and racing the two remaining blocks to the Bauer house. Without even knocking, she flew through the front door, past the entry hallway and living room, past Oma Bauer peeling potatoes in the kitchen, and into the garden in back, where Fritz, dressed in the simple clothes of the farm boy he was, had jumped out of his canvas chair at the sound of the commotion in the house.

They almost hurt each other hugging so hard. Ingrid could only cry; Fritz could only laugh. His mother and father just sat there beaming, letting their son and daughter-in-law savor the reunion.

"When did you get here?" Ingrid finally asked, still holding tight.

"Last night," Fritz said. "I walked most of the way from Aachen. It wasn't too bad."

That's all he wanted to say. He was enjoying the feel of his wife draped all over him, her short, straight black hair tickling his cheek.

But Ingrid could not stop geography from creeping into her racing mind, and she pulled her head away from his and gave him a slightly chagrined look.

"Karlsruhe would have been closer," she said. "Why didn't you go there?"

"Your last letter was from here," he said, almost defensively, not knowing he had just verified her own earlier speculation.

"How's Elisabeth?" he asked, happy to change the subject.

"She's been cranky with new teeth, but she's healthy," Ingrid replied, stroking the back of her husband's neck as she held on to him. She didn't think she would ever let go.

But Fritz's rural German genes started taking over. He was always shy, and displays of emotion were for women only. So he gently separated from Ingrid, and still grinning, took her hand and sat down, pulling her onto his lap in the process.

"Would you like something to eat or drink?" Fritz's mother asked, rising in anticipation of the answer.

Ingrid only shook her head, keeping her arms around Fritz's neck and enjoying the sight she had fantasized for nearly a year. She briefly came to her senses enough to remember the two suitcases, but a neighbor had picked them up and left them at the front door.

They spent the later afternoon and evening sharing stories of their separation. He told of being caught in the huge Ruhr pocket where more than 100,000 soldiers ended their war as prisoners. He recalled the endless days of sitting in an open compound, surrounded by barbed wire, under armed guard, doing absolutely nothing but waiting for the end and for the word to go home.

Some Waffen SS members had been detained for questioning, but Fritz was a simple Wehrmacht soldier who drew little attention from his captors.

His one interview with a German-speaking allied officer was cut short after Fritz proudly identified himself as his unit's band leader. He had taken the job seriously all through the war; he genuinely believed he had helped boost his comrades' morale more than all the Nazi propaganda rolled together.

The British interrogator's reaction, however, was not what Fritz expected, or wanted. He laughed. Hard.

Collecting himself, the officer switched to grinning condescension.

"Superman's band leader," he sneered. "What will you tell your children about what you did in the war?"

Fritz stiffened, sat up in his wooden chair, and replied, "I will tell them I never killed anyone. Can you say the same?"

The Briton flinched but stayed seated, then angrily ordered Fritz out with a silent, dismissive wave of his hand. After weeks of anxious boredom, the compound gates opened, the prisoners were handed papers and were told to leave. Whether the Germans had homes and families waiting was of no interest to the camp supervisors. The sooner the prisoners were gone, they reckoned, the sooner they could go too.

Fritz, keeping his story simple, told of hitching a few rides but mostly walking nearly a week before reaching Gmuend. Then he asked about Ingrid and her family and what they had experienced.

Ingrid was too happy and too drained emotionally to talk about the last days of the war, the trek from Gmuend, the daily struggle for survival at home. So she said not much had happened, and Fritz let it pass.

They spent the rest of the evening talking about the end of the war, the occupation, the loss of many of the things they thought had defined German society. They avoided two topics—the Nazis and the unthinkable stories emerging about the death camps. There would be time for those discussions later.

Opa Bauer was generous with his wine that night, and when Fritz and Ingrid finally retired to an upstairs bedroom, they undressed, hugged, kissed, caressed, fell into bed....and fell sound asleep. Their physical reunion would have to wait another night.

The next morning Fritz found some old clothes that still fit him, helped Ingrid bargain away the crystal in trade for a gunny sack full of vegetables and a fine blood sausage, and then said goodbye to his parents and grandparents as he joined Ingrid for the walk to the train station and the ride back to Karlsruhe.

At dusk that day, the Baumann house experienced another explosion of celebration after Monica ran out to greet her sister and saw Fritz with her. Ingrid had not sent word ahead about his return, so the family was joyously shocked as Fritz rushed past his sister-in-law and into the main downstairs living room where his daughter was playing on the floor. More hugs, more tears, more questions, more stories and more wine. Even Axel seemed to enjoy the evening as they all shared experiences while Fritz let Elisabeth bounce in his lap or play at his feet.

Max and Emma were the first to fade. They retired for the evening while Axel, knowing he would be spared the usual admonishment from his father, left to meet his drinking buddies at the local gasthaus down the road.

Elisabeth was out for the count in her crib, and Fritz and Ingrid had decided without saying a word that they would not miss the next opportunity to renew their physical relationship.

But Monica was talking too much to think. So she babbled on, asking questions, getting no response, and just moving on to the next subject she thought was equally riveting.

Fritz yawned.

Monica talked about news of the frightful weapon the Americans had just used against the Japanese.

Ingrid stretched.

Monica forged ahead with her tales of Vienna.

Ingrid moved from her chair to Fritz's lap, leaning her head on his shoulder and nipping at his ear.

Monica poured her brother-in-law and sister another glass of wine, not missing a beat as she shared the latest gossip about the neighbors.

Fritz was already past his limit when Monica launched into her analysis of options available for coping with the lack of functioning toilets.

He gently pushed his wife to her feet, stood up, muttered the traditional German farewell of "Good night, sleep well," and walked hand-in-hand with Ingrid up the stairs to their second floor bedroom.

Monica stopped in mid-sentence, cast a puzzled look at both of them as they walked away, and then got it. She blushed, thought about apologizing, then decided to say nothing as she watched them go.

When she heard their door close, she raced up the stairs, clomping past their room to signal her passing presence and to mask any sounds that might leak from behind their door, and on up to her top-floor room, where she turned on the radio as an audio cocoon shielding her from any other sounds of the night.

Next morning, at the breakfast table, small talk was in far better supply than the meager selection of weak tea, bread, butter and jam. Monica allowed herself one inquiring glance at her sister, but it was not acknowledged. So talk turned to the future.

The question was not so much what it would bring. As the first post-war winter approached, they all wondered if they had any kind of future at all.

GOLDEN TIMES III

Mike Falwell struggled with his bag, his typewriter case and his emotions as he approached the dirty brick building that was about to become the center of his life.

It was raining, and he was hoping that his few meager possessions crammed into the canvas bag over his shoulder would stay dry. He knew his portable Royal typewriter nestled into its battered aluminum case would be fine. It had survived more than a year in the field with Mike following the First Army from Normandy, across France and into Germany as a correspondent for the Military News Service. He had languished a few weeks after VE Day in the Frankfurt regional hub before the orders to Karlsruhe.

Now he was covering the occupation, still stuck in the Army but no longer living the glory of a war correspondent. The thought of covering such mundane stories as school re-openings, refugee relocation or army demobilization was depressing. What could possibly get his journalistic juices flowing in this battered city that most of the world had never even heard of?

Nevertheless, he was still a soldier, so orders were orders. He hitched his bag up firmly onto his broad shoulders and trudged up the stone steps to the entrance of HQ 7TH ARMY BADEN and started searching for the MNS office.

Mercifully, it was close to the main entrance on the ground floor. He squeezed through the already open door and was greeted by several upturned faces, distracted momentarily from their typewriters and wire machines by the new arrival.

"Sergeant Mike Falwell," he said to the person closest to the door, mustering all the cheeriness he could manage. "Where's the bureau chief?"

"That's me," came the answer from behind a low partition separating the writing desks from the wire machine area. George Martin raised his 280-pound civilian frame from the task of changing a roll of paper on one machine, clumped into the open entry area and stuck out his inky, sweating right hand.

"Mike, right?" Martin said as they shook hands. "I'm really glad to see you. We need a ton of help right now. There's way too much happening around here, and Frankfurt is all over my ass to get the story count up for this bureau."

Mike wondered whether his new boss was just hyping the town's news value for his benefit. But as he went station to station for introductions to the two American staffers on duty plus an office manager and technician, both German, he got the idea there could be more to Karlsruhe than he imagined.

"What's so hot about this place?" he asked, dropping his bag and typewriter case to sit down for a second in Martin's cramped, steamy office. "This is a far cry from Berlin, or Frankfurt or even Stuttgart. What's happening here?"

George, like all good bureau chiefs, got defensive about his town.

"What were you reading in Frankfurt? The funnies? We've got ex-Nazis hiding from the French. We've got denazification that makes the Spanish Inquisition sound like a radio quiz show. We have a town full of displaced refugees, released POWs, widows, orphans, disabled German veterans, bored GIs, sanctimonious socialists who think they should run the place and spotty basic services for us or the Germans. Take your pick. There's a 400-word piece on every corner. You just have to go out and start looking. Your file says you speak German. Fluent?"

"It's fair," Mike said, downplaying the fact that it was nearly fluent. "I just need to brush up a bit."

"Well, you'll get it here. I'm surprised how many of the locals don't speak English. But being right next to France, I guess that makes sense. Anyway, read the German newspapers and listen to the radio as much as you can. That's the best way to learn. You single?"

Surprised by the sudden change in the conversation's direction, Mike just nodded.

George said lowered his glance to take a paternalistic pose.

"Don't think you can polish your German or anything else with the young ladies in this town. Ike is really pushing the non-fraternization thing. Chat up some local cutie, and your next conversation might be with an MP or a review board. So stay clean. And just for the record, allied female officers are off limits too. If you can find an American non-com worth chasing, she's fair game. But you won't. I've seen 'em all. The ones still available could make a freight train take a dirt road."

Wonderful, Mike thought. A 23-year-old single guy in the best shape of his life and with bucks to burn, and for what? His thoughts drifted to images of a medieval monk, living a solitary life of enforced denial while slaving to transcribe some obscure manuscript for most of his adult life.

He looked around the poorly lit bureau with its dark wood desks, battered wooden chairs, dirty windows draped on the outside with sheets of rainwater, blue haze of old smoke mixing with the aroma of unwashed bodies, and he wondered what had ever prompted him to re-up for another hitch. A quick flashback to a scene from home reminded him why. Anything would be better than going back to that.

"Been to your quarters yet?" George asked, snapping Mike back to the present. "They're just across the street. Not bad, actually. Generator power, working phone, running water, even a stove and fridge. We took over the building as soon as we got here and spruced it up as best we could. A German would kill for a place like that right now."

Mike reacted to his boss's odd choice of words with a sharp, inquiring glance.

"Not really," George quickly added. "Just a figure of speech. What do you think about the Japs throwing in the towel? A lot of guys over here are loving that. I guess the war really is over now."

Mike had heard the news but was too tired to talk about it. With a weary grunt, he got up from his chair, hoisted his bag over his shoulder, picked up the typewriter case and trudged out of the office, out the front door and across the remarkably well-paved four-lane road to the five-story red brick structure identified only with a standard Army-issue sign: "BILLETS."

Officers were living in commandeered or abandoned homes around town, leaving the small apartments to the enlisted men. The irony was that in some cases, the apartment buildings were in better shape than the homes. As Mike checked in with the housing officer in the narrow lobby, he wasn't sure what to expect. The hallway and stairwell were dark. Paint was peeling from the walls, and the tiled steps had chunks missing, making the walk up to the first floor adventurous, if not treacherous.

But once he turned the heavy key in the lock and pushed on the typical heavy brass handle of the front door, he relaxed. Inside, it was pretty much as George had described. Nothing fancy, but all the conveniences he could hope for under the circumstances. The bathroom had a tub, but no shower. That would take some getting used to, and not a little dexterity. A couple of thin towels were hanging from hooks screwed into the plaster wall. A bare bulb stuck out above a mirror over the sink. Next to the bulb was a socket that accepted the round prongs of a European plug. Mike was ready for that.

The toilet was the old German version, with a platform configuration in the bowl rather than a pool of water. For Mike, this was one of the many mysteries of German living. Why the platform? What did the Germans do, study it before flushing? The flush cord unleashed a reassuring surge of water strong enough to keep the bowl relatively clean. The ubiquitous bowl brush sat in a holder next to the toilet, and on the other side was a stack of folded toilet paper that would do nicely as sandpaper in a pinch. Mike was ready for that too.

In the bedroom, the curse of German households was immediately apparent. No closet, just a small armoire and a cabinet big enough to hold a few things on hangars. The furniture crowded the double bed, leaving no room for a chair. A cheap lamp sat on an even cheaper table at the side of the bed. The bulb was just strong enough to serve as a night light. Reading in bed was out of the question.

Mike dumped his bag on the bed and strolled into the main room. A musty couch and matching chair, an ash coffee table, a small but ornate walnut wall unit with a few books and glassware, carpets on the polished pine floor, thin curtains over the one picture window that looked out over the street at the bureau building. An overhead light fixture, more like a chandelier, cast a yellow glow into the room. A table next to the stuffed chair held a lamp that would be enough for reading. A desk at the other end of the room could serve well as a workspace, if Mike needed one.

A left turn at the desk took Mike into the combined kitchen and eating area, the latter nothing more than a small round table and two café chairs.

Again, George had been true to his word. A small refrigerator sat at the end of a counter that held the sink and a few drawers and cabinets. More cabinets were bolted to the wall. At the other end of the cabinet, the stove. Mike froze when he saw it. It was gas. He had long feared gas appliances, ever since the horror at home decades earlier, but now he'd have to learn to live with it.

So this simple apartment was to be Mike's home away from home. By American standards, it was not much. By German postwar standards, it was a palace.

Mike stashed his clothes and other belongings in the bedroom and bathroom. The afternoon rain had stopped, and the sun emerged from behind the clouds, pouring light and heat into the apartment. Opening a screenless window did not create much of a breeze, but it did admit a wave of mosquitoes. Swatting at the thirsty pests while slamming the window shut, Mike wondered where he would find a fan.

It was still bright outside when Mike decided he needed something to eat before turning in. He had noticed a small bierstube in a bomb-scarred building next to his, so he figured a beer and a snack would do for the night.

He stuck some Reichsmarks in his pocket and strolled into the small establishment, a bleak hole in the wall with a small bar on one side and a few small round tables with uncomfortably tiny chairs on the other.

The bar at that moment had one other customer—an old man with bad teeth drinking schnaps and trying to gum a boiled egg.

"What would you like?" the middle-aged bartender said in passable English with an even tone that was neither hostile nor friendly.

"A beer and something light to eat," said Mike, annoyed that his uniform had preempted a chance to work on his German.

"We have sausages with potato salad or a small plate of cold cuts and bread," the bartender said as he put the beer in front of his new customer.

Mike ordered the sausages, hoping they were the wiener kind and not some exotic local variation full of odd colors and unknown ingredients.

The old man looked at Mike, gave his uniform some notice, and then turned away to quietly concentrate on the consumption of his egg.

Having nothing to read and nobody to talk to, Mike just studied the meager selection of spirits behind the bar as he waited for his meal. The bartender was in the small kitchen at the back of the place, leaving just the old man for company. Mike thought about trying to start a conversation but decided it would get him nowhere.

The bartender was mercifully quick with the sausages. They were the long, thin, pink kind he liked, and the potato salad was authentic. Mike toyed with the idea of becoming a regular in the place.

The old man, having finished his battle with the egg, turned again toward Mike.

"Why are you here?" the man slurred in a local dialect that Mike barely understood.

"I'm an American journalist with the Army," Mike said as pleasantly as his German would allow. "I'm here to report on the occupation and Germany's recovery from the war."

"An American and a journalist," growled the old man. "What a terrible combination."

Mike's startled gaze followed the old man as he slid off his bar stool and shuffled out the door.

"He was a local politician before the Nazis," the bartender explained with a shrug. "You Americans killed his son in Remagen."

Mike threw a handful of Reichsmarks on the bar without counting and hurried out the door. The depression set in even before Mike could make it back to his apartment and the bourbon he had found in Frankfurt.

"If this is what it's going to be like," he said out loud as he brought the bottle to his lips, "I'm in trouble."

Mike's depression was nothing like the mood in the Baumann household that night.

Riding past the PX as he arrived in town, Mike had noticed a long line of German civilians at the base theater across the parking lot. As the line was moving in, another group was filing out. Mike was surprised that the theater was open to Germans but let it pass.

He did not know until later that the presentation that day was anything but entertaining. He had not been close enough to see the looks on the faces of the people leaving the theater. Some were stone-faced and pale. Others were crying. One woman walked around to the side of the theater and vomited.

The district populace was following orders from the American occupation command to view the film showing the grotesque scenes shot by Army cameramen at liberated concentration camps. As the theater filled and the film started, some thought they knew what was coming. They had heard rumors during the war and read accounts of the camps after the surrender, but the 45-minute silent film, even in black and white, hammered each viewer's conscience. Gasps and groans filled the theater in the first few minutes, then a numb shock brought silence broken only periodically by a whisper or a sob. People leaving the theater were too upset to even warn those entering for the next showing. They all just went home to confront their collective shame. Some thought about Jewish friends, colleagues and neighbors who had vanished. Now they knew. That's what happened to them. It became personal, further magnifying the horror and revulsion.

The Baumann home was no different. Around a dinner table where nobody ate, they spoke in a whisper about how it could have happened, why nobody stopped it and what it would mean for Germans and Germany.

Max knew the answer to the last part.

"We will be branded forever," he said. "The world will see those pictures and hear the stories and say 'Look what the Germans did.' Not what Hitler or Himmler or the Nazis did. It's what the Germans did. And no matter how honorable and generous and tolerant we become as a nation or a people, this will always taint our image. And that's as it should be. Every generation will carry this burden, and every generation will have to make sure it is never forgotten and it never happens again."

Everyone nodded, said nothing more and went to bed, leaving the table to be cleared in the morning.

Mike's first few days at work were routine as he settled into the pace of wire service work in a town not exactly hopping with news. He covered the typical traffic accidents, fires and petty crimes, plus the activities and pronouncements of the American occupation authorities. The Stars and Stripes picked up a few of his stories, but there was nothing to attract the attention of editors at the major stateside papers that also subscribed to MNS.

One warm September afternoon he got a chance to break the monotony.

"Hey Mike, you doin' anything?" George yelled from across the room and over the clacking teletype machines. Mike was sitting at his desk, feet up, reading a month-old Saturday Evening Post, so George didn't wait for an answer.

"They found a dud next to the train station," George hollered with a glee only a news hound could savor. "They're gonna have to defuse it right there. Wanna check it out? It's dangerous stuff."

George didn't have to ask twice. Mike grabbed a notebook and jacket, commandeered a jeep waiting outside, and roared off to the station area about two miles away.

When he got to the cordon set up by MPs, he was surprised at how few people had gathered. He thought it would lure a crowd of curious thrill-seekers eager to watch the specialists take the 500-pound bomb apart.

"These things aren't much of a draw," an MP said as if talking about a rodeo or the circus. "If those guys do their job right, there's not much to see. If it goes off, nobody wants to be around for that either."

Mike, however, found the whole process riveting. Two Germans, volunteers for the high-paying and risky job, approached the bomb that was pointed upward, easing access to the fusing device. As the work began, one of the men waved a flag, and everyone in the area stopped moving and went silent.

Mike was too far away to see exactly what was happening, but he could see one man working at the tip of the bomb while the other stood next to him, ready to take any supporting action that would help prevent the fuse from activating and setting off the the quarter ton of high explosives.

It seemed to Mike that they were taking forever, but it was only 10 minutes before both men visibly relaxed and backed away from the bomb. One had the fusing device in his hands. There would be no disaster today, and as far as Mike was concerned, no story.

"Too bad," George said with no hint of shame for his callous attitude when Mike told him what had happened. "Nothing ruins a good story like a happy ending."

Mike surrendered to George's cynicism and his own disappointment and called it a day. After dropping by his apartment to freshen up, Mike hitched a ride to the commissary and PX on the west edge of town to stock up on razor blades, booze and other necessities that were running low. The two warehouse-style buildings once housed machine shops for the small air strip used by the Luftwaffe early in the war. They had been patched up and converted to merchandise marts that were a touch of home for those with privileges and the object of intense curiosity and envy for the Germans who saw Gis and American civilians waddle out the front gate loaded down with coffee, liquor, chocolate, sugar, flour and, most importantly, cigarettes. Such commodities, once taken for granted by all Germans, were nearly impossible to find in German shops and commanded staggering prices on the black market that had long ago established itself in Karlsruhe, like every other German city.

It had turned dark when Mike walked through the main gate with his relatively modest cache in the typically American brown paper bag. Hookers had already set up shop a discreet distance from the entrance, as they did every night. Mike usually steered clear of the pathetic collection of women, most of whom were either desperate to feed their children or fooling themselves into thinking they could parlay a liaison with a lonely American into a ticket to the good life.

This night, however, there was no ride for him at the gate. So he lowered his head and doggedly marched past the chorus line of come-ons and down the road lit only by moonlight, past rows of nearly identical German houses for his half hour walk home.

GOLDEN TIMES IV

A wire service reporter endures days of tedium while waiting for a story he can really get excited about. Mike worked a five-day week, but he was on call during weekends. The phone could ring at any time, and he had to be ready. After all, he was still in uniform, and to miss an assignment without a bulletproof excuse could cause him far more trouble than a similar transgression as a civilian journalist in the states.

One brisk fall Saturday (Mike thought it a perfect day for a football game), the phone rang in his apartment with an assignment that would eventually change his life.

The office assistant was calling to say George wanted Mike to cover the arrival of a train full of POWs released from Russia. These men, mostly Wehrmacht soldiers, had suffered the misfortune of falling into the hands of the Red Army. After years of captivity, they had languished another several months after the war ended while the Soviet Union squeezed one last bit of work out of them in POW camps that were little more than slave labor operations. As Moscow slowly released these miserable wretches, they were making their way back home by rail, truck or even on foot.

The train due in Karlsruhe that day was carrying hundreds of recently freed POWs, all from Baden, who had been rounded up by the Red Cross and sent home in special rail cars. Despite the short notice, the platform was crawling with relatives, many of them women with young children, hoping that their husbands, fathers and brothers would be among the returnees.

As he waded into the crowd, Mike knew he had a great human interest story on his hands, maybe even good enough to make the stateside papers. He fantasized about bylines and kudos and even awards, and in the process he mishandled the story and missed the best angle.

As the train slid into the station and bumped to a stop, haggard German POWs stepped or jumped or hobbled off the train and into the arms of waiting families. Emotional reunions like Mike had anticipated were happening all around him. But instead of focusing on one or two families for his story, he took a general approach. He would later realize he had a few paragraphs of description but no real emotion in his story. There were quotes, but no narrative to link them.

While trying to edit the piece into something useable, George ripped into Mike for missing an angle that could have been a better story, or at least a sidebar.

"I've covered a few of these homecomings too," George sighed with sadness clouding his face. He sat back from desk and lit a cigarette that Mike mistakenly took as a sign the boss was giving up on his copy.

"You're in the middle of all this hugging and kissing and crying, but there is always a guy who gets off the train ready to celebrate, and there's nobody there. Either they're dead, or they moved on and didn't get word the guy was coming home. Watching that face dissolve from joy to confusion to dejection is a story by itself, even if you never talk to the guy. I did, once. It made the Sunday New York Times. It's the only time I ever cried with a person I was interviewing."

Mike had been waiting to see the softer side that he suspected lurked beneath his hulking boss's tough exterior. He thought about apologizing for botching the story, or offering to rewrite it. Instead, he just nodded, mumbled something about trying better next time, and headed for the door. As bad as he felt, he had no idea that he had missed yet another story or that he was on the verge of a career-making reprieve.

While Mike had focused on the good news and overlooked the story about the POWs with nobody waiting at the station, he had also failed to notice a curious phenomenon transpiring in a few of the reunions.

But Ingrid hadn't.

She was at the station that day to get on a train for one of her periodic trips to Gmuend for provisions that were still scarce in Karlsruhe shops. She was trying to hold her ground on the other side of the platform where the POW train was arriving, when she literally bumped into Lisle Mueller, a neighbor from a few doors down. Ingrid knew that Lisle's husband had been reported as captured after Stalingrad, but she had no idea he was coming home until Lisle excitedly told her he was on the train due in any minute.

They hugged briefly in celebration, and Lisle then hurried to get a good spot on the arrival platform. Ingrid watched as Lisle studied every window in every carriage until she spotted Wolfgang, standing at an open window, smiling but with little genuine joy in his face.

As Wolfgang stepped off the train, Lisle pushed and elbowed her way toward him, not seeing the other man step onto the platform and quickly grab Wolfgang's arm. This other man, also in a tattered Wehrmacht uniform, seemed dazed, unsure about what to do and determined above all else not to lose contact with his comrade.

Lisle finally reached Wolfgang and slammed into him with a passionate hug and an equally passionate kiss, pausing only to suck in some air and babble some welcoming silliness before kissing him again. It took a minute or so for Lisle to sense a lack of reciprocity on Wolfgang's part. Then she noticed the stranger standing very close to her husband.

"Who's this?" she asked, trying to be cheerful and polite while resenting the intrusion.

"I'd like you to meet Peter Hauer," Wolfgang said, putting his hand on his comrade's shoulder. "We shared a lot together in the camp, and he'll be staying with us for a while. We both need some time to adjust."

Lisle couldn't hide her disappointment and confusion.

"You don't mind, do you?" Wolfgang asked, not seeming too interested in the answer.

"Of course not," Lisle lied, trying to preserve the spirit of the reunion. "We have room for him, and I want you to feel good about being home. If Peter helps you do that, then that's all I care about."

"I knew you'd understand," Wolfgang said, putting his free arm around his wife's shoulders. "We won't bother you with stories about our time in the camp. We'll be trying to forget as much of that as we can."

So off the three of them went, Wolfgang and Lisle arm-in-arm while Peter followed, carrying two small bags of clothing and other basic items that the Red Cross had provided.

Ingrid, having been too far away to hear the exchange, nevertheless saw the expression on her neighbor's face as she turned to leave. Ingrid sensed that the homecoming had not turned out as Lisle had hoped.

Mike never saw this little drama on the platform, but it didn't matter. He would learn the whole story soon enough.

Ingrid returned home the next day and after carefully storing away all her farmland treasures from Gmuend and checking on Elisabeth, sat down in the kitchen with her mother and sister to recite the strange tale of Lisle and Wolfgang Mueller's reunion.

"I don't know who that other man was," Ingrid said, "but he didn't move from Wolfgang's side the whole time, and Lisle didn't look at all happy about it."

"I've seen them," Monica chimed in. "I was sweeping the sidewalk this morning and Lisle and Wolfgang came out of the house. And that other man was right there with them. They walked somewhere, I don't know. But that man was walking as close to Wolfgang on one side as Lisle was on the other. It did look strange."

"Don't judge," Emma snapped. She suspected ugly speculation was about to surface, and she wasn't in any mood to hear it.

"We're not," Monica snapped back, shooting a quizzical glance at her mother and then her sister. "It just looks strange. The man's gone three years and comes back to his nice young wife and insists on having a fellow prisoner stay with them. If that man was a gentleman, he'd leave Wolfgang and Lisle alone."

"I don't want it discussed again in this house," Emma snapped again. "I hate neighborhood gossip. I'm sure people talk about us too."

"What's to gossip about us?" Monica answered with a wry smirk on her face. "We're the dullest family in Karlsruhe. We never do anything."

Emma looked down at the pile of potatoes on the table in front of her, started peeling, and said nothing.

The topic never was raised again during the next few weeks, although Emma would occasionally see her older daughter chatting with Lisle on the sidewalk. Ingrid, heeding her mother's banishment of the subject, never discussed what Lisle had said. When Monica would pump her sister for information, Ingrid would appear ready to say something, then wave off the topic with an annoyed glance or a brief word of dismissal. Ingrid's behavior convinced Monica that the subject was not a happy one, nor was the Mueller household.

Soon, rumors of loud arguments and late night door-slamming started filtering through the neighborhood. Peter Hauer was still living there. He never spoke to anyone in the neighborhood and rarely even ventured beyond the front gate of the two-story stucco cube. Wolfgang might spend a moment in idle conversation with a neighbor, but he also seemed preoccupied. The couple never socialized, even though the neighbors were eager to make Wolfgang feel at home after his ordeal.

As might be expected, the rumors had taken a sexual turn with speculation about the true relationship between Wolfgang and Peter. Nobody dared to discuss it openly, but it featured prominently in plenty of kitchen chatter and pillow talk.

Ingrid, still honoring her mother's prohibition of the subject, steadfastly refused to join in the gossip, even though she seemed to have more contact with Lisle than anyone. When someone tried to pry information from her, Ingrid would fix an icy glare on the interrogator and turn away.

Clearly, there was trouble in that little beige house, but nobody, not even Ingrid, could do anything about it.

Something nudged Mike awake. It wasn't a sound, more like a feeling. He looked at the clock, and seeing that it was only 2:12am, rolled over and tried to get back to sleep.

After 20 minutes he was roused again, this time by the clear, jarring ring of the telephone.

"Sorry, Mike." It was the bureau's young night shift writer, Jimmy Montgomery. "There's been some kind of an explosion out near the PX."

"The PX blew up?" Mike said in an unintended high voice as he jerked into a sitting position in bed.

"No, no. We think it was a house or a shop. It's in a residential area. George wants you to get out there right now. A jeep will be waiting for you at your door by the time you're ready. He says find out what happened and then come right back to the bureau to file your story. Don't try to phone it in."

Mike jumped out of bed, rummaged through his wardrobe for a relatively clean uniform and went through his best fireman routine that he saved for emergency calls. What's this all about, he wondered. Maybe another dud went off. But he had been through those neighborhoods, and they hadn't suffered much bombing during the war.

He jogged out the front door of the building in 15 minutes and hopped into the waiting jeep. In no time the jeep was turning the corner onto Rosmarinstrasse, where a German policeman and American MP were blocking the way.

Mike flashed his ID, rushed passed the police line and toward a small crowd of Germans, all wearing coats over nightclothes. They were whispering quietly or silently staring at what was left of a house illuminated by the lights of a few emergency vehicles. The exterior walls were still standing, but all the windows and doors had been blown out. Black flash marks framed every opening. Much of the roof was gone, but exposed rafters did not show signs of a major fire. The area around the house looked like someone had picked it up and shaken out all the contents. Furniture, curtains, books, a radio, silverware—anything that a modest German home of the day might hold littered the garden, driveway and landscaped walkway that led to the now missing front door.

Mike's stomach tightened and turned all at once. Gas. O God. Not again. Please, please, no charred flesh this time. Just let me get what I need and get out of here.

The thought had barely finished when the ambulance workers carried out the first stretcher. The body was covered, but a slender, blackened arm dangled from under the sheet. Mike, trying to fake professional indifference while battling nausea, guessed out loud to nobody that it was a woman. A few minutes later, another stretcher came out, then another. An ambulance attendant told a firefighter standing next to Mike that the last two were males. They had been found dead in separate rooms. Both had minor burns, not serious enough to cause death. Mike reckoned the attendant saw his uniform and assumed he didn't speak German. Mike wanted to preserve that mistaken assumption, so he eavesdropped on their German conversation but didn't take notes. He'd get it all down later.

After that chat broke up, Mike decided to find out more. The German police and fire personnel were no help, so he walked over to the cluster of civilians across the street.

Blowing his cover by speaking in German, he asked if anyone knew what had happened.

"We had been in bed a couple of hours," an elderly man said, "when we woke up to the explosion in this house. I thought it was a bomb. It broke some of our windows."

Neighbors validated his version of events with "us too" murmurs and nods. So Mike, clearing his head to focus on the job, walked back across the street to talk to one of the ambulance workers who carried the first body out.

"We found her in the kitchen," the worker said in the matter of fact tone common for that profession. "Her head was in the oven. It looks like a suicide."

Mike asked about the two men.

"I don't think they died from the explosion," he said. "I'd say they were asleep and died from the gas before something touched it off. A pilot light maybe. There was a gas water heater near the kitchen."

Now Mike's journalistic juices were flowing. Something gnawed at him. Women killing themselves in gas ovens were not that unusual in the desperate times of postwar Germany. But they usually lived alone and died alone. She wasn't alone. She had a home, and presumably a husband. That would be one of the dead men. But who was the other guy?

Mike returned to the dwindling group of neighbors. Ingrid was standing there in a wool overcoat, her hair tied in a bun the way she wore it to bed each night. Monica was there too, her reddish hair flowing freely over a shawl that covered her hastily donned housecoat that she clutched tightly at her throat, as if she had something to hide. Both women wore slippers, but the horrid sight made them oblivious to the fall night's chill.

"Did anyone know these people?" he asked. "Does anyone know why this would happen?"

"Maybe my sister does," Monica said, pointing to Ingrid next to her.

Ingrid flashed with anger at her sister. "Keep quiet."

"Did you know the people in that house?" Mike asked gently, hoping not to intimidate this witness. "Can you tell me something that would make sense out of this?"

"Who are you?"

"Mike Falwell, Military News Service. I'm a reporter. There seems to be a tragic story here, and I'd like you to tell me about it, if you can. What's your name?"

Without her mother at her side, Ingrid started to weaken. She knew the whole awful truth, and something told her it should come out. With Monica's unspoken prodding at her side, Ingrid opened up.

"I'm Ingrid Bauer. I live with my husband and little girl in that house up the street," she said, pointing to the Baumann home. "I knew Lisle well. Maybe better than anyone in the neighborhood."

Mike started taking notes, but he was smart enough to keep quiet. He just wanted to story to flow out of Ingrid in her own words, at her own pace, slowed only by periodic pauses to fight back tears.

"I guess I'm not surprised she did this," Ingrid said, unable to utter the word "suicide." "She started talking about it a few days ago. I begged her to go see someone who could help, a doctor or a priest or someone. But she said she didn't think that would do any good. I felt so helpless, but I couldn't tell anyone. Lisle told me everything because she knew I'm not a gossip."

Mike had to ask. "What did she tell you?"

Ingrid battled her conscience one more time, then gave up.

"Her husband, Wolfgang, came back from Russia, where he was a prisoner for three years. He brought this other man, Peter, who had no family left. They were comrades in the camp. Lisle said they endured terrible times together. Wolfgang told her that they could not have survived without each other. They stole food for each other, took care of each other when they were sick, protected each other from the guards and other prisoners. She said they were like one being. And when they were freed, they couldn't imagine being separated. So Wolfgang brought Peter home.

"Lisle wanted to resume her marriage with Wolfgang, but she felt like Peter was always in the way. She tried very hard to tolerate Peter, but eventually she told Wolfgang that Peter had to go. Wolfgang refused and would not even discuss it. Lisle got more and more depressed, and finally I guess it was too much to bear. So this is how it ended."

Mike's professionalism required the next question. He groped for the proper words in German and did the best he could.

"Ingrid, was the relationship between Wolfgang and Peter, uh, more than a deep friendship?"

He braced himself for Ingrid's denunciation of such a crude question but was relieved when she replied in a matter of fact manner that even surprised her.

"We never talked about that," Ingrid said, "but in so many words Lisle said it was very different from the kind of relationship I think you are asking about."

Ingrid was clearly getting uncomfortable with Mike's questioning, so he decided to let her off the hook. The fact that the men had died in separate rooms seemed to support Ingrid's analysis. Besides, Mike didn't want to go any farther with that awkward topic anyway. He thanked Ingrid, gently warned her he might come back later with more questions, and gave her the bureau's telephone number in case she had anything further to tell him.

Mike knew he had two stories to work on. The first was the fatal explosion. He limited the "why" of the story to a vague mention of domestic problems. He talked to a few other neighbors to get the standard "they were nice but somewhat reserved" quotes, collected the usual forensic details from the authorities, and went back to the bureau. His tight, well-written 500-word story made page 3 of the Stars and Stripes but didn't get much play beyond that.

The second story was another matter.

Ingrid's description of the strange relationships in the small stucco house whetted Mike's news instincts. He sensed that he might have stumbled onto an unusual sociological phenomenon unique to POWs returning from the appalling ordeal of survival in Stalin's vengeance camps. Bonds formed there, Mike theorized, might be far more intense and indivisible than any male friendship or homosexual relationship.

To test his theory, he telephoned a psychologist he had met at Heidelberg University while covering a conference there a month earlier. Heinz Melk had fled Germany when the Nazis took power but had returned from America to help the prestigious German institution recover from the war.

When Mike started telling the story of the house explosion, Melk bantered cordially and seemed to almost be patronizing the reporter. However, when Mike turned the conversation toward the strange relationship between the two men in the house, Melk grew silent.

Mike finished his oral dissertation and waited for Melk to knock it down and tell him to stop playing amateur analyst. But he heard no such rebuttal. Instead, for what seemed to be several minutes, he heard nothing.

He asked whether his conversation partner was OK.

"Yes, I'm fine," Melk answered in a distracted tone worthy of any absent-minded professor. Then his tone turned clear and direct.

"Mike, what do you plan to do with this?" Melk asked.

"This what?" Mike answered. "I'm not sure what I've got."

"Can you come to Heidelberg tomorrow to discuss this further?"

"Of course I can. Is 11am OK?"

"That'll be fine. We can meet at the Golden Knight restaurant and then walk to my office."

"OK, " Mike said, wondering what that was all about.

The next morning Mike took the short train ride to the old university town and took advantage of the sunny day to walk along the Neckar River to the restaurant. Melk was already there, so they strolled down the picturesque old street that was spared the ravages of war, turned left into the main campus area and entered one of the classical limestone structures that all universities cherish.

In Melk's cluttered, professorial office, Mike had to clear a stack of papers from a chair to sit down. Melk, strangely preoccupied by now, sat behind his simple walnut desk and shoved aside papers and reports until he had a clear space. Then he reached into a drawer, pulled out a bulging file, and placed it in the clearing.

"This is why I asked you to come here," Melk said, tapping the file. "Several of us have been aware for several months of a strange pattern of behavior shown by prisoners of war returning from Soviet camps. Only those prisoners, not the ones from North America or British camps, where conditions were more than tolerable, sometimes even pleasant.

"We have studied scores of cases where prisoners return home with their camp comrades and cannot stand the thought of separating from those men. This is not homosexuality in the classic sense. This is a bond far deeper than that. We have documented murder-suicides and double suicides caused by conflict these bonds create with spouses and entire families.

"The story you told me is another manifestation of the problem—spousal suicide. The woman cannot understand the relationship and cannot tolerate the intrusion of the comrade into her marriage just as it is supposed to resume after years of disruption.

"What made your story unusual is that the two men died as well. Based on our preliminary studies, this was not the intended consequence. The woman obviously succumbed to severe depression, but I doubt she had any thought of physically harming those men. If anything, she may have only wanted to inflict severe emotional trauma—remorse or guilt, perhaps.

"Several of my colleagues and I have been wondering how to give this phenomenon wider exposure. I talked to some of them after our conversation yesterday, and we agreed that you had been very clever to suspect that something unusual happened in that house. We decided to give you access to our files on cases we have documented so far. If you think it's a story, we will help you."

Mike tried hard to keep his professional demeanor, but he didn't do very well.

"I want to start right now," Mike said, reaching for the thick file.

"One caveat," Melk said as he handed the file to Mike. "We hope you will consult with me before you publish the story. We don't want to be censors, but we want to make sure your story has a solid scientific foundation.

"Don't worry," Mike said, "I don't want to do anything stupid either. I'll check my facts with you before the story goes out."

The story became as series. First, Mike rewrote the story of the house explosion to include Ingrid's saga of Lisle's agony. He used that vignette to introduce the subject of what he called the "Gulag Syndrome", quoting Melk for an explanation of the condition and why it was unique.

The second part was a description of some of the cases in Melk's file. Names were withheld, but the odd and sometimes tragic social situations created by the return of inseparable POW pairs were told in a narrative style that was both coldly clinical and delicately empathetic.

Finally, Mike persuaded two former POWs named in the Melk file to talk on the record about their experiences in war and captivity and the relationship that had formed between them. Both had divorced soon after returning home, sparing Mike the ordeal of trying to interview one or two wives ravaged emotionally by the unexpected intrusions on their marriages after their husbands returned.

Without showing Melk his copy, Mike rigorously checked every fact and conclusion with the psychologist. George Martin also red-penciled the pieces, with a particular eye toward any wording that might be confusing, vague or judgmental. The two POWs even agreed to George's request for signed releases, just as a legal precaution.

All three parts of the series went onto the wire at the same time, with embargoes to give editors time to find places for the 1,500-word stories that were to run on consecutive days, starting on a Sunday. Stars and Stripes played all three parts on the front page. So did several major American newspapers and scores of smaller ones. Even British papers requested rights to the series, which were granted.

The Soviet occupation headquarters in Berlin protested the series as anti-Soviet propaganda and questioned why Mike had not reported the wartime activities of the two POWs he interviewed. Mike had verified that they were Wehrmacht infantrymen and decided that was all he needed to say. Had they been members of the vicious Waffen SS, it would have been another matter.

As a primary source in the series, Melk gained priceless publicity that raised his status among his peers and established his preeminence in his profession. The file he loaned to Mike became the grist for his doctoral dissertation.

Mike's personnel file overflowed with letters of commendation and praise from superiors, mental health professionals, readers in America and Germany and even one from the two POWs he interviewed. He won two press awards for the series, and someone nominated it for a Pulitzer Prize.

For a story that Mike had first missed at the train station and almost ran from the night the little stucco house blew up, it turned out to be the cornerstone of his reporting career. But it didn't get him out of Karlsruhe. All it did was ensure that he got all the best stories in that region. It wasn't the big time, but Mike was satisfied for the time being.

Besides, other forces were starting to stir.

Whenever he was asked about the Gulag Syndrome story or reflected on all the good it had done, he would always think back to that scene across the street from that shattered house, to his conversation with the surprisingly candid and helpful Ingrid Bauer. And inevitably, he'd recompose the image of her younger sister studiously watching him take notes. Although he didn't need her name for the story, he did make a mental note of one fact—she was a doll.

GOLDEN TIMES V

The best and worst times of Monica's life started on the same morning in December, 1945. As Emma, Ingrid and Monica labored to make the house as festive as possible in the austere times of Germany's first post-war holiday season, Max was outside checking the winter proofing in the garden when an elderly neighbor, Walter Meier, called from the low fence separating the property from the street.

"Good morning Max," Meier chirped in his annoyingly faux-friendly way. They chatted a while about the latest news but just touched lightly on the Nuremberg trial of the top Nazis that had opened two weeks earlier. Some things were still to sensitive to discuss with casual acquaintances.

Meier found a pause in the banter to come to the point of his visit.

"Does that pretty young daughter of yours still remember her English?"

"Monica? Naturally," Max replied, barely able to mask his annoyance at the question. Monica would never forget six years of English studies, or even the four years of French. Max wouldn't tolerate that. "Why?"

"I hear the Americans are looking for translators and telephone operators who know English," Walter said with a shrug. "I just thought maybe Monica would like to find some work."

"Where are these jobs?," Max asked, ready to squelch the conversation if he didn't like the answer. "What do they pay? What are the working hours? Who exactly would she be working for?"

"Wait a minute," Walter interrupted, holding up his hands in mock defense. "I just heard the rumor. I guess she'd have to go down there and find out. I do know that some of the offices are around Bismarck Square. She can almost walk there, or ride a bicycle."

That's all Max needed to hear. He knew the area and knew something about the American activities there. They were all fine with him. And the thought of extra income sealed the idea in his mind. After all, he was still waiting to be reinstated as school rector, so any financial support would help their shrinking cash supply. Maybe they could even stop haggling with goods from Gmuend and keep more for themselves.

Fritz was doing his part, but he had been victimized by postwar political realities. After settling back into civilian life in the now-crowded Baumann home, Fritz quickly realized he would have to find work, any work, as the only viable breadwinner in the extended family. He had always counted on returning to his accounting job with the city government. In fact, his boss had promised him exactly that when he left for Wehrmacht service.

One Monday in October, Fritz walked by his old workplace to find it in fairly good condition. So he took a chance and walked in unannounced to the office of his old boss, Ernst Markel, who was trying to sort out the city's tangled financial condition. Markel recognized Fritz, warmly welcomed him into his surprisingly roomy and orderly office and, after some obligatory small talk, assured him he could start just as soon as Markel was ready to reassemble a staff. And that was just days away.

Fritz thanked his boss with a warmth and enthusiasm rare for the Swaebish farm boy. He was sure the entire family was headed for better times.

That feeling lasted just seven days.

The following Monday, Fred had not heard again from Markel and was eager to start earning a paycheck. So he decided to risk offending his former supervisor and future benefactor by dropping by for a quick visit.

He bounded up the tiled steps of the old brick municipal building, knocked on the accounting office door and walked in without waiting for a reply.

Sitting at the desk was a total stranger.

"What can I do for you?" the occupant asked, trying to cover his annoyance with formal politeness.

"I'm looking for Ernst Markel," Fred said with shy deference. "He was going to give me my old job back here. I just wanted to see how long I might have to wait."

Without moving from his chair, the occupant introduced himself. "I'm Albert Horstbauer. I run this office now. I'm afraid there is nothing here for you."

Resisting the curt brush-off, Fritz asked for – almost demanded – an explanation. And he got it.

Markel had been part of the old regime. He was not a Nazi Party activist, but he served the regime, and that was all the new German administrators working under occupation needed to know. The orders were clear. Anyone who had opposed the Nazis would get preference in hiring over those who had worked for them. Denazification would determine who could return to public service and who would be relegated to common labor.

Horstbauer, a Social Democrat, had been forced out of his private accountancy because of his political activities and even spent a short time in detention. Now it was his turn, and he had seized it. And no friend of Markel was welcome.

Fritz realized he had no chance and retreated from the now icy city accountant's office. He visited a few accounting firms he had known before the war, but only two were even in business and they didn't need any help. Fritz had no English, so the Americans were not an option.

He trooped home that night to report the bad news and silently endured the tantrums Ingrid and Emma unleashed against the stranger Horstbauer. Monica said nothing, while Max started thinking of alternatives. None came to mind.

So after a few frustrating days exploring dead ends at the Karlsruhe labor office, Fritz and the family agreed that he should take a sure source of income until something better came along.

The next day, he went to the local office hiring workers who earned a meager hourly wage clearing rubble. As a group, they became known as "truemmer Frauen" – rubble women – because most were female. But not all. And Fritz was man enough to swallow his pride for the sake of his family. So the Baumann household's only income was from Fritz the brick-stacker.

"I'll talk it over with Monica," Max said to his neighbor still standing at the fence. "Thanks for thinking of her, and Merry Christmas."

"Same to you, and gladly done," Walter replied in the typical German phrase. "But if she gets into that PX, remember who told you."

Max nodded, at first annoyed by the parasitic implication of Walter's parting comment. But then he quickly got over it, thinking if the roles were reversed he'd probably say the same thing.

He immediately went into the house through the back door leading into Ingrid's kitchen. Emma and Ingrid were washing peas. Monica was playing with Elisabeth, who was fussing with a cold and general crankiness.

Max told them about the opportunity Monica might be able to find with the Americans. He didn't like them, but he was worried about his steadily shrinking bank account and knew Fritz's small wages barely covered the cost of rationed goods for his own family.

The idea made Monica nervous.

"I'm not sure my English is good enough," she said. "It's been years since I studied." Her linguistic errors with the Americans during the trek from Gmuend a few months earlier had bothered her ever since. "When I try, I make mistakes."

"It will all come back to you very quickly when you work in a totally English workplace," Max said. "You need to get out of this house, and we need the money. And if you can find your way to some American things at..."

"I won't go there as a scavanger," Monica snapped, interrupting her father for one of the few times in her life. "If that's why you want me to do it, forget it."

Max held his temper, for once, and tried to steer the conversation back to basics.

"Fine, never mind about all that. You're right. It's not important. What is important is that you find something safe, useful and dignified, perfect your English and help this family by earning some money. At least go down there and see what they have to offer."

Monica knew she had no further defense and agreed to stop by their employment office after she bicycled to Axel's place later in the day to take him some fruit preserves scrounged from Emma's scrawny orchard as a Christmas treat.

As she went upstairs to get ready for the day, someone rang the front door bell. Max lumbered through the hallway, down the stairs and opened the door to find two American MPs standing there. One spoke heavily accented German. The other just stood there holding a large envelope.

"Max Baumann?"

"Yes," Max answered, slightly intimidated by the uniformed occupiers standing on his doorstep.

"We have orders to deliver this to you personally. These documents confirm that you will be undergoing a denazification investigation and hearing. The reasons for this are listed in the documents. You will be notified later about how the case will proceed. We suggest that you get the help of a lawyer familiar with this process. Please sign here."

The speaking MP held out a clipboard with a simple delivery confirmation note in English and German. Max, utterly dumbfounded, could only sign and accept the white envelope from the other GI. Then, in a profoundly shocking final gesture, both saluted as they said goodbye. Why would they do that, Max wondered. I wasn't a military man, at least not in this war.

Max turned and shuffled slowly back to the kitchen, where his wife, daughter and granddaughter all went still, sensing something serious had just taken place.

Max sat down at the only place left at the table and carefully opened the envelope.

"What's that?" Emma asked, suspecting she was not going to like its contents. "Who was at the door? Who gave you that?"

"Be quiet," snapped Max, with instant effect. He was trying to concentrate on the cover letter that had all the markings of an official legal document. As he read it, his ruddy face lost all color.

"They think I was an important Nazi," Max said in almost a whisper. The women gasped in unison but said nothing, waiting for more. "It says somebody has identified me as a 'Nazi authority figure.' It also talks about some of my answers in the questionnaire we all had to fill out. It says that after further investigation, I must go before a denazification tribunal to determine if I am to be punished."

Ingrid was ready to explode. As far as she knew, all he had ever done was follow orders from the regime during a war and go to Strasbourg to convert the schools to German administration.

"That's utter madness," she blurted out, slapping her hands on the table, which startled Elisabeth and got her crying. "How could they…"

"Be still," Emma snapped before Max could say anything. His wife was frightened by this sudden crisis, but she maintained her composure for the sake of her family sitting around her.

"I've heard about this process. It has already started with Goering and Hess and all the other big shots in Nuremberg. Then they'll work their way down through German society, trying to weed out anyone who did anything to help the Nazis."

Nobody spoke for a few seconds as Ingrid got Elisabeth quiet again.

"Who are they to judge?" Emma hissed, her anger rising. "Are they so innocent? Look what they did in Dresden, in Hamburg. Look at what the French and the Russians did when they occupied us. How many people did they kill?"

"They won the war," Max said in almost a whisper, thinking about the threatening future while trying to calm his wife down. "The Nazis did things we couldn't even imagine."

As Max sorted through the documents, Monica came bouncing into the kitchen with a growing enthusiasm for the job search she was about to start. The mood in the room stopped her cold.

Her father was staring at some papers. Her mother was looking out the kitchen window, close to tears. Ingrid was fussing with Elisabeth, but her mind was miles away.

"What's wrong?" Monica asked in a voice blending excitement with dread.

As Max went over the implications of the documents from the large white envelope, Monica blanched. Like Ingrid, she was astonished that some school reorganization five long years ago could have such potentially devastating ramifications.

"Well then to hell with the Americans and their jobs," she replied, stomping her foot and startling Elisabeth again. "I don't want to have anything to do with them if this is their idea of justice and fairness and how Germany is supposed to recover from the war."

Her father started shaking his head slowly as he looked down at the incindiary papers on the table.

"No, now you have to go," he said. "This means I can't return to the school. I have no work. We'll need the money you can earn from the Americans. I'm sure I can straighten this all out. As soon as I find out more about the accusations against me…" and here his brow tightened…"and the people making them, everything will turn out fine."

Monica was secretly relieved that her father gave her the green light to look for work. Her rage had been genuine but evaporated as she thought more about working outside the home, earning her own money and meeting new people, not just Germans either. She really did want to work for the Americans, even if they had decided to put her entire family through corrosive uncertainty for months to come.

She had found her favorite green wool skirt and had borrowed, without asking, an off-white silk blouse from her sister, a Christmas present from Fritz just before he went to war. Nothing fancy or gaudy, but business-like and stylish for the scaled-back standards of postwar Germany. Ingrid flinched when she saw her sister's outfit but calmed down when she realized it did indeed look good on Monica. And that was all that mattered right now as the family's financial wellbeing rested on her padded silk shoulders.

Monica looked at her still pale father and nodded. "All right, I'll see what I can find."

She walked past Ingrid and Elisabeth, leaned over her father and kissed him on the forehead. "You're a good man," she said with a daughter's confidence. "You didn't do anything wrong. This will turn out to be nothing."

Monica pecked her mother on her cheek and said goodbye as she headed out the kitchen door for her visits to Axel and the Americans. She expected to see a nod or a word of agreement from her mother, but Emma just stared at the floor and said nothing.

Monica tied a pale green scarf over her head to keep her flowing strawberry blond hair in place, just in case it might make a difference with the Americans. She put the two jars of preserves – peach and black cherry, Axel's favorite – into the basket on the back of her sturdy bicycle and headed off for his small apartment in the heart of town.

Axel's split with his father had widened just after Fritz had come home. Max tried to tolerate the wild mood swings and occasional drinking binges of his handicapped son, but he had little patience for all that when Axel further eroded his welcome with frequent political tirades against the Americans, the British, the French, and above all else the Germans helping to manage the occupation. He had hated the Nazis and anyone who worked with them (causing his first big break with his father over the Strasbourg episode). He went to war only out of a sense of duty instilled by his father, the decorated World War I officer.

Listening to his son's bitter, self-pitying and liquor-fueled rants as they became almost daily performances, Max started detecting a curious hole in Axel's litany of evils. The Russians were never mentioned. For some reason, Axel always gave them a pass, even though it was one of their shells that had blown away two of his limbs, four of his comrades and all of his future ambitions in a Ukraine bunker on a warm spring day in 1943. Physical rehabilitation had given him a prosthetic right hand and left leg, but it could not restore his ability to play the piano or pound out music reviews and newspaper columns on his sturdy Olivetti typewriter.

So day after day he sulked, smoked, ranted and drank until Max had had enough. One day, for no particular reason, their regular argument escalated into a towering rage on both sides. The shouting was heard throughout the neighborhood, even through closed doors and windows. The course of the conversation was usual – stop feeling sorry for yourself, what else am I supposed to do, get a job like Fritz did, nobody will hire a cripple like me, especially the damned Americans, maybe they would if you wouldn't drink so much, that's easy for you to say, and so on.

Maybe it was the full moon, or Max's frustration about his own unemployment finally getting to him, or just the logical outcome of the ever-intensifying storm. As Emma, Ingrid and Monica cowered in the Baumann's upstairs living room, Max this time went the final step and blurted out the inevitable ultimatum – change or leave this house.

Axel was getting a small stipend as a handicapped veteran and he still had friends in town, so that's all he needed to hear. He threw a few necessities into a bag he could carry with his one good arm, slammed every door he walked through from his third floor room to the main floor hallway, and stormed out. He never said a word of goodbye to the rest of the family. He just left Max steaming in the downstairs living room while the women looked at each other with perplexed frowns, wondering what had happened but knowing this was something new.

When they found the nerve to go downstairs, they found Max sitting in the Bauers' living room pouring a brandy. That was a wild extravagance for the times, alerting the women to the fact that something momentous had happened.

"Axel's gone," Max said matter-of-factly, as if he were reporting some routine news headline. "He won't be back. I just couldn't take it anymore. I guess he couldn't either. So it's done. He can find somebody else to listen to his political nonsense and drunken tirades. At least we'll have peace in this house."

Somehow, Max didn't seem as relieved as he tried to sound. The women knew there would be no further discussion, at least for now. Max knew Emma would eventually chew his head off, but he had weathered those storms before.

When Fritz came home that evening from a quick Gmuend trip, he heard the news from his wife. In a sense, he was relieved. He had sometimes been caught between the two volcanoes and never relished that role. Mediation was out of the question. The best he could ever do was separate the combatants and arrange a truce that never survived more than a day or two. And Fritz certainly had no time for Axel's politics.

But Fritz, as a veteran, also had deep sympathy for Axel. He knew his brother-in-law was a supremely talented young man who had been robbed of almost everything important to him except life itself. And now that life was miserable and apparently aimless. Fritz thought he might have to secretly ensure Axel's wellbeing by finding him a place to live and something to do. But Axel showed astonishing resilience once he was out from under the crushing domination of his imperious father.

As Monica peddled toward town, she was eager to finally see where Axel had taken refuge. She had a much different view of her brother—she idolized him. She still saw the whole Axel in him and was able to look past his physical problems and hear the discourse of a keen, active mind searching for far more answers than any one human being can ever find, even healthy ones. His parents had no time or patience for long, rambling discussions on politics and culture ranging from Hegel to Harlowe. Ingrid and Fritz didn't either and wouldn't have understood anyway. But Monica loved the casual chats, challenging debates and good-natured arguments she still managed to have with her brother, even if he lost her by swerving onto some obscure philosophical or theoretical tangents.

She held the key to the mystery her father had detected concerning the Russians. Only she knew that Axel now considered himself a Marxist. He saw capitalism in any form as evil. It was capitalists who had allowed Hitler to rise to power. Capitalists on all sides had profited from the war. And Germans were the worst. IG Farben, Bosch, Siemens – all had done well by the Nazis and were positioned to do even better now.

The Soviet Union, on the other hand, endured suffering greater than any country invaded by Germany. And yet its people and system were resilient enough to take a crushing military blow, respond to it with unshakeable patriotism and determination and eventually snuff out the Nazi regime, in Axel's view, with precious little help from Moscow's so-called allies. The true enemies of Nazism, the Communists, were being installed as the new bosses in the Soviet occupation zone, as they should be in Axel's eyes. In the western zones, he saw closet Nazis make self-serving loyalty pledges to the new system and get on with their lives. Some with vital skills were even shielded from rigorous denazification for the sake of rapid reconstruction. He formed those opinions before general denazification was in place, and no subsequent judicial or social reckoning with history could change his mind.

Communism looked after everyone, he argued, and it was the way of the future. He was sure he'd have much better care and more opportunities for a profession in the eastern zone than under American occupation. With the conveniently narrow view of a zealot, he chose to ignore how the Soviet Union had treated his captured comrades, or even its own forces, during the war. He brushed off horror stories about atrocities committed against Germans in the Soviet zone, fabricating an alibi that the same awful things had happened in the other zones as well, including his family's own neighborhood. Comparing the extent of atrocities and the occupying forces' reactions to them did not come into play in Axel's mind. And never mind Stalin's genocidal campaigns against his own people, such as the forced starvation campaign in the early thirties that killed 10 million Ukrainians. If confronted with those facts, Axel conveniently brushed them off as anti-Soviet propaganda. His selective memory and self-deceiving choice of facts and events would shape – some said warp – his beliefs the rest of his life.

Monica did not have strong political views and never would. She found politics boring or infuriating, depending on the issue. She tolerated Axel's views because he was her brother and, while strange and even illogical to her, his ideas at least seemed harmless. Let him spout his political nonsense if it made him feel better. That's how she dealt with it. She was more worried about the practical matter of his survival on his own.

She tried to envision his new abode as she peddled through Karlsruhe, following part of her path out of town on that fateful April day when she fled to Gmuend. Much of the rubble had been cleared away, leaving barren gaps where buildings once stood. A few shops were open and trying to look festive for the time of year, but their holiday wares were sparse or of poor quality, mostly wooden or cardboard toys, cards, colored pencils and ornaments. Some people attempted festive decoration to suit the Christmas season, but most of it only magnified the depravation in the town. Apartments were still an acute shortage. As winter deepened, people desperate for shelter occupied apartments with doors, windows or walls missing.

A few had pathetic little Christmas trees set up for the holidays, a remarkable devotion to tradition when heating and cooking material was in such short supply. Monica noticed some of the trees as well as outdoor decorations were draped with thin metallic strips clearly meant as a poor substitute for tinsel. It was chaff, the radar-deflecting material dropped by bombers during the war to confuse German air defenses. Some enterprising and inventive holiday devotees had found enough of the stuff to festoon a few trees, bushes and facades.

Germans considered themselves the creators of many holiday customs and traditions – the Christmas tree, Father Christmas, "Silent Night," and so on. The barren trees, paltry gifts, sparse holiday meals and general lack of cheer weighed particularly heavy on every German household. Some made the point that the weather was milder than usual or that they were at peace for the first Christmas in six years, but that didn't help much.

The city's German administration had started fixing the main streets, so Monica's bike ride was less jarring than usual. Streetcars were running again along Kaiserstrasse. As she pedaled past the train station, she noticed a small crowd, mostly children, aimlessly standing near a curve in one of the tracks carrying intercity rail traffic. Even though Axel was waiting, her curiosity got the better of her and she stopped. A few adults were mingling with the children, and one wore an American military overcoat and cap. Strange, she thought, why would he be there, nevermind what they're doing.

Axel was waiting, so she climbed back onto the bike and pedaled away.

Mike didn't see Monica in the distance. He was on assignment. He had heard about the gatherings at the rail sidings and decided to see for himself. Children were always a good story, so his concentration was on them as the motly gathering prepared to leap into action.

A freight train pulling several coal cars rumbled by, slowing for the curve. Suddenly, adults scurried dangerously close to the slow-moving rail cars, picking up pieces of coal that centrifugal force and rough tracks jarred from the gondolas.

Even more alarming to Mike, some adults were tossing children onto the cars, where they scooped coal over the side as fast as their small hands could work. Others ran alongside the cars, grabbing coal and stuffing it into bags, buckets and even, in one case, a small tin bathtub with two old women holding each end. When the train picked up speed, adults barked warnings and children hopped off the cars, rolling to break their falls as they landed on the grading. Two of the children, fearing the train was moving too fast, couldn't find the nerve to jump. So off they rode to who-knew-where.

Fighting to keep his professional demeanor intact, Mike anxiously asked one of the adults how the children would be rescued.

"Don't worry," a middle-aged man said, sorting through his precious collection of coal. "That happens all the time. They wait for the train to slow down, then they jump. They either walk home or get a ride from some sympathetic stranger. German or American. To the children, it's a game."

Mike's subsequent research for his story confirmed that Germans desperately short of coal for the winter participated in such trackside adventures every day throughout the occupation zones.

Authorities tolerated the petty thievery for awhile. But when the scavengers got bolder and started shoveling coal from railcars, steps were taken to stop the pilfering. In a followup story,

Mike reported how police stakeouts waited for the coal collectors to finish their work, and then swooped in to arrest them on charges of stealing coal. Even suspects who hastily discarded their ill-gotten goods were done in by a simple look at their hands. Dirty meant guilty. A few clever ones heard of the busts and did the deed wearing gloves. In case of a raid, they jettisoned the incriminating coal plus the blackened gloves and, as a wirephoto by Mike illustrated, asserted their innocence by showing policemen remarkably clean hands.

Meanwhile, Monica was seeing yet another part of her hometown for the first time since the war ended. Axel's part of town had been spared heavy war damage, but maybe that wasn't such a great thing. The buildings were century-old, rundown hulks. Not quite slums, but close. Dirty vagrants and listless residents sat on doorsteps and curbs, owning nothing, doing nothing. They just stared at Monica as she rode by. It took considerable courage for her to stop at one point and ask for directions. A young man in a tattered wool coat over the remains of a uniform told her the way in a dialect she had never heard and barely understood. But eventually she found Axel in his new home – little more than a shed behind a commercial building now overcrowded with squatters. Axel was working under a lean-to next to the shed when he heard Monica walk up behind him, the jars of preservatives clinking in the basket.

"Well, Herr Lenin, so this is your idea of worker's paradise?" she chirped, drawing a smile from Axel.

"Some day the bosses will live here and we'll be in the palace," he said, waving to the waifs loitering in the courtyard in front of his shed. "What did you bring?"

"Preserves – peach and cherry. Mother and Ingrid send their greetings. So does Fritz. They worry about you.

"And father?"

"He has his own problems right now." Monica didn't want to get into it.

"What problems?" Axel asked, showing genuine concern.

With a sigh, Monica decided to give him the main points. She told him about the MPs, the envelope's contents and what it meant for his future and that of the entire family.

"Well, what did he expect?" Axel said with disdain. "He did some work for them, in France no less. He had to know it would come back to haunt him."

"He didn't do any harm," Monica shot back defensively. "He just worked in the school system for awhile."

"Right," Axel said, ready to end the topic. "There was no harm to the minds of children forced almost overnight to adjust to a German school system – designed by Nazis—instead of the French one they had known all their lives."

Monica didn't have a quick answer and shared Axel's interest in dropping the subject. So she looked around quickly, spotted a wooden armoire that Axel was working on as she arrived, and seized the chance for a new topic.

"What's this? Were you doing something with this?"

"I'm repairing it," Axel said with some pride. "I found some old tools and supplies in the sheds back here, and I've started working on furniture. Not just repairs, but restoring antiques too. People seem to like my work. They pay me for it. And I like it because I'm my own boss and, well, in some ways I find it creative."

Monica didn't want to embarrass her brother, so she held her delight in check. She instantly saw what this could mean, not only to his survival, but also to his financial future and self esteem. He had shown real artistic talent as a child, but never tried to develop it. Maybe this would be that outlet he needed to find his own way.

"But don't tell father," Axel said, cutting off her next line of conversation.

"Why not? He should know you've found something to do, something you can build on for the future. You should be proud of this. I am.

"That's nice, little sister," Axel said, warmed by her approval. "But I just would like this to keep going on its own. I don't want him down here snooping around or telling me it's not good enough or whatever he'd do. I'm content here, he has me out of his house, so let's just leave it for now."

Monica didn't understand the logic but agreed to honor his wishes. She went no further, leaving herself a rationalization for at least confiding in Ingrid. After all, Axel didn't say she couldn't tell their sister.

The siblings chatted a bit longer about life on Rosemarinstrasse and other small talk before Monica decided she needed to move on to her second big task of the day.

When Axel asked her where she was headed next, she made some noncommittal response. She knew any mention of her quest for a job with the Americans would set Axel off. Why spoil a pleasant visit with something that may never amount to anything?

So with an awkward hug and promises to visit again soon, Monica pedaled out of the rundown section east of the train station and on to the relatively well-heeled neighborhood occupied, in all senses of that word, by the Americans.

GOLDEN TIMES VI

After Axel, next stop for Monica was the German Labor Office which advertised openings for all enterprises – German, American and French. Monica chained her bicycle to a cellar grate and walked into a narrow, poorly lit foyer lined on both sides by bulletin boards covered with notices pinned in chaotic patterns.

Monica slowly sifted through the job postings with their brief descriptions of duties, requirements for applicants and hiring offices.

She counted 20, far fewer than she had hoped for. Some were technical – electricians, plumbers, engineers and so on. Those had no language requirements, only experience levels that could be verified. Monica felt sorry for those applicants. What were the chances of verifying previous employment if many of the previous supervisors were dead or untraceable? The posting dates indicated those jobs were not being filled too rapidly.

A few of the listings sought professionals – lawyers, bankers and even a physician. Monica saw “accountant” and thought of Fritz. But he had no English.

A few translator jobs were on the list, but Monica was disappointed to see they were in smaller towns around Karlsruhe. Commuting would be impossible.

Then she saw it. “Telephone operator. Level 3. Listing 33227-A. Hiring officer: telephone exchange manager. Duties: operating telephone switchboard for Karlsruhe HQ, OMG (Office of Military Government) Western District. Shift work—possible evening and weekend work. Requirements: fluency in German and English, French also preferred; previous switchboard experience preferred but not required. German citizens must pass background checks and English proficiency test. Salary negotiable. Housing available. See Mr. Avril, Room B-226 to apply. Closing date: open.

Monica didn't stop to write down the details. She knew she could do that job. No, she had never worked a switchboard, but how difficult could that be? She worried about her English proficiency but decided it was probably good enough and would improve quickly with practice. The salary would help offset her father's enforced unemployment, and she thought the working conditions would be good. Shift work might cause trouble with her father, but she would worry about that later.

She got back on her bicycle and pedaled as quickly as conditions would allow to the west end of the city center, where the Americans had set up their headquarters in a cluster of former banks, insurance companies and apartment buildings.

Surveying the area, she guessed that the largest building with a large sign reading OMGUS over two sentries at the entrance must be the place she was seeking. So she chained her bike again, smoothed her skirt and hair, hurried past the two indifferent sentries who ogled her more as an opportunity than a threat and headed for the central staircase. She was momentarily distracted by the clatter of strange machines in a grungy, smoke-filled office to her right, full of gritty looking characters with bad postures and gruff voices. She was glad the job wasn't there.

She climbed the stairs in a deliberate but quick pace, found B-226 and knocked on the metal door with a small pane of frosted glass at eye level. Nobody answered, so she just opened the door and walked in. A secretary, definitely German, looked up from her typewriter, seeming almost annoyed by the distraction.

"Yes?"

"Meine Name…." Monica started, then stopped, aware that she was making the wrong first impression.

"My name is Monica Baumann. I am here to apply for the telephone operator position."

Monica thought her English sounded pretty good. She was glad she had taken time once in awhile to listen to BBC and American Forces Radio and repeat aloud what she heard. It helped both comprehension and pronunciation.

"Sorry?"

So much for great pronunciation.

"The telephone operator position. I would like to apply."

"There is no opening for a telephone operator."

"But the job list at the Labor Office…"

"We always keep that posting up. That way, when we have an opening, we can fill it right away. We can't afford to have a vacancy for too long. The staff cannot cover all the shifts that way."

Monica's confident optimism deflated as she listened to the officious secretary knock down her hopes.

"Well, can I apply for the job so that I'm considered when you do have an opening?"

"Mr. Avril will have to decide that."

"Can I talk to Mr. Avril?"

"Do you have an appointment?"

What a bitchy question, Monica thought as her annoyance rose with her frustration.

"Of course not. You know I don't. Why even ask?"

"You'll have to make an appointment," the secretary declared, ignoring Monica's line of questioning.

"All right then. When can I have an appointment?"

"Mr. Avril is not taking appointments right now."

"Why not?" Monica shot back, trying to keep her voice at a businesslike level.

"We have no openings." The secretary turned toward her typewriter, signaling an end to Monica's audience.

Monica tried to challenge the load of nonsense that had just been dumped on her, but the secretary started typing as if Monica wasn't there.

In a move that would have made her father proud, she did not show her anger and did not storm out of the office. She held her ground and tried again in a matter-of-fact tone she had perfected arguing with her friends about far less serious things. Any hint of tears was out of the question.

"Please. I am here to find a job. You can hear my English. I have a good voice for phone work. I can handle pressure. I come from a good family and have a good education and background. I have never had a fulltime job before. In fact, this is the first time I have ever tried to find one. I need work. Can't you help me?"

The secretary turned, looked at Monica and a small smile appeared. Just then Monica noticed the office door adjacent to the secretary's desk was ajar. If Mr. Avril was in there, he probably heard the whole thing.

He had. And he liked what he heard.

Avril, a balding, pudgy, middle-aged man with a penchant for bow ties and mind games, was a career bureaucrat with stints at a half dozen government personnel offices in Washington. He had never risen to the management level, but that didn't stop him from fantasizing – for years – about how he would run a personnel office if he got the chance. The occupation gave him that chance. At his request and with no regrets, the Agriculture Department detailed him to Karlsruhe. He was given the telephone exchange to run. No matter that he didn't know a jack from a plug. The technical staff would handle all that. Avril's job was to make sure the phone system was properly working, fully staffed and on budget.

He stuck his cue-ball head past the door and just looked at Monica for a moment, grinning – or maybe leering. Nobody was ever sure with him.

"Would you like to step into my office, please?" Avril said, pulling his door wide open for Monica. She stepped into small but almost shockingly fastidious corner office. Books were neatly stored on floor-to-ceiling shelves. Curtains of a quality Monica had not seen for years adorned the windows. In the center of the room was Avril's desk, a fine piece, maybe even an antique. He sat in a brown leather chair, and another soft, upholstered chair faced his desk. Monica heeded his gesture to sit down.

"I think we owe you an explanation," Avril said, leaning forward and folding his hands on his desk.

"I like to test people to see how they handle stress and adverse situations. My many years of experience have helped me develop my own ways of vetting prospective employees. They may not be by the book, but here nobody cares. As long as this place runs right, I am the book."

Monica struggled with the "book" cliche but let it pass.

"Telephone operators here sometimes work under great duress. They have to speak in several languages, sometimes translating as they go, and they have to maintain a professional demeanor at all times. If they get excited or nervous or angry or frustrated, they don't do their jobs well.

"So I came up with this little screening exercise you just went through. With the able dramatics of Frau Strauss, my secretary out there, we put prospective applicants through that little ordeal to see how they handle adverse situations. Some start crying, some start yelling at Frau Strauss, and some just storm out. Thankfully, we never see them again. But the ones like you, who stand their ground and don't give up, those are the ones I want to see applying for the operator jobs."

"So you have openings? Monica interrupted, skipping all the other questions that had bubbled up during Avril's soliloquy.

"Uh, no," he replied, looking down for a second at his hands. "But we do have a rather high turnover rate. Girls find something better or get tired of the hours or get married. We average about one a week.

"So part of what Frau Strauss said was true. We do accept applications and hold the best ones for when a vacancy occurs. Would you like to apply?"

Monica at once said yes, choosing to postpone for now any contemplation of what it might be like working for this nut case. She didn't appreciate his pseudo-psychological theatrics. But she saw an opportunity and didn't want to miss it.

Avril led her back out to Frau Strauss, whose attitude was this time far more collegial. Monica was seated at a small desk opposite Frau Strauss and was given a one-page government-issue application form. She breezed through the application, happy to document the extent of her English and French studies in school.

She handed the application to Frau Strauss, who immediately took it into Avril. Monica wasn't sure whether to stay or leave, so she didn't move. Several minutes later Frau Strauss returned, giving Monica a smiling, reassuring look as she sat down at her desk.

"You did fine," she said. "If a suitable position opens up, we will contact you using the information on your application."

Suitable? Monica chose to skip a clarification and felt drained by the whole ordeal.

What she wasn't told was that Avril's scope of responsibility was about to explode. His bureaucratic realm was gaining a transient hotel for GI's heading home, a canteen to feed them, a large pool of translators for more than a dozen languages and an expanded telephone exchange. Anyone who could talk English decently was an automatic hire. He was just awaiting the final word so he could hire Monica and dozens like her. But he wasn't going to promise her anything. That was his motto: careless now, sorry later.

After a cordial thank you, she walked out of the office, not really sure what the future might hold. After all she had been through with the brain-teasing system in B-226, Monica wasn't convinced she could trust either of them. But now she just wanted to go home, tell her mother about her day, play with Elisabeth or escape into a good book.

Monica didn't have long to wait. A week later a note was delivered, inviting her to another chat with Mr. Avril. The next day she was in his office to receive a formal offer of employment. Her wage would be at the lower end of the pay scale but fair. She would work Tuesday through Saturday 2pm to 10pm. She would get a half hour break but could not leave the premises. She could bring a meal from home or purchase something from a blind German war veteran (the victim of a grenade fragment in Normandy) who had a license to sell snacks and sandwiches in the lobby. She would be paid on the last day of each month in cash. There was no talk of vacation, holidays or benefits, nor did she expect any of that. But if she passed a brief probation period, she would be eligible for agency housing in an apartment block across the divided boulevard in front of the headquarters building.

When Avril slid the offer sheet across his desk to her with a pen, she didn't hesitate to sign it. Evening hours would be awkward, but the route between the office and home was well patrolled and only 10 minutes by bike. Her work week meant

Fridays and Saturdays on duty. She shook off her gnawing concern about the effects on her social life by coldly reminding herself she didn't have one. At least she would have Sunday for the family and Monday for doing chores and running errands.

As she skipped down the stairs, out the door, unchained her bike and peddled home, she talked herself into the idea that she was really going to like this job.

"Evenings? In that district? Surrounded by those people? Unheard of! Out of the question!"

Max was in full song in his living room, raging at the news that his younger daughter was expected to work for the Americans as a telephone operator, at night. Stomping around the room, flailing his arms up and down for emphasis in front of a thoroughly intimidated quartet of Emma, Ingrid, Fritz and Monica, Max fairly gushed reasons why this could not happen. There was no way to escort her properly to and especially from work. It was undignified. She had not gone to school to talk to strangers on a telephone. It was beneath her. It would be bad for her health. How could he be sure she would meet the right kind of people there? What would the neighbors think of him as a father, forcing his pretty young daughter into menial work for a paltry wage – from the Americans, no less? It could only be worse if it was the French.

When he finally ran out of steam, he just walked to the picture window and stared out, hands in pockets, periodically shaking his head in total disbelief his favorite child could cheapen herself in this way.

Emma drew on more than 30 years of marital experience to pick the right moment to speak up.

"She needs to get out in the world. She needs to meet people. She needs to work."

"What world? That one?" Max yelled back, gesturing to the nighttime world on the other side of the picture window. "What people? Americans? How many Germans will she meet there? And what kind? And as for work, we don't need the money that badly yet. We can wait for something else."

Turning directly to his daughter, he issued his final word on the matter: "Tell them no."

An emotional stew of anger, resentment, disappointment and frustration coursed through Monica. As tears started, she jumped up from the sofa and hurried out of the room and up the stairs to her attic bedroom. She allowed herself a good cry while searching for a way to appeal the verdict her father had just rendered – a decision that inexplicably countered his earlier blessing.

Her mother helped her cause as she poured Max a glass of his favorite white wine as a combination peace offering and tranquilizer. They were alone now. She waited for him to take a few sips, then started the counterattack in a low-key but matter-of-fact voice.

"She is 21 years old now. An adult in many ways. She has no life outside this house. She will never have the opportunity for university studies. She needs to learn how to work. You gave your permission without any conditions, and now you are taking it back. That's not fair.

"From what I have seen and heard, the Americans are mostly good people. And they have strict rules about contacts with Germans. This will be good for her. Let her try. If it does not seem right, she will know very soon and will quit. She knows what to do."

Max slowly shook his head as his wife's soothing tone delivered disturbing challenges to his way of thinking. She had done it before. It usually worked – Axel being an unfortunate exception.

"The wage is decent," she continued cautiously, knowing she could sabotage her argument with one careless word. "Not much, but it will help. If things get better for us and you go back to school, maybe she can even find a flat with a friend."

Max jerked his head toward her and his face snapped into a menacing frown. Emma searched for a new tack to douse the fuse she had just lit.

"But that's probably not wise for some time to come," she continued in the same even tone. "The main thing is to let her grow a little as a person. She's ready. We're here to protect her. But we have to start letting go. Just a little for now."

One of the many reasons Max loved his wife was her knack for talking sense at just the right moment. He had done well listening to her at key times in their lives. Maybe this was time to do so again. But the idea of his little girl confined to a small dark room and talking into a headset while staring at a console of plugs and cords and lights – for Americans!—was more than he could manage at that moment. He finished his wine, patted his wife on her hand and shuffled off to bed. He didn't want to think about it anymore tonight.

Monica had a little over a week before she was expected to show up for orientation and training, so she decided to buy some time. She sat down to breakfast with her parents the next morning as if nothing had happened the previous day or evening. She knew the issue would not die, but maybe it could hibernate while she devised a way to save the job.

Max and Emma appeared to favor the same short-term strategy. The topic never came up during breakfast, or, for that matter the rest of the day.

Late that afternoon, Monica learned a whole new appreciation for the unique German concept of *schadenfreude*, finding joy in someone else's misfortune. The victim was Fritz.

Months of strenuous rubble clearing had been good for Fritz. He was getting to know all walks of Karlsruhe citizenry, and his avuncular personality made him popular with his crews. He was in the best physical condition of his life, something Ingrid noticed with approval, admiration and a regular affirmation of their excellent sex life. Contrary to barely repressed concerns her parents had when they got married, Fritz was turning out to be a fine husband, father and provider, as much as the rubble work would allow.

One act of tragically naïve curiosity changed all that.

Eva Grutz was a farm girl from near Dresden who had been dispatched by her fearful parents to relatives in Karlsruhe as the Red Army approached. She had made the grueling journey mostly on foot, except for a short truck ride that ended when the driver tried to coerce payment from the full-figured, round-faced blonde in the form of physical gratification. She left him lying in the road next to his truck, clutching his groin and gasping for air between wretches of vomiting. Farm work had given her deceptive strength, and her cautious father's martial arts lessons had rounded out her formidable self-defense skills.

Eva arrived in Karlsruhe just after the armistice to find her relatives either dead or missing. So she took refuge in a displaced persons camp and found work as a "truemmerfrau", which led her to the old slaughterhouse where Eva, Fritz and a small group of coworkers were assigned that day to start clearing rubble from the battered façade of the local landmark.

As Fritz was handing salvageable bricks to another worker, he noticed Eva about 50 yards away stop her work and sift aside smaller stones, as if to unearth something of value. With rural innocence, she lifted an 80-millimeter mortar shell that had failed to detonate. The olive-green projectile still had its fuse intact, but Eva had no idea what that signified.

Fritz did and frantically yelled to Eva to put the shell down and get away. She gave Fritz a puzzled look, shrugged, and tossed it aside.

The next thing she knew was the last thing she ever knew. The anti-personnel shell exploded before hitting the rocks, decapitating Eva and spraying the immediate area with shrapnel. Fritz and several others had jumped for cover as Eva was still holding the shell, so the survivors suffered little more than minor shrapnel wounds and assorted cuts and scrapes diving into the rubble.

Except for Fritz. The fear of the moment and the impact of lunging onto the rocks had masked the otherwise audible pop that eminated from the left side of his lower back, just below the beltline.

As he rose to rush to the others to help, he felt the first surge of crippling pain. He immediately fell back onto the rocks, leaving some of his coworkers thinking he had been seriously wounded by the exploding mortar shell. He waved them off and tried to sit up, hoping the pain was a passing cramp or at worst a minor strain.

His back quickly told him otherwise.

The ache grew sharper. Stretching in his seated position made it worse. When he tried to stand up, the full force of the injury hit him. The pain buckled his knees. He saw stars but stayed conscious, groaned and fell to the ground. Coworkers rushed to his side, and when he told them what had happened, they helped him into the back of a horse-drawn cart, the only transportation on hand at that moment. Its driver walked the horse to a clinic a half mile away. For Fritz, lying prone in the cart, every bump was hell. The clinic staff put him in a wheelchair and rolled him into an examination room, where the elderly doctor had little trouble making a diagnosis, especially with the emergence of bruising where the pain was centered.

Fritz had sprained his back severely enough to rule out any work for months. He was ordered to rest, avoid stairs, apply heat to it whenever possible and wear a girdle-like brace to protect the damaged area from sudden movement. He was given pills for the pain, a board to sleep on, and was sent home.

With the foreman's approval, another crew partner borrowed a small truck and drove Fritz home lying flat on his back in the truck bed. The pills helped, but the consequences of losing work created a different kind of anguish for Fritz. He knew what this would mean to the family.

When the truck reached the house, the colleague backed it into the driveway to give Fritz the shortest walk to bed. He helped Fritz out of the truck and then propped him up as Ingrid opened the front door to see why a truck had stopped in their driveway. Fritz's face spoke of disaster before she knew what had happened. A short explanation followed by a tortured walk up a few steps and into their bedroom ended Fritz's day, his job and, as it turned out, his career as a rubble worker.

Ingrid pulled the down comforter off the bed, put the board on top of the sheets and helped Fritz gingerly sit and then lie down. The position at first was agony for him, but as his damaged muscles settled down and another pain pill took effect, he could at least breathe easily and talk with his wife.

"What are we going to do?" he said in almost a whisper. "That money wasn't much, but it made all the difference for us.

With your father not working, and now this, we'll be in trouble pretty soon."

"Don't worry about that," Ingrid said, sitting on the edge of the double bed, holding his hand. "Money always takes care of itself. We just have to make you well again. Then everything will be fine."

"I'm not so sure," Fritz said as the pills reached their full effect. He was drowsy, and Ingrid knew any sleep would be good for him. It would be difficult to come by in the painful days and nights ahead. So she let him doze off, checked on a napping Elisabeth and then went upstairs to see her parents, who were about to have a light dinner of cheese, bread and potato salad cobbled together with bartered goods that had cost Emma some preserves and a homemade pair of knit gloves. She had already started unraveling an old wool blanket for yarn to weave replacements.

"What was all that commotion a few minutes ago," Max asked with little real interest in the answer.

"Fritz had a small accident today," Ingrid said. Both parents came to riveted attention.

"He hurt his back," she said, leaning against a kitchen cabinet and looking at the floor. "He can't work for awhile."

"How long?" Max and Emma blurted in unintended unison.

"Two, maybe three months." Ingrid was trying not to lose her composure. But she was failing miserably.

"What are we going to do?" she sobbed. "We have nothing."

"That's not quite right," Max said, not meaning to sound like a correcting schoolmaster. "We have some cash left, a few things to barter."

That's where his list ran out. So he put a piece of cheese on a slice of brown bread and munched in contemplative silence. Emma knew she had nothing to offer at that point, so she just poked at her potato salad.

"We'll work something out," Emma finally said, not sounding too convinced. "Go back downstairs and make sure Elisabeth doesn't bother Fritz."

Max nodded as Ingrid went back downstairs, just missing Monica who was coming down from her room. She walked into her parents' kitchen expecting to find dinner and instead found her salvation. Fritz's predicament forced everyone in the family, especially Max, to see what had to happen.

When Monica heard the news, she wanted to run downstairs to console her sister and brother-in-law. But her parents stopped her, saying the couple needed time together. As Monica sat down in the third chair at the kitchen table and reached for some potato salad, the consequences for her hit her like a ton of Fritz's bricks.

For once, she squelched her impulsive nature and didn't blurt out the obvious conclusion. She waited to see whether her father would walk down that path on his own. Slowly, as they batted the effects and options around the table, the solution became inescapable.

"Maybe," Max said, trying to sound nonchalant and noncommittal, "you could take that job with the Americans – just until Fritz can work again."

Emma stifled a smile and Monica flinched but kept her glee bottled up inside. She stole a glance toward her mother, who was just finishing her salad.

"It would only be as long as necessary," Emma agreed, knowing inside that this was just a momentary concession to seal the deal."

"Well, if you really think it's a good idea," he said without looking at his wife or his daughter, "I guess it will be fine. But just until Fritz can work again or I can return to school. Agreed?"

Monica allowed herself a beaming smile, nodded emphatically and said, "Agreed."

Emma cleared the table, Max went into his living room for some wine and radio, and Monica went upstairs to jump around her room, clap, laugh and cry as she celebrated the opening act of the rest of her life.

Just three days before Monica was to start her new job, Max suffered another blow to his self esteem and his family's well being. It was denazification again.

Another MP, this time alone, delivered the bad news in person around dinner time. It was a regular envelope with nothing on it other than Max's name and address.

He took it upstairs into his living room, turned on the light on his desk, put on his glasses and opened the sealed envelope.

It's message in German and English on standard white paper was brief:

"Herr Max Baumann,

"Because of the allegations made against you under denazification, the U.S. Military Government has ordered all your financial assets frozen pending the outcome of your case. Effective immediately, you will be denied access to all bank accounts and other financial assets. When it is determined that these assets were acquired legally and honorably, your access to them will be reinstated."

It was signed by some faceless official with a suitably imposing title. It gave contact information if he had questions, but there was no mention of an appeal option. Except for whatever he had in the house, he was now officially penniless. Emma walked into the room, saw that something awful was afoot and walked toward her husband. He handed her the letter.

She read it, slumped into her overstuffed chair and just stared at nothing.

"What can we do?" she finally asked, breaking a long silence.

"I have to find work. Monica will help. We can figure out something for Fritz to do when he gets better – something without physical labor. We need to look at everything we own – furniture, silver, crystal, carpets, artwork, everything – to see what we can use to barter for things we need."

Emma saw the treasures of a lifetime slipping away into some black market void, never to be seen or touched again. That started her crying. All Max could do was get out of his chair, walk over to her, sit on the arm of her chair and put his arm around her as she cried as hard as he had ever seen her cry. Maybe, he thought, this might be what finally breaks her mentally. She has been so strong, endured so many things. He could only sit there, saying nothing, contemplating various scenarios that might help them survive.

When Emma calmed down enough to stop crying, Max walked downstairs and asked Ingrid and Monica to join him in the bedroom where Fritz was trying to read while lying flat on his back.

His news shocked them, then almost panicked Fritz and Ingrid. While still relatively young, they too had collected valuables they were expecting to keep for a lifetime. They saw all that evaporating in the black market so they could feed and clothe themselves and especially Elisabeth. It was too heartbreaking to even talk about.

Monica, however, tried to find a bright spot. She reminded the assembled mourners that she was about to start a job with decent pay that could keep the whole family going, at least for the necessities. Then Fritz surprised them all by saying that he had been thinking a lot about his own future, and he thought maybe it was in Gmuend with his family's silversmithing business. It was starting to show some life, and he could do bookkeeping and other clerical tasks that required no physical strain. He could work there during the week and take the train or hitchhike home on weekends. Just until good accounting jobs opened up again in Karlsruhe.

"That would leave me alone with Elisabeth all week, " Ingrid blurted out, realizing instantly that she was not helping things.

"I'll be here," Monica chimed in, "and mother and father can help with her too if they have to."

Max chose not to contemplate a return engagement as father for a diapered toddler. More pressing matters were at hand.

As they kicked these and other ideas around, they all started feeling at least they had a basic survival plan for the months – or God forbid years – before Max was cleared by his denazification process.

Next week, when Monica started work, Max would look around for some way to make some money.

Monica's first day started with infuriating weather. She had two ways to get to work, bicycle or walking. The latter took too long, especially at night. Max would not hear of it. He had already made too many concessions.

So Monica spent her morning getting ready. She wanted her hair just right, her outfit perfectly pressed, her black low-heeled shoes shined, everything perfect. But there was one thing she could not control – December in Karlsruhe. The day started dark and wet and didn't change. As her time to leave approached, she looked out the window repeatedly, looking to the west for any break in the clouds carrying the steady cold shower. But nothing changed. So at 1:45pm, she put an ugly raincoat she detested over her favorite outfit, added a hideous canvas hat her father had used for fishing along the Rhine, and pedaled off to her new career.

Ten minutes later she was at work, cold, soaked and angry at the weather gods. Even her wavy hair had gnarled into curly clumps. She felt like going home and never coming back.

She walked past a different pair of sentries from her application day. They had the same stupid stares, even though she was not nearly as presentable this time. Up the staircase she went, leaving a drippy trail on the tiled steps, and into B-226 to report for duty.

"Where have you been?" Avril asked with a hint of exasperation as she closed the door.

"I am very sorry. The weather is awful and I ride a bike to work and..."

"I don't care about all that," he snapped, cutting her off. "We expected you this morning."

Monica flushed with embarrassment and confusion. How could that be?

"But you told me my shift would start at 2 p.m. Evenings, remember?"

"I did?" Avril looked flustered, and it was his turn for a red face. He thought for a second, and then quickly apologized.

"I guess I did. I've hired so many lately I tend to forget these things."

He turned to Frau Strauss, and tried to deflect the embarrassment onto his secretary.

"Frau Strauss, I thought we had notified Fraulein Baumann of her new situation."

"I guess not," was the icy reply as she kept her gaze on a partially typed letter in her typewriter. There had been several foul-ups as Avril's responsibilities exceeded his capabilities. She was getting the blame far too often to suit her. So she had decided to stop accepting it.

Avril's expression soured as he took the verbal shot. But he quickly recovered his equilibrium and formally welcomed Monica to her new job.

"You need to go downstairs right away to the canteen and help wait on the soldiers," he said as if it was the most logical of requests.

"Canteen?" The word, shaded with equal parts surprise and disdain, spewed from her mouth before she could stop it. "What about the switchboard?"

"O, I guess we didn't tell you that either," he said defensively, as if there was any doubt left about failed communication. "The building next door is now a billet for GI's rotating back to the states. They come here for a few days waiting for their rides home, and then when their time comes they leave and others take their place. That'll be going on for some time. The canteen in this building is where they eat. It's always busy, and we don't have nearly enough waitresses.'

Monica was getting angry. She had the feeling she had been duped, the victim of a shameful scam.

"What about the switchboard," she asked again, with more edge in her voice.

"Ah, yes. Well, we had to expand the call center to serve several new offices in this complex, and it's not done quite yet. It'll just be a few more weeks. But when it's ready, we'll put you there straight away."

Monica was livid. She was ready to launch into a ferocious denunciation of Avril, his silly mind games, his poor management style, his crazy ideas, and whatever else she could think of, but she was fortunate enough to catch the eye of Frau Strauss, who very subtly shook her head no. It could only be a warning she was about to go too far.

She thought of her father, the family's need for the money, the fact that she really had no alternative, and she ratcheted her rage down below seething.

"Who should I see in the canteen?" Monica asked, signaling an exasperated surrender.

"It's 'whom,' not 'who.' Frau Portmann. She's expecting you."

Noting the quick English lesson, Monica turned, gave Frau Strauss a resigned smile, and walked out the door, down two flights of the central staircase and into a basement facility holding about 50 folding tables with matching folding chairs, way too much smoke and the unmistakable smell of old grease in older fryers. A sad Christmas tree and paltry garlands on the walls hinted at the holidays.

Karlsruhe had become a major routing point for leave trains to Paris and redeployment to the United States. Dubbed Hotel Karlsruhe, the transit center could billet 1,000 men a night, and the canteen could serve 5,000 a day.

As Monica surveyed her new workplace, it wasn't even half full. Men in uniforms were slurping soup, munching burgers chasing meatballs around plates with dull forks, hacking away at cheap steaks with dull knives, or boring each other with dull conversation.

At the door, a plump middle-aged lady with silver hair sported a flowery dress that Monica judged totally inappropriate for winter. But the name tag was helpful.

"Frau Portmann, I'm Monica Baumann. Mr. Avril sent me here to start working."

"Ah, Fraulein Baumann. We were expecting you earlier."

"Yes, I know. I'm sorry. Nobody told me my hours or duties had changed."

Frau Portmann rolled her eyes and nodded.

"Yes, I've heard that too often in the past few days to think it's not true. I fear our poor Mr. Avril may be in over his head."

Monica didn't quite understand that phrase but guessed correctly at its meaning. That's when the first ray of acceptance hit her. She'll surely improve her English working here for a while.

Frau Portmann, a widow who had taught English and ran a cafe in Mannheim before the war, showed Monica around, introduced her to the other canteen help, and gave her rudimentary training on the menu's content, how they determined wait stations for the staff, and most importantly how to serve the customers. The meals were free, so at least she didn't have to handle money and cope with all the hassles that entailed.

Monica forgot her angst about her appearance as she started taking orders from American servicemen sitting alone or in small groups. One of the more experienced waitresses would handle any large group. Monica found the routine easy, but she soon felt an intensifying conflict between her previously pampered feet and her rain-warped shoes. Only during her brief break did her feet stop hurting that first day.

She was mercifully allowed to leave early so she could come to work "on time" at 10 a.m. the next morning. Those would be her hours, the lunch and dinner period, until further notice.

It was already dark, when she pedaled home. At least the rain had stopped. Her night vision, first noted during the pathetic antiaircraft artillery training she endured during the war, was still with her. She had no trouble steering around potholes and puddles and other obstacles, but she could not avoid the evening chill. When she got home, she hurried up the stairs and asked her mother for some tea.

"Well, how did it go?" her mother asked as her father walked in from the living room.

"O fine. I learned the difference between a frankfurter and a hamburger today."

"On the telephone?" blurted her incredulous father.

Monica then took them through the entire day, explaining the change in signals and describing her new duties as a waitress, while faithfully repeating Avril's assurance that she would work in the telephone exchange as soon as the expansion was finished.

"A waitress," huffed Max. "That's even worse."

"What was I supposed to do?" Monica fired back. "Quit? The money and everything else is the same. I can get used to it. I don't have any choice, do I?"

Max hated when his daughter was right. He had no retort, so he just went back to his living room to continue reading his newspaper.

"I'm sure it will be fine," Emma said, pouring the tea. "It could be worse."

Monica didn't respond, but she knew what her mother meant. She had seen them as she rode past the PX gate on the way home.

In the succeeding weeks, Monica settled into her routine. She actually enjoyed talking to the GI's. She found most of them nice guys with interesting stories about home. And her English was showing steady improvement every day. It was more like American, though. She picked up the Yank pronunciations for schedule, tomato, aluminum and a host of other words shared by the British. Later she would learn that even spellings differed for words like defense and color. Within a month, any vestige of BBC school English was gone from both the sound of her speech and its content. A few mischievous boys taught her some words she never heard in school, sometimes not telling her the meanings. That would later cause her a few awkward moments.

And there was the other issue she always had to keep in mind. Fraternization was legal after Oct. 1 but was still discouraged. It was a tough sell, even to pragmatic commanding officers knowing that boys would be boys, especially uniformed ones thousands of miles from home who had just emerged unscathed from a war. They were a frisky bunch, and Monica was a favorite target of teasing, compliments and not very well disguised come-ons. She learned quickly to pretend she didn't understand. If some guy pushed the limits of acceptable behavior, others in the canteen would come to her rescue, or once in awhile, particularly when a friendly pat strayed out of bounds, Frau Portmann would have to assert her authority with threats of ouster and permanent refusal of service.

The system worked, partly because the men still had some sense of military discipline, and partly because they never stayed long enough to get familiar with the staff. A few days at most, and then they were gone. Monica made sure she didn't get too friendly with any customer and kept her attire neat and respectable. She didn't want to give the wrong impression.

She usually took her breaks at the community staff table in the kitchen. It was the most quiet, most relaxed and least polluted part of the canteen. Through the holidays and into the new year, she got to know the cooks and dish washers. They were all men and either had worked in restaurants before the war or were professionals desperate for income while waiting for denazification.

And that's how Monica got the idea for Max.

GOLDEN TIMES VII

It was now 1946, but the new year brought little happiness with it. Mike's reporting was a daily litany of depressing news. The cold, damp German winter exacerbated the already miserable living conditions. Fuel for heating and cooking was hard to find. Armed guards had been assigned to coal trains to stop looting. Parks were scarred by barren patches once filled with trees. Millions were looking for shelter, work or loved ones. Failure was one of the few abundant commodities.

Adding to the gloom from day to day were the revelations from the Nuremberg trial. Germans had mixed feelings about the goals and motivations for the trial, but there was no sympathy for the defendants. Newspapers and the radio, needing no prodding from occupation authorities, gave blanket coverage to the evidence unfolding in Courtroom 600 of the Justice Palace against Goering, Hess, Speer, and 18 others. Accounts of each crime or atrocity documented by the chief American prosecutor Robert Jackson awoke memories of the 45-minute black and white film and brought on new pangs of revulsion and shame.

However, signs of recovery were starting to flicker. There were stirrings of commercial activities as small shops reopened and tradesmen found tools and materials to resume their crafts. The military government was trying to process background checks fast enough to clear Germans to run the power plants, water and sewage systems, phone network and other basic services that would help get the pulverized society back on its feet. But only one word dominated the thoughts of nearly every German that winter – survival.

Against that backdrop, Monica's idea was just about the only bright thing to be found in the Baumann household when she got home one mid-January evening. Max was still without work and could not touch his assets while waiting for denazification to run its course. Fritz was able to walk around the house for short periods of time, but he was still months away from going back to the rubble piles. Elisabeth was walking, creating a whole new set of challenges for Ingrid as she tried to help Fritz through the boredom and uncertainty of enforced idleness.

Emma kept her household in order, putting food on the table with a spartan selection of produce and dairy products donated by Fritz's family in Gmuend. When that wasn't enough, she would painfully select something from her collection of household treasures and find one of her black market contacts.

Jewelry for vegetables, a brass candlestick for bacon, a rare book for butter, whatever the market would bear.

The military government had set up its own bartering center in an old military barracks not far from the PX in an attempt to counter the black market trade. Items brought to the center for barter would be appraised on the spot and assigned a points value. The owner would then get a coupon for those points and could exchange it for anything of equal or lesser points value.

Emma had tried it a few times just before Christmas, using some of her older Belgian-made linens to trade for gifts. But she felt she had not gotten her fair share of goods in return – some new sewing scissors, a doll for Elisabeth, two woolen shawls and an off-white blouse for Monica made with silk recycled from a discarded American parachute. So she stuck to the black market contacts she trusted.

Ration cards were still a lifeline. They were supposed to ensure a daily diet of 1,500 calories. That worked out to five slices of bread, three potatoes, three tablespoons of cereal, one teaspoon of fat and one teaspoon of sugar. But transportation failures, import restrictions and a worldwide food shortage made even that meager allotment more of a target than a reality. Black market purchases, usually meat, on average brought the daily calorie total in the U.S. zone to around 1,900 calories, well short of what displaced persons received in camps and even what imprisoned Nazis could count on.

In this increasingly desperate environment, Monica plotted a strategy and mentally rehearsed her sales pitch for her father's next line of work. She had been mulling the idea through the holidays and had let them pass before testing her plan.

One evening, a week into the new year, she waited until after dinner, when Emma and Max were sitting in their living room, Max reading a newspaper and Emma knitting socks. Monica walked in uninvited, sat down on the sofa next to her mother, and launched her dissertation.

"I've been talking to the people I work with in the canteen," she said, starting slowly in an indifferent tone of voice. "They are some very nice people."

"What sort of people?" Max asked in a perfunctory acknowledgement of the topic while reading the paper.

"Older, well educated men. Many of them professional people waiting to return to their line of work, just like you."

Monica's emphasis of the last phrase caused Max to slowly put down his newspaper and look at his daughter. Now what?

"It's not very difficult work. Some of them cook. Others wash dishes. They get decent pay, and they don't have to know English or any other language. They don't even have to deal with the customers. We do all that."

Monica paused, searching for just the right path to take the conversation. Her father just stared at her, waiting for his daughter to get to the point, if there was one. He could never be sure with Monica.

"Well, I started thinking," Monica continued.

"O dear Lord," Emma interjected.

"Mother, I'm serious. I started thinking that maybe, if there was nothing else in sight for father, he might want to see about taking one of the jobs."

Max rolled his eyes, Emma slowly shook her head and Monica, anticipating their reactions, just plowed ahead.

"I know it's not the kind of work father likes to do. I know it's far below his station. But with Fritz not working and your assets frozen and Axel gone and just my salary to live on, we can't go on like this."

Pointing to the black wooden china cabinet with conspicuous gaps in the glassware, silverware and other keepsakes where bartered items once stood, Monica turned to her mother.

"Before long that cabinet will be empty. All the treasures of your life together will be gone. And even if you replace them some day, it won't be the same."

Monica quickly turned back to her father, now with urgent pleading in her voice.

"Father, you are wasting away here. Every day you mope around this house doing little chores, reading old newspapers and listening to that radio. You get no exercise, physical, intellectual or social. You can't keep going this way. The canteen would just be something to keep you active and make a little money until everything gets better."

To Monica's amazement, and Emma's too, Max did not shut down the conversation with a curt rejection of the idea. He just stared at his daughter, thinking. He glanced at the cabinet. He let his eyes drift to his wife, but didn't dare make eye contact. Then back to Monica.

"What kind of people are there?" he asked again, and Monica gave more detail this time about their backgrounds, their family situations and how some shared the problems Max was facing. She added that they even seem to support each other as they all go through the tough times. In truth, she didn't know that for sure, but she thought it probably was the case. At least it should be.

Max set aside the newspaper, leaned back and looked at the ceiling. He closed his eyes and tried to imagine himself standing at a sink washing and drying canteen dishes and glasses. Max Baumann. School rector. Respected community figure. Dish washer. He looked again at Emma, who was keeping an eye on her knitting, afraid to do or say anything else. Max had seen the strain weighing down his wife in the past few months and she scraped to keep the family and home in order. The Axel explosion had hurt her deeply, although she never challenged Max on the issue. She also had trouble keeping up with Elisabeth when Ingrid had to run an errand and Fritz was bed-ridden. She was losing weight and energy. She had endured life as an army officer's wife at the start of their marriage, then the first war, then the inflation times, the depression, the Strasbourg mess, the second war. Now this. My God, he thought, she really is amazing. But how much more can she take?

Max needed time to sort out all his feelings about his daughter's proposal. So he told her he'd think about it and they would talk about it again some other time.

Emma fought the start of a smile, and Monica masked her own astonishment and relief that she had gotten this far. She wasn't going to push it, so she merely thanked her father, kissed both parents on the forehead and said good night.

The littlest member of the family had the biggest role in getting Max to make a decision. For several days, the idea of Max washing dishes for the Americans had not been raised. Ingrid and Fritz knew nothing about it because Max felt they didn't have to know. Monica and Emma bided their time as well, not wanting to kill the prospects with a premature revival of the topic.

Elisabeth was the catalyst, along with a virus that pushed her temperature to dangerous levels and congested her lungs so badly her crying lacked the usual attention-grabbing pitch. After trying home remedies for a couple of days, Ingrid told Fritz that Elisabeth needed a doctor. Now. Fritz wondered out loud what that would cost, but all Ingrid cared about at that moment was the health of their only child.

Without further input from Fritz, Ingrid went outside in the mid-January cold without a coat and asked a passing neighborhood child to run to Dr. Karl Huber's house, tell him that Elisabeth was very sick with a fever and cough, and ask him to come to the Baumann house as soon as possible. Huber, a fixture in the district for decades, happened to be unoccupied when the message arrived, so he packed the usual necessities in his black physician's bag, dressed against the morning chill, and hurried the three blocks on foot to see what he could do for Elisabeth. It was a common flu racing through Germany that winter, helped along by homes with little or no heat and substandard diets. Children were particularly susceptible, so that was one reason Huber didn't hesitate to make a house call.

He rang the lower of the two bells at the front door, greeted Ingrid in a perfunctory manner as she opened the door, and headed straight for the small bedroom where Elisabeth was cranky and coughing. Emma had heard the visitor's arrival and came downstairs to see what was going on. When she saw Huber sorting through his bag for a thermometer, she knew why he was there and was relieved Ingrid had finally called a doctor for Elisabeth.

Huber instantly recognized the symptoms. After listening to Elisabeth's labored breathing through his stethoscope and verifying her fever, he got Elisabeth howling with a quick injection and gave Ingrid a bottle of liquid medicine with instructions on size and frequency of dosage. He assured her that in a few days, Elisabeth would lose the fever and cough her lungs clear. If not, he should be summoned again.

A relieved Ingrid thanked the physician and walked him into the foyer, where she offered him a cup of tea. He politely declined, but then they all stood there – Ingrid, Emma and the doctor – as if something was left to be done.

Ingrid took a guess.

"Naturally, we'll pay you for this," she said, trying not to sound too servile. "We don't have much cash right now, but when Fritz starts working again we'll be sure your bill is the first one we pay."

Instead of graciously accepting the verbal IOU, Huber surprised them with a different reaction. In a polite but matter of fact tone, he made it clear that would not work.

"I prefer something other than cash," he said, smiling at Ingrid and looking her in the eye. "We don't know how long it will have any real value. I prefer other arrangements with tangible goods – something that carries a value far more stable than money."

Then he stopped, still smiling, waiting for Ingrid's offer.

But Ingrid was speechless. She had not expected this, especially from the man who had treated the family since Axel, Ingrid and Monica were children. Financial arrangements had never been a problem, even during the inflation time when a wheelbarrow full of marks couldn't buy a loaf of bread.

"I, I don't quite understand," Ingrid stammered. "I mean, I'm not sure I understand what you have in mind. We don't have very much. Not even things that would have value in the black market. All that has been handled by my…"

Ingrid started to gesture toward her mother, but stopped short, realizing what she had just done. But Huber jumped at the opening.

"Well, of course, I would accept something from Frau Baumann. It makes no difference to me who takes care of the matter."

He turned to look at Emma. She instantly lost her liking for this so-called healer who seemed more like a parasite now. He didn't say anything, again preferring to give her the first word.

"I'm not sure I have anything suitable," Emma said defensively, hoping to turn the matter back onto her daughter. "I've already had to give away some of the best things we have."

Not hearing what he was hoping for, Huber lost patience and pounced.

"Frau Baumann, I remember seeing a fine Majolica sculpture of a young horse in your living room the last time I was here. It's been some time since I was here, but I remember it very well. I thought it was a fine piece."

Emma briefly let her thoughts drift to wondering whether his reference to the long time between visits meant he had expected more frequent invitations. But then the horror of his point hit her. He wanted the horse figurine. It was a fifth wedding anniversary gift from Max. He had scrimped to set aside enough from his paltry military pay to buy it for her. It was her favorite memento of the early years of their marriage. She paled at the thought of losing it, especially to this suddenly loathsome man.

"O, I couldn't part with that," she said. "It means too much to Max and me. Surely we have something else you might want."

She gestured toward the stairs, in effect inviting him up to their living room to plunder something else from what was left of their treasures. At least Max had gone for a walk, so she had time to work this out on her own.

Emma followed him up the stairs and into the living room. Huber spotted the sculpture exactly where he had first seen it atop the china cabinet. He furtively scanned the glass-enclosed upper part of the cabinet for something else but saw nothing of interest. His gaze returned to the horse sculpture.

"That is a classic piece of work," he said. "It would be the prize of my collection. I collect Majolica, you know. Have for years. It survived the war and now really is worth something. I have no plans to sell it. I just want to make my collection as complete as possible…just in case."

Ingrid had followed them into the room. She saw her mother's anguish. She had to try something else.

"What if we can't give you this piece," Ingrid said, deciding that no other option was left. "We would just pay you with something else for your collection later when we could."

"No, I'm afraid that's not acceptable. None of us knows what the future holds in these difficult times. I have to think of the present, to protect my own family. I'm afraid I'll have to insist on this sculpture. I assure you it will have a prominent and honored place in my home."

As if that mattered. Ingrid pressed on as Emma just stared at her favorite possession.

"And if we say no?"

For the first time, Huber added menace to the conversation.

"Frau Bauer, we have laws about such things. Even under occupation, people must pay their bills. With everything else happening, I doubt you would want the added inconvenience of a legal action against you. I don't think that would help Herr Baumann's situation either."

Everyone in the area knew about Max's denazification case. They felt sorry for him, but they had their own concerns to deal with right now. For Huber, it was another bargaining chip.

Ingrid's resolve crumbled. Emma saw the inevitable approaching and tears started down her wrinkled cheeks. She fought to hold herself together, but lost. She sat on the couch, covered her face with her hands and quietly started crying.

Ingrid tried one last stretch of rationalization.

"If at some later date we are able to buy the piece back from you, would that be possible?"

"I doubt I would ever want to sell it, but I suppose anything is possible in the future."

That's the best Ingrid could hope for. She rushed to her mother's side, put her arm around her shoulders and consoled her with the faint hope of someday recovering the little pale brown horse. Emma just gave a quick, dismissive wave, all that was needed to seal the deal. Ingrid got up, found some plain wrapping paper in her father's desk, and bundled up the little sculpture for Huber to carry home. He took it without saying a word, nodded in Emma's direction as he left the room, and walked downstairs. He peaked into Elisabeth's room for a quick last look, saw she had fallen asleep, repeated his assurance of a quick recovery and left. Ingrid refused to offer the usual thank you or any other farewell. She just was glad to get him out of the house. After checking on her mother, now in the kitchen and sniffling as she started peeling carrots. Ingrid went back downstairs and into the bedroom to tell Fritz what had happened. He was relieved to hear Elisabeth would be fine, but when Ingrid revealed the price they had paid, he started to bolt upright in anger, only to have his back remind him that such moves were not to be tolerated right now. He could only grimace, lie back down on his board, hold his upset wife's hand, and yet again curse his inability to provide properly for his family.

"We'll get it back," he vowed through clinched teeth. "I don't know how, but we will. Meanwhile, find another doctor. I don't ever want that pig in our house again."

Within the hour, Max returned from his walk. He had passed the house of an old friend who had found some bean coffee and invited Max to share a cup. Max saw no reason to hurry through the rare luxury of a real cup of coffee, so that's how he had missed the Huber atrocity.

Ingrid intercepted her father as he started upstairs and took him into her living room. He rarely visited that part of the house because his living room was larger, better furnished and didn't have a small child as a distraction. So when Ingrid asked him to sit down in Fritz's favorite chair, he braced for trouble.

His daughter was not as adept as Monica in shaping a conversation, so she rattled off what had happened. The figurine was gone, and Emma was very upset. Ingrid told her father not to make matters worse.

Max jumped up and started shouting shocking invectives aimed at the despicable Dr. Huber. Ingrid tried to shush him, fearing Elisabeth and Fritz would both wake up and her mother would hear his explosion from upstairs.

"I'll go see him right now," Max said in a slightly lower voice, with no less anger. "He can't do that. He talks about laws. I'll show him laws. That's nothing but extortion. How dare he play such a game. And after all the years we've known him, and trusted him. (Slight pause.) Has the whole world gone mad?"

Ingrid gently guided her father back to his seat and explained all the reasons why he should do no such thing right now. She noted how Huber had left the door open for recovering the sculpture some day and begged her father to let the matter drop for now.

Max was not mollified. He wanted a showdown. He and his wife had endured enough. This was the final straw. He wasn't going to tolerate such abuse anymore. Period.

He hurried out of Ingrid's living room and went upstairs to tell Emma what he planned to do for her. But when he saw her, he stopped in his tracks. She was still in the kitchen, partly peeled carrots on the table in front of her. Her hands held a carrot in one hand, peeling knife in the other. Both were motionless. Emma's head didn't even turn when he entered the kitchen. Tears were rolling down her face, but she wasn't crying. She was just sitting there.

Max spoke her name, but she didn't react. He walked over to her and put his hand on her shoulder. No response. He stepped behind her, took the carrot and knife out of her hands and then wrapped his arms around her shoulders, kissing her cheek, his hands caressing hers.

"We'll get it back," he whispered. "I promise."

"What's the point," she whispered without moving. "We're going to lose everything. We won't have anything left. We will lose this house. We can do nothing now. We are finished."

Max had never heard his wife surrender to any setback in their lives. Even Strasbourg, the greatest crisis of their marriage. He forgot about the figurine, Huber, everything else. For the first time in his life, he was frightened. If she gives up, what then?

He needed to think, alone. He gently pulled Emma up out of her chair, guided her to their bedroom, and helped her lie down in their bed. He put a cover over her, told her to rest, closed the curtains, and swung the door shut as he walked out. It was the middle of the day, but it was time for a cognac. He poured a stiff dram into a crystal snifter they had manage to keep, sat down in his favorite chair and tried to sort it all out.

He glanced momentarily at the spot on the cabinet now vacated by the little horse, and he marveled that such a small thing could be the catalyst for such a huge crisis. But, he reasoned, that's usually the way it goes. Now he needed to figure out a solution. The family needs money. Not a lot, just enough to cover vital expenses. More cash would not have blocked Huber's style of extortion, but with more cash, maybe they could have bought a small stash of barter goods for better protection from a vulture like Huber.

One solution kept drifting into his thoughts, and he kept pushing it out in search of better ones, or at least more palatable ones. But nothing else came to mind. So there was only one option. Every time he imagined himself in such degrading circumstances, he reminded himself of the scene at the kitchen table as his wife slipped into near total emotional disintegration. She came first. He would save her.

GOLDEN TIMES VIII

Max wasted no time putting his plan in action. That evening, after Ingrid had prepared a communal meal and made sure Elisabeth was asleep, everyone convened in the Bauers' family room. Emma was still in a daze and had hardly eaten anything. The tears had stopped, but the mournful gaze was still there. Fritz, who was actually showing signs of real recovery, was able to step slowly into the living room and sit on a dining room chair that was not as low as one of the upholstered seats. Ingrid had briefed Monica on the day's events but cautioned her to let others do the talking. Monica took the advice, but it didn't stop her imagination from racing ahead to where all this might lead. Especially for her father.

So when everyone was settled in with a glass of wine, they waited for Max to savor the first sip and then start.

"This has been a terrible day, especially for your mother," Max said, nodding toward Emma, who showed no expression. "Things cannot go on like this any longer. We are not financially strong enough to prevent people like Huber from picking us apart, exploiting our situation until we have nothing left. Only one person can do something about it. And that's me."

He looked to Monica as he announced he would seek work. He would explore all opportunities, and he would consider working for the Americans. However, he would do this only as long as necessary. When the family was on better financial footing, either because of Fritz or himself, he would quit and wait to be reinstated in his old job as school rector.

The day's events had been too traumatic for anyone, even Monica, to celebrate Max's decision. They knew it was painful and would cause him still more pain if the work he found did not suit his station in life, as was likely. So they settled for perfunctory small talk about what Max might find and how much it would help, and after one more round of wine they all went to their rooms for the night. Emma said nothing during the entire gathering, did not touch her wine, and leaned on Max as they went upstairs to bed. She had just shut down for the day, and would stay that way until the routine tasks of daily life slowly brought her out of it. Everyone gave her time and space, letting that process happen at its own pace. Sometimes she would show signs of returning to normal. Then she would glance at the empty spot on top of the china cabinet and she'd slip backward for awhile.

As everyone expected, Max had no luck testing the job market. Monica held her tongue, letting other opportunities play out to the predictable disappointment.

Two weeks after Max started his search, the canteen kitchen reached a crisis of its own when two of the dish washers quit at the same time with little notice to return to their pre-war occupations with local German firms. Frau Portmann went to Avril for immediate replacements, but he had none. The creeping economic recovery in town had started eroding the labor pool for the relatively poor paying jobs Avril had to offer. The thought of unwashed dishes piling up in her canteen kitchen panicked Frau Portmann, which in turn distressed the overmatched Avril to the point he promised new staff that he was not sure he could deliver. At least Frau Portmann calmed down. But Avril needed a break, if not a miracle.

He circulated a call for volunteers in the other units he supervised, and that turned up one man, a motor pool mechanic who had no experience working on anything built since the war started. That made him fairly useless to the well-equipped American motor pool. So he accepted a transfer to the kitchen. It was a slight cut in pay, but he had four mouths at home to feed, and he had been warned unofficially that his days in the motor pool might be short.

Monica saw Avril's laconic cry for help and rushed to his office.

"I know somebody who would love to have that kitchen job," Monica announced to Avril, as Frau Strauss pretended not to listen through the open door. "He can start right away. He's an intelligent, conscientious man with a good reputation. He's just what you need."

Avril suspected from Monica's energetic sales pitch that there might be a hidden agenda at work. But anything would be better than having Frau Portmann on his back.

"Do you know this person?"

"Of course I do," Monica chirped. "It's my father."

Avril's cautious nature kicked in.

"I don't know, Monica. Didn't you tell me he was a school principal or something? I'm not sure he'd like that kind of work."

"O, I'm sure he'd be fine with it." Monica knew she was treading on thin ice but didn't want to lose the opportunity. "He'd just be there until his old school job opens up again."

Denazification didn't enter into the conversation. Monica reckoned that if that was an issue, somebody else could bring it up. And besides, other Germans had worked in the kitchen while waiting to be cleared.

Seeing a way out of his own dilemma, Avril capitulated. He told Monica to have her father report to Frau Portmann as soon as possible. She would take care of the paperwork so he could start right away. Monica confirmed Avril's assumption that Max had no English, but he said that was not a problem with an all-German kitchen staff.

Monica thanked Avril with a hearty handshake, neglecting to mention that she still had to sell the deal to her father. She was sure that would be a snap.

Three sentences into her announcement to her father, she sensed it might not be so simple.

"I still think I could find something better," Max said, shaking his head.

"But you've been trying, and there's nothing out there."

"These things take time. I'm not sure I can see myself washing dishes for the Americans. What would people think?"

"They would think you are sacrificing your pride to take care of your family. There's nothing wrong with working there. And it would just be for a brief time anyway, just like the other men who've left as soon as they found something better or were denazified."

Max thought for a few minutes, weighing his embarrassment as a kitchen worker against the memories of his shattered wife trying to cope with a life collapsing around her. He happened to glance up toward the ceiling and stopped instead on the void that once held their favorite possession. He saw no way to avoid it. So he made up his mind.

"But with one condition," Max said, short-circuiting any exultation by Monica. "I don't want you working in the canteen too. That would just be too much for me to work under those conditions in front of my own daughter. I must insist on this. We can't work together."

Monica saw her carefully crafted deal about to disintegrate.

"Father, I'm not sure that's possible. We can't give Mr. Avril such an ultimatum. What if I just work different hours, so we're not there at the same time?"

"No, that's not going to work. Our shifts might overlap, or you may have to work extra hours when I'm there. I just can't bear the idea of you being there while I'm washing dishes. I have a right to salvage a little of my pride with my own family."

Monica saw no way around this complication and promised to talk to Avril the next day.

She went to work early and found Avril pouring over some budget documents and droning gibberish to himself.

"So, when is your father coming to work," Avril said cheerfully, grateful for the distraction.

"Well, something has come up," Monica said.

"He found another job?"

"O no, he's ready to start work here any day now."

"So what's the problem. We can't change the pay scale."

"It's not the money. It's who he'll be working with."

"He has a problem with the kitchen guys? How does he know them?"

Avril was starting to wonder whether Monica's father was worth all this.

"It's not them. It's me. He doesn't want to wash dishes with me there."

Avril looked puzzled for a second, then got it. No matter where you go, some things about fathers never change. Like preserving their stature with their children.

Avril slowly nodded once as he mulled the latest staffing puzzle. He wasn't about to do anything to risk losing Monica. He felt fortunate to have kept her in the canteen for so long. The telephone exchange was nearing completion, and he had plans for this sharp, multilingual young lady when that system got up and running.

So it boiled down to a matter of where to put Monica so her father would take the kitchen job. He looked down at the papers on his desk, pretended to thumb through them while thinking, and then noticed a memo he had first seen two days before. Having no instant response, he had just set it aside.

Military News Service downstairs was begging for someone who could work as translator, secretary and occasional teletype operator. George Martin never cried wolf. He had added some staff lately, and it made sense that he would need some support help. His memo said someone with French and English would be perfect.

"I think I may have a solution," Avril said, jerking the memo out from under the mound of papers. "Another office needs some help, and you might be perfect. How would you like to finally get out of the canteen?"

Monica didn't expect to become the subject of the discussion.

"But what about the telephone operator job? I thought I was going there next."

"You'll end up there all right. You're perfect for that. But it's not ready yet. You could take this other job just until the call center is ready. Then I promise you a good position in that unit."

Avril shocked himself by the uncharacteristic guarantee he was making. But that was the extent of his desperation.

"This way, your father can work in the kitchen, you're in a completely different job so he doesn't have to work under his daughter's gaze, so to speak. You get a little more money, a different experience in an exciting place to work, and even if you don't like it you only have to spend a little time there before moving on to the call center."

"How much time," Monica asked, skipping the tasty bait of more money for now.

"A few weeks, no more. I'm sure it will be fine. And since you have English and French, I know they will love to have you down there."

Monica did some quick thinking, decided to take a chance for her father, and took the deal.

"What is the place called again?"

"Military News Service – MNS – it's a wire service run by the military government to cover news about the occupation and the recovery. It's a very interesting place. And very interesting people."

Avril skipped elaborating on the interesting people part. No need to ruin things now.

"All right," Monica said, choosing to concentrate more on the prospect of her father finally getting some work. "When does all this happen?"

"Just to make things tidy, next Monday. I'll tell Frau Portmann that you are being reassigned but that your father will join her kitchen staff. She needs a dish washer right now more than a waitress. And I'll send your file to MNS. The bureau chief is George Martin. Look for him when you come to work Monday. The office is just downstairs, inside the front entrance. You've passed it a million times, I'm sure."

Monica needed to get to work, so she thanked Avril, said a quick hello to Frau Strauss and bounced down the stairs on her way to the canteen. She stopped on a dime on the main floor when she saw "Military News Service" stenciled on the glass window of the bureau's main entrance. O no, not that place. It looks like a pig sty and smells almost as bad.

She lingered by the door to listen. Above the clatter of wire machines, a large man chewing on an unlit cigar stood up and yelled across the room.

"Hey Mike, what the fuck does that second line mean?"

"How the fuck would I know, George," came the sarcastic response from some man she couldn't see. "You're the goddam editor. You tell me."

Monica hurried downstairs, wondering if she had made a terrible mistake.

The following Monday, Monica decided that if she couldn't work with her father, she could at least escort him to his first day on the job. Ingrid and Fritz got a chuckle out of the reversal of traditional roles. Emma saw no humor in anything yet, but she did seem more lively as she fixed breakfast for her newly employed husband.

Max, proper as ever, put on his best three-piece suit for his first day. When Monica came down from her bedroom and saw him dressed that way, she immediately ordered him to change into something more suitable for a grimy kitchen. He found an old sports coat, checked shirt and casual slacks in his armoire, and that passed Monica's inspection. She also made sure he had comfortable shoes.

Wearing overcoats and hats against the March cold, they rode their bicycles in single file to the American complex. Monica took her father to the unmarked staff entrance of the kitchen, where she summoned Frau Portmann for a discrete introduction. The hostess greeted Max cordially, happy to have her dishwashing crisis over. She showed him where to hang his coat, gave him a clean apron and asked one of the other kitchen workers to show Max his new duties. It was just like kitchen duty in the barracks in Munich, Max thought as he started his new line of work. I can do this.

For Monica, a far more intimidating and stressful workplace awaited her on the main floor.

She had dressed for the occasion by reverting to her favorite business attire – her sister's blouse, again borrowed under protest, and the wool skirt. She would learn to regret the choice.

She entered the MNS office to find no receptionist, nobody remotely looking like a secretary or someone to function as a greeter and gatekeeper. So she wandered farther into the office, ignoring and being ignored by a few people at clustered metal desks pounding on Royal typewriters or reading newspapers.

The large, middle-aged man she had seen a few days earlier walked out of a side office and toward a row of rattling black machines. Each had a black hood with signs labeling the content pouring out of them on wide ribbons of rolled yellow paper. MNS. UP. INS. AP. She trailed the man as he went to one machine, raised its hood and appeared to be fiddling with its innards.

"Good morning. My name is Monica Baumann. Are you George Martin?"

"That's me," George said, turning toward Monica and extending a welcoming hand. She almost made the mistake of shaking it.

George glanced at the hand, saw the blue splotches and quickly withdrew it.

"Sorry, I was changing a ribbon. You must be Monica. I saw your file and we sure are glad to have you joining us."

Monica thanked her new boss, not wishing to spoil the moment by reminding him that she was only temporary. George closed the lid on the AP machine and showed Monica where she would be working. It was a smallish desk toward the front, with a typewriter, phone, a few basic office supplies and a medieval looking spike that, as she would learn, had a myriad of uses, some job related, some not. A battered tin ashtray took up one corner of the desk, so she quickly moved it to an adjacent table.

"The job's pretty simple," George said as Monica hung up her coat on the wooden coat rack by the door and returned to her new work site. "If your phone rings, you answer it. Say MNS. Everybody knows what that means. If they speak German, English or French, you talk in their language. You are ok with that, right?"

Monica nodded, sorting through her desk things.

"If they ask for somebody, just yell their name. If they're here, they'll see what line it's on and just pick up. Or just tell them which line. You also need to watch those machines to make sure they don't run out of paper or need new ribbons. We'll show you how to change all that stuff. If we need something translated, we'll give it to you to type up. How's your typing?"

"Fine," Monica said, neglecting to mention she hadn't typed in years.

"Good. I'll introduce you to the guys that are here right now. There are a couple out on stories, and we have a night shift too. We're on call during overnight hours. Frankfurt is our headquarters. Any time somebody calls from there, no matter who they ask for, I want to talk to them first. I don't want some idiot editor going around me to my staff."

Monica was starting to lose the thread of George's instructions but figured they would eventually make sense. He then took her around the office, introducing her to an American reporter, Sam Buchanan, and a German technician who kept the machines working. Mort Sexton and Mike Falwell were out on assignments, and Jimmy Montgomery would come in later for the night shift. The new photographer, Gary Easterly, was out of town.

Missing from all this was an explanation of just what this office did. Monica asked, and George laughed at his failure to explain the most important thing. He gave Monica a tour of the wire machines while explaining over their clatter that the bureau covered news in southwest Germany for the military news agency that was set up during the war. Any news of interest to Stars and Stripes, Armed Forces Radio, clients in allied countries or major U.S. newspapers was written in the bureau and sent out by teletype to Frankfurt, where it was then channeled onto various MNS wires, depending on its news value. Local stories stayed on the MNS German wire. More important or interesting ones were edited by Frankfurt staffers and relayed onto wires that went to clients in Europe or the United States. A really big story would go on all wires.

"We've had a few of those," George said. "One guy here, Mike Falwell, has had some real blockbusters. He'll be here later in the day. Nice guy. Speaks fluent German. Best reporter I've ever worked with."

Monica hardly paid attention as she looked at the machines spewing out news of the day. The MNS wire had datelines she recognized from all over occupied Germany. But the others carried news from around the world, much of it from America. At least she'd have plenty to read in this job.

George heard some bells ring on the regional wire from Frankfurt and excused himself, as Monica returned to her desk. George checked the wire and then waddled to the back room where Manfred Hoep, the technician, was working on a stripped-down wire machine. George said something to Manfred, who nodded, cleaned his hands and walked out toward Monica.

"Good day," he said with a literal translation of the traditional German greeting. "I'm Manfred Hoep. I'm the bureau's technical director."

You're wearing a mechanic's blue shop coat, Monica thought, and you still give yourself a title. How German.

"Mr. Martin asked me to show you how to take care of the machines over there. You need to know how to change the paper and the ribbons."

Monica thought of George's blue hands, looked at Ingrid's favorite white blouse, and saw trouble.

Manfred showed her where the paper rolls were stored in cabinets below the machines. He picked one running low, opened the hood and showed her how to take the old roll off the spindle, slide a new one onto it, feed the paper through the roller, under the ribbon carriage mechanism and up high enough to emerge from the closed hood lid. She got that right away.

He then went to a separate cabinet, returned with a small white box and opened it to pull out two spools holding a ribbon. After switching the machine off, he deftly pulled an old ribbon out of one machine, put one spool in its holder, led the ribbon through the carriage mechanism, put the other spool in the opposite holder and tightened the ribbon before turning the machine back on.

He then gave Monica a ribbon and told her to change the adjacent wire machine. It was ugly. The ribbon unwound as she was trying to put one spool in its holder. So she rewound it again. Then she couldn't get the ribbon straight in its carriage. It took three times and some help from Manfred to get that right. The ribbon then snagged as she was trying to lock in the other spool. More digging into the works of the teletype machine finally freed the ribbon and got it working properly.

Manfred made some consoling comments about how easy it would become and walked away, leaving Monica looking aghast at the ink stains on the sleeves of Ingrid's ruined blouse. She hoped her mother could alter it for short sleeves, and she hoped for an early spring.

Monica went out to the women's room and washed her hands as best she could. The blue would not vanish, no matter how hard she rubbed. But at least it wouldn't smear on anything else.

She rolled up her soiled sleeves, went back at her desk and spent the rest of the morning looking at the wires, answering an occasional telephone call and translating a French newspaper article for George.

Just before lunch time, Monica heard the front door open and turned as Mike Falwell walked in. Right away he saw an attractive young lady sitting at a front desk and decided he had better say hello.

"Hi, I'm Mike Falwell," he said, offering a handshake.

Monica looked for ink and then shook it.

"Hello. I'm Monica Baumann. I'm just filling in for awhile until Mr. Avril finds someone permanent for this job. Mr. Martin thinks very highly of you."

"He's full of shit," Mike said, but his mind was taking him elsewhere.

Where have I seen this girl before? The face was very familiar, and the long reddish-blond hair added to the déjà vu sensation. But he had learned the hard way that the "Haven't we met before?" line was a guaranteed conversation killer, so he let it pass.

"Well, I sit right over there. So if I can help in any way, just ask. Thanks for helping us out."

He went to his desk to file his story, not seeing that Monica was staring at him from her desk. She had seen him before. She was sure of it. But she was hungry and she wanted to sneak a check on her father, so she shrugged it off and went down to the canteen for lunch.

Mike turned to watch her leave and stared at the door when she had gone. Then, with a slight shrug, he turned to his typewriter and started writing.

GOLDEN TIMES IX

Within days, the new jobs for Max and Monica were heading in opposite directions. Max had no trouble washing and drying dishes, even at meal times when the stacks were their dirtiest and highest.

What did surprise Max was how much he enjoyed the comraderie of the work place. His kitchen cohorts were men with similar interests and backgrounds, mostly professionals waiting to go back to real work. One was a teacher Max had met at school conferences before the war. They all told stories about life during the war and how their families were handling the post-war deprivations, and they soon bonded into a social club that happened to cook and clean in a kitchen.

Monica, however, was miserable. She had no interest in the news business. After just a few days she found that she did not like the noise, smoky haze and the grime of keeping wire machines fed with paper and inky, serpentine ribbons. She had learned how to strip the wires and hang copy on the appropriate spikes on the wall behind each machine. All that did was add paper cuts to her list of complaints.

Even the spike on her desk was a menace. It was supposed to hold papers she had finished translating or transcribing, but she managed to poke herself a few times, drawing more blood. On her third day, an angry officer foolishly demanding a retraction in an MNS story tried to slap Monica's desk for emphasis. He spiked his hand. The shaft poked through and didn't stop until his palm hit the lead base. He cursed and stormed out with the spike still in his hand. Monica never replaced it.

Worst of all was "punching" teletype copy. The keyboard was a problem because it was American, with a few annoying differences like the y and z transposed and no keys for umlaut vowels. It had fewer keys than a typewriter. And instead of typing directly onto paper, her key strokes punched holes in a yellow tape that was fed into a reader that decoded the holes and typed the text on the machine in front of her and any other machine on that phone line. Monica found all this nerve-wracking. Sometimes the tape would jam. Or, because her typing produced a tape but no text, she would lose her place and have to start over at the beginning of a paragraph. To type a number or punctuation, she had to remember to hit the shift key with her little finger, and then she had to remember to hit it again to return to letters, or the machine would spew out figures and symbols as it read the tape in the wrong shift mode.

The regional wire, carrying both news and messages, taught her new levels of insults and rudeness. Wire time was precious, so staffers had no time for verbal gentility. She got that message one day when Frankfurt was pressing Munich to complete a breaking story. The hub repeatedly asked the Munich writer for the lead. The harried writer finally reached his limit.

> WORKING AS FAST AS I CAN. ONLY HAVE TWO HANDS.

From an unknown bureau came the anonymous response:

> FIRE THE CRIPPLED BASTARD

Monica found no humor in such exchanges and no satisfaction in bureau work.

Her frustration was obvious to everyone in the room, but most of all to Mike. He had still not figured out where he had seen her. But he felt sorry for her or anyone new to a job. So when she was having a particularly bad time at the teletype, he walked over and offered to help.

"I don't think anybody can help," Monica said. "It's this bloody machine."

"That's British."

"This machine? So what?"

"No, the word 'bloody' as an expletive. The Brits use that. Americans have other words for that purpose."

Who cares, was her first reaction. I need help and I get an English lesson. But she was still the office neophyte so she just nodded and asked what was wrong with the tape she was trying to run through the reader. The text was all garble.

"It's backward and upside down," Mike said. "You put the wrong end of the tape in first."

He coiled the tape into a figure-eight spool by using the thumb and pinkie of his left hand as the holder while the right hand wrapped it in a smooth alternating motion. Then he put the tape into the reader at the spot where her text was supposed to begin (he had learned to read the five-hole patterns that the machine translated into text) and started the tape feed. Everything printed out on the yellow paper exactly as Monica had typed it, including a few typos.

"Don't worry, they can fix those in Frankfurt. The wire can be a pretty scary thing, but you'll get used to it."

Monica never did. Nor was she very impressed with the people around her. Other than Mike, the bureau's reporters were an odd lot. Mort Sexton was a middle-aged veteran of the American newspaper wars who had tired of the copy desk and signed up with MNS toward the end of the war. His wife worked for the Red Cross in Frankfurt, and they commuted between billets on weekends.

Sam Buchanan, in his late 20s, had returned to the United States just before the war ended. But his wartime marriage quickly fell apart and he moved back to Germany for MNS just to get away and start over.

Jimmy Montgomery, a German-speaking southern boy, was barely 21 when he mustered out of the army. But he stayed on as a local hire translator and was quickly picking up the news business. He worked the night shift, so Monica didn't see much of him. Gary Easterly was a 37-year-old former AP photographer who had left that agency for unexplained reasons. MNS didn't care; it was having trouble finding and keeping talented photographers.

A few teletype operators would float through the bureau, but the hours and the pay usually drove them out after a few weeks. Holding that part of the operation together was Manfred Hoep, a 42-year-old Sudeten German who had learned his trade as a wartime exile in London, mostly with SHAEF headquarters. He settled in Karlsruhe after the war and talked his way into the bureau job as technician and chief teletype operator.

Manfred knew his business, but he seemed to be accident prone – snake bit as the Americans would say. He caused no major disasters, but his life was one little mishap after another. He bought a car and wrecked it. He found a flat for himself and his wife and lost it to a family of displaced persons. Another flat was ruled unsafe and was torn down. He had to settle for a former garage with no plumbing. His wife hauled water from a nearby spigot every day, and for basic necessities, there was a bucket. Every wintry morning, Manfred would leave home with two bundles wrapped in newspapers. One was his lunch. The other was the solid waste from the bucket, which he would toss onto a pile of rubble or trash. Wintry temperatures would freeze it before it was carted away.

On her first Thursday, Monica was sitting at a desk in the back of the bureau near Manfred's small and cluttered workshop. As the morning passed, first Monica and then others noticed a foul odor spreading through the bureau. Office sleuths traced the source to Manfred's area. When he returned from an errand, the entire bureau staff complained in unison about the stench.

He entered the reeking room, reached under his desk and trotted through the bureau and out the back door with a newspaper bundle held at arms length.

That morning, on his way to work, he had tossed the wrong bundle.

George, Mike, Morton an Sam amused themselves for days afterward with one-liners and inside jokes, all at poor Manfred's expense.

Monica marveled at how immature they could act. Nevertheless, she found herself talking to Mike frequently when he was alone. And easily. He was 6-1, in fighting trim, with dark blond hair and an angular face. He was rather shy and obviously talented. She could tell that by reading his copy on the wire. She noticed him staring at her once in awhile, but he would quickly look away if she made eye contact.

Toward the end of her second week in the bureau, Mike covered a fire at a school that had reopened a few months earlier. Children were shivering on a sidewalk across the street from the smoking structure as fire crews labored to keep hoses from freezing while trying to douse the flames, mostly in the roof. An electrical short caused by hasty reconstruction was too blame, but Mike sensed a better story was with the children.

They were a heartbreaking bunch, some sobbing, others with blank looks of dejection on their round faces irrigated by tears and runny noses. Mike approached a young, heavy woman with thick glasses and short black hair. He correctly guessed she was a teacher.

"Good day," he said in German as she finished consoling one of the students. "My name is Mike Falwell. I am a reporter for the Military News Service."

The teacher introduced herself as Karin Martens, offering her hand to shake but otherwise wary of the uniformed American wanting to ask questions.

"Where I come from, children would be cheering to see their school burning," Mike said, hoping to break the ice. He failed.

Without overt rancor, Fraulein Martens set him straight.

"These children are devastated. This school is the only bright spot in their lives. It is a place of shelter, warmth, a good meal, protection, friends to play with. Most of them live in ruined buildings. Some have lost parents, or even whole families."

Mike knew better than to interrupt. He took notes and let her talk.

"Every morning they have to bring a piece of wood or coal to school to help with the heating. This is a huge sacrifice for some of them. It means they sleep without heat part of the night. But they do it.

"They never complain. They know everyone has the same problems, or worse. They try to look their best, even if their mothers have to tear up their own dresses to make something nice for the child. A few weeks ago we discovered that twins had been coming to schools on alternating days. They only had one pair of shoes."

Mike had always dreaded covering stories of children suffering. It hit him harder than he wanted to admit. This was no exception. He wanted to talk to a few of the children, but Fraulein Martens asked him not to.

"These children have been through a hell that was not their fault. They survived the bombings and the street fighting. Some of them start shaking if they just smell wood burning in a trash pile. A few from the east saw things no child should ever see. You Americans have been nice. But they still are intimidated by military uniforms. Leave them alone, please. I will give you any information you want, if I can."

Mike looked at the children and saw gut-wrenching quotes there for the taking. But the teacher's concern for her students trumped his reporter's instincts, so he left them alone.

After a few more routine questions, he thanked Fraulein Martens and started walking back to his jeep. The way took him past the children once more. He didn't dare look at them because he didn't know how he would handle it. They all watched him walk by and then returned their attention to their smoldering school.

Except for one boy no older than eight at the end of the sad gantlet. As Mike passed by, he looked up, quickly dug into the pocket of his tattered coat, held out a packet wrapped in newsprint and asked in a firm, clear voice, "Cigarettes?"

Mike was startled by the offer, and curious.

"How much?"

"Ten for one dollar."

Despite his freckled round face and his age, Willi Geiger had the hard look of a veteran haggler. Mike wanted to know more?

"These don't look very good. Are they homemade?"

"I make them myself," Willi said with unbridled pride. "You Americans waste a lot of cigarettes. They're never finished. So I pick them up, shake out the tobacco and then use tissue paper to make new ones. My customers say they're good."

Customers. Mike was fascinated, but Fraulein Martens had seen them talking and was moving over to shield what she thought was a frail, vulnerable child from the American reporter.

Mike abruptly pulled out a dollar bill, gave it to the boy and hid the packet of cigarettes in his coat pocket.

Trying to mask the true content of their conversation, Mike asked the first thing that came to mind as the teacher reached them.

"And what does your mother do?"

Willi thought for a second and then shrugged.

"Cry, mostly."

Manhood is no match for moments like that. Mike turned away to fight the tearing up and lump in his throat. He walked away without a word to the child or the teacher.

He drove directly to the bureau, draped his coat over the back of his chair, spooled paper into his typewriter and started typing. As he wrote, he noticed that the fire had impregnated his jacket with the smell of burning timbers. The odor reminded him of the children, particularly Willi, forcing him to concentrate even harder on the story clacking onto the off-white copy paper almost as fast as he could think.

Mike gave his copy to George for editing, but the boss didn't change much. Mike had written with emotion, something rare for a hard-nosed wire service guy. George had expected a routine fire story and instead got a fine feature, a vignette of life for children in postwar Germany, with Willi the star character.

George walked out of his office looking for a teletype operator, but none was on duty at the moment. So he asked Monica, who agreed despite her dread of the evil black contraption.

She started punching Mike's story, and when she reached his description of the burned school, she spun to look at Mike, who was hunched over some paperwork at his desk.

Now she remembered. He was the reporter who had covered the tragic explosion down the street from the Baumann home last summer. He was the reporter who got Ingrid to talk about the sad goings on in the Mueller house.

After Monica finished punching Mike's story and dispatched it on the wire, she walked over to his desk and leaned against it, interrupting his paperwork.

"You know, we've seen each other before."

Mike saw no reason to play dumb.

"Ever since Monday morning," he said, "I have been wracking my brain to figure out where I've seen you. You looked familiar, but I didn't want to ask and sound like a come-on line."

Monica added decency to her mental Mike list.

"You covered the explosion at the house in my neighborhood last summer. The lady whose husband came home with his POW comrade. You talked to my sister."

"That's it! I knew it. She got me onto a story that ended up being very big – the biggest in my career. How is she?"

"Fine, thanks. Her husband hurt his back and can't work right now, and they have a small child. But they do OK. Just like all of us, I guess."

As Monica walked away to answer a phone, Mike pretended to check his paperwork one more time. Instead, he savored the memory of the cute reddish-blonde gal watching him write down her sister's comments. Damn, I got to meet her after all.

Monica's recollection of that meeting was not as clear, because her concentration had been mostly on the tragedy itself. But she did remember thinking how serious and sensitive that reporter seemed to be. Much nicer than the pipe-smoking pompous journalists her brother had worked with before the war.

They both got back to work. But neither concentrated very well the rest of the day.

Mike started looking for excuses to chat with Monica, or have a cup of coffee with her in the bureau's small break area. It was always shop talk or banter about news of the day. But she always stayed with him in the conversation, never acting bored or disinterested or faking interest either. She had not traveled or read much, but she was bright and could make surprising literary references at times, repeating what she had learned from her father, her brother or well-read friends.

Monica had no problem with Mike either. He treated her as a colleague, not as an underling or a potential source for some good times. As the conversations got longer and more personal, she learned he could be funny, especially telling stories on himself or making fun of his hometown, some place called Kansas City. It sounded dreadful, the way he talked. She didn't know that he liked Kansas City in many ways. His problem was with one of the town's leading couples.

In her third week in the bureau, her attitude toward the job didn't change. But she was working on a genuine friendship with Mike, and it was mutual. George noticed all this and called Mike into his office late one afternoon for George's version of career counseling.

"Mike, I see you're getting along pretty well with Monica."

"Yeah, she's nice."

"Uh huh. And she works in this bureau."

Mike's expression told George he had no idea where this was headed.

"Look, Mike. Here's the deal. The fraternization rules are long gone, but I still have an office to run. Your personal life is your business, and I like both of you. But I have to watch what happens in this office. So, uh, just be careful. OK?"

That chat was well ahead of its time. And that's why Mike was confused and a little annoyed. Some bosses would declare any skirt in the office fair game and let the staff act accordingly. He wasn't sure what George's problem was, but respect and friendship overruled any resentment, and Mike said he'd keep it in mind.

That Friday, solutions sprang up for an assortment of problems. Avril had found a French university dropout who was fluent in five languages, could write English like a pro and was willing to work for the salary George could pay. He could start Monday.

Avril first told George, who hated to see Monica go but was relieved to have a permanent solution to his staffing need. Then Avril asked to see Monica. She joined the two men in George's messy office and stood rather than taking a seat in a grimy ink-stained chair. Avril told her the call center would become operational in a week. He needed her to start training on Monday. She was done with the news business and could finally take the job she had first applied for almost three months earlier.

She thanked Avril, thanked George for the experience (fudging what she really meant) and went home to tell everyone the good news. Good for everyone but Mike. He was surprised by how unhappy the news made him, but out of his funk sprang a revelation. She was no longer a bureau employee. George's odd rules didn't apply anymore. That kept him thinking all weekend.

On Monday, Monica reported to the newly expanded and recently painted call center. Four rows of consoles could keep 30 operators busy at one time. And eventually they would. But for now, it was only Monica, one other young woman, and the telephone center manager, Paul Royce. He was a retired army colonel who lived with his wife in a government apartment across the street. She was a nurse assigned to the local military clinic. They enjoyed living and working in the same place, a luxury for a military lifer and his spouse.

Paul had seen Monica's employment application, particularly her language skills. He agreed with Avril she had potential to rise higher than switchboard operator.

Monica, however, gave Paul just a brief, courteous hello before rushing over to hug the other young woman. Gisela Salzenberger had been a classmate until her family moved to Mannheim just before the war started. They had tried to keep in touch by writing, but the war eventually severed all contacts. Monica was thrilled that she had found a good friend and that they would be working together as well.

Gisela had taken a small flat in the American housing block, so after their first day of training they went straight to her place for coffee and conversation. They caught up on their lives to such an extent Monica almost stayed past dinner time and had to rush home, leaving many questions for another time.

Gisela knew how to have a good time. She had been socially active since moving back to Karlsruhe, meaning she knew the best clubs and had loads of new acquaintances to share with Monica. If Gisela had her way, Monica would be a regular companion. But Monica wasn't used to that much of a social life, so she told Gisela she had responsibilities at home and would have to limit her night life to few select outings.

Gisela took this in stride, but she insisted that Monica accompany her to the annual Press Ball, once a highlight of Karlsruhe's social calendar. Monica remembered Axel's exciting tales of the flamboyant and famous at prewar balls and had always yearned for a chance to go some day. So she gave Gisela a quick yes, but only if her friend would help find something suitable to wear. A black market search yielded a dark green satin gown that complimented Monica's reddish hair and her movie star figure. Gisela was a little jealous, but she consoled herself by counting on Monica to attract plenty of fine young men as dancing partners.

For Mike, the Press Ball had been a story to cover, marking its return as a sign of Karlsruhe's recovery. Monica changed his priorities. He saw this local tradition as the perfect opportunity to ask her out. He might have to mask his motives by telling her he was just going to cover the party and thought she might like to come along. When he thought it over, that seemed gutless. But he still might play that card if it felt right.

Mike loitered around the stairwell that Friday evening waiting for Monica to come upstairs from the phone center, which shared the basement with the canteen. He didn't want to bother her at work. Right on time, at just after 5 p.m., Monica came walking up the stairs with another young woman—taller, a little heavier with short brown hair and something of a horsy face but still nice looking. As George was fond of saying, you could drink her pretty. But Mike was focused on Monica.

She saw him at the top of the stairs and sped up for the last few steps, glad to see him. Gisela knew the rules and said hi to Mike, whom she had never met, and walked on home, expecting Monica to follow after her chat with the nice looking young American.

"How's the new job?" Mike started.

"Well, we just finished our training. We'll know for sure how it's going Monday."

"Ah, right. Maybe we should cover the center opening."

Lame, Michael. She doesn't care what we cover anymore. So he forged ahead.

"Um, I was wondering. Now that the Press Ball is back, I thought it might be interesting to see how it's done."

No reaction.

"Uh, maybe we could go to a couple of receptions too."

Her look was discouraging. Next track.

"I might write something about it, that's all. You could help me understand the tradition. If it wouldn't be too much trouble."

Monica got that "you're sweet but no way" look that deflates even the most confident lady's man.

"Mike, I would love to. But I promised Gisela I would go with her. She already bought tickets."

Mike assumed Gisela was the other woman who had just left them alone. No matter. He tried to think of a quick way to save the idea.

"Couldn't she find someone else? Maybe I could fix her up with someone I know and we could make it a double date."

Monica was no help.

"I think it's probably too late for that."

Mike saw no other avenue to explore. She had plans and that was it.

"O, OK," Mike said, trying not to overcompensate for his disappointment by sounding like an indifferent idiot. "Well, maybe we can try some other time."

"I would really like that," Monica said, trying to be encouraging but not overanxious. "Thanks for asking."

She patted him on the shoulder as she walked past him and out the door. When Gisela heard what happened, she railed at Monica for not seizing the moment.

"I could find someone else to go with," she said. "Plenty of people. If you like this guy, go with him. When's the last time you had a real date?"

Monica couldn't remember. High school some time, she guessed. But it was too late, and besides, she had made a deal with her friend and wouldn't renege on it. But she hoped he would try again. She liked being asked.

Mike, on the other hand, felt equal parts embarrassment and disappointment. He chastised himself for even thinking she might accept. Then he shook it all off and decided he would try again. After all, she said she'd like that.

GOLDEN TIMES X

As the first peaceful spring in seven years approached following a mercifully mild winter, Monica was starting to feel stirrings of independence. She loved her family and appreciated their support, but she was well past her 21st birthday and developing an irresistible urge to leave the nest.

Her employment with the Americans helped feed the impulse. Relaxed rules meant she was eligible for housing across the street in the same mid-rise brick apartment building where Gisela lived. Her best friend even had space for a roommate and had initially planted the relocation idea of by inviting her to move in. As their friendship grew, and Monica's contacts with young men, mostly Americans, increased thanks to her gregarious friend, the idea of moving out of the Baumann home grew to an unstoppable obsession.

This was not a concept to spring on her parents without careful planning. So with Gisela as a role player, Monica rehearsed how she would break the news. Gisela was good at this game and tossed out a realistic array of objections and arguments that Monica could expect from her parents, mostly her father. Even though his attitude toward Americans had softened a bit because of his canteen work, he would surely recoil at the thought of his daughter living unsupervised among strangers, open to the questionable influence of that party girl Gisela.

So on the last Sunday of winter in 1946, Monica came down from her attic room to the midday feast in the first floor dining room, wearing a properly conservative cotton dress. Fritz and Ingrid would be hosts and could be counted on for morale support, or at least she hoped so, even though they knew nothing of Monica's plan.

Most of the meal featured small talk and the usual assortment of political and social commentaries by Max and Fritz, who never disagreed on the major issues. As Ingrid and Emma cleared away Ingrid's fine porcelain dinner plates, which had been declared off limits for barter, Monica waited for a lull or cue to make her announcement.

Max obliged. "Monica, you haven't said much. Is something on your mind?"

"Well, actually father, there is."

Emma and Ingrid, back from the kitchen, sensed something important was unfolding and sat down. Max and Fritz stared at Monica, almost daring her to continue.

"Ever since the war ended, I have been living in this house, placing a burden on all of you. I know that my earnings help buy rationed goods, but I still feel like I am in the way or distracting you from more important things.

Monica had no idea what those could be, but she kept to the script she had rehearsed with Gisela.

"I am almost 22. I have been through a war. I know how to take care of myself. I have my own job and earn my own money. I think I am ready to live on my own."

Without looking up to see the frowns bearing down on her from around the table, she forged ahead.

"I am eligible for housing across the street from my work. My good friend Gisela has asked me to move in with her. I will be safe there. I should be close to my work in case I am needed at the call center for an emergency. I will still be able to help you financially because I will have no rent to pay. I would still be close to home and would come here often. I don't want to abandon you. I just think it is time for me to move on and start a life of my own."

That was it. She stared at the empty table in front of her for a few seconds, waiting for some kind of reaction. When silence persisted a few more seconds, she slowly raised her head to look at her father. She was braced for an explosion.

Instead, she saw his large, balding heading nodding slowly as he thought about her proposition. Everyone else was looking at him too. What they thought was of no consequence at that moment. Max would have the first word.

Monica stole quick glances at the others around the table and then locked her gaze back on her father.

After what seemed like a lifetime, Max finally spoke.

"I wondered when this would happen. I've been expecting it. Your mother and I have talked about it. This is very difficult for us. We don't like the idea of you leaving this house."

Monica's heart sank, but not for long.

"However, we think it is time for you to go your own way. We know you won't abandon your family. But you are a grown woman, and living here prevents you from finding your own life. You know you can come back any time. But if you want to be Gisela's roommate, then do so. She may be flighty, but I think she is a good girl from a good family. I trust both of you to behave properly."

Monica knew a whoop of celebration would be inappropriate. So she lunged at her father to hug him. He smiled and patted on her shoulder without saying a word. Emma fought tears, knowing several family milestones had just been passed. Monica had declared and won her independence, and Max had suppressed grave misgivings to let his youngest child have her way – just as he always did.

"What's for dessert?" Fritz chimed in, hoping to preempt further discussion and thereby seal the deal. Ingrid rose to prepare the fresh fruit concoction without saying a word. She was not in a celebrating mood. Once again, Monica had gotten her way without a fight. If Ingrid had tried something like that before she got married, Max would have handed her head to her. Now Monica can go off and live the party life while I'm left here with a baby and a damaged husband. So what if she contributes to the household budget. That's just her way of buying her independence.

Ingrid caught herself in mid-thought and was started feeling guilty about her jealousy. But she shrugged off the guilt. Sometimes life isn't fair, she thought, and this is one of those times.

The following Saturday, the season's first warm, clear day, Mike happened to be walking by when he saw Gisela and Monica unloading some clothing and other personal items from a jeep driven by one of Gisela's growing band of American friends. Gisela and the GI each grabbed a box and headed into Gisela's building, leaving Monica struggling to control an unruly pile of dresses on hangers.

"Need help?"

"Hi Michael," Monica said with a grateful smile. "I can't seem to get hold of these things. Thanks."

She grasped a few dresses and thrust the pile at him, keeping her other hand on the remaining mess. He trapped them with a hugging motion that made him feel slightly silly. She got control of the rest, and they both headed inside.

"What's happening here?" Mike asked as he walked through the open door of Gisela's place and saw the clutter. "Are you moving in?"

"Yes. I wanted to get out on my own, and my family agreed. Gisela invited me to room with her, so that's what I'm doing. It's time I have my own life."

With that final declaration and a curt introduction for Mike and the GI, Gisela pulled out some glasses and a bottle of wine, and they toasted Monica's liberation.

As the others chatted, Mike started plotting. Now she lives just a block away. We'll see a lot of each other for sure.

"We have places to go this evening," Gisela said, bringing Mike back to reality. "We should be getting ready."

That was courteous but unmistakable – time for Mike and the other guy to go.

"I live in the next block," Mike said to Monica as he turned to leave. "Maybe we can get together once you're settled here."

"That would be nice," Monica replied with an easy smile and forced neutrality.

Nice, maybe, but not easy. In their first week as roomies, Gisela kept Monica busy. They went out almost every night to a club or bar or party. Gisela collected invitations at will, and she liked having her pretty roommate along as guy magnet and, when needed, a shield.

This pace was something new for Monica. At first, it was exciting. Then it started to wear her down. She liked socializing and meeting new people, but not every night. Weekends provided more than enough time for such things. During the week, her work was strenuous enough. At night, she just wanted to relax, reading or listening to the staid, almost bombastic American-run Radio Luxembourg or, more often and more surprisingly, Soviet-run Radio Berlin with its superior blend of modern music and interesting news about the rest of Germany.

Gisela didn't argue, respecting Monica's different social habits and not wanting to jeopardize their friendship.

Mike knew nothing of this when, while walking back from dinner one evening, he saw Gisela leave the building and jump into a Chevrolet with American plates, but without Monica.

On pure impulse, he entered the building without ringing the apartment's bell first and walked up the flight of stairs to the apartment. He knocked, not knowing what to expect or even what he might say.

Monica opened the door a crack, saw who it was and opened it further.

"Hi Mike. What brings you hear?"

"I saw Gisela go out without you, and I thought you might be home. So I figured I'd just drop by and say hi."

Monica was wearing a housecoat and slippers, and her hair was knotted in a bun. Hardly her A package.

"That's nice of you, but I'm really a mess right now. I wasn't expecting visitors."

"O, well that's OK. I just wanted to make sure you're all right." Lame, but the best retreat he could think of.

"If you're not doing anything Saturday night, maybe we can go see a movie. The American theater has a great one – The Maltese Falcon."

"Sure, that sounds like fun. I've heard about it."

"OK then. I'll be by about 7."

"OK, see you then," she said as she slowly closed the door.

And that's how it started.

They sat through "The Maltese Falcon" and then talked about it for more than an hour at an American club near the theater. Prompted by the film's unsavory characters and dark plot, she asked question after question about life in America. When Mike realized that she was getting the wrong impression, he countered the film's message with balancing stories about his time growing up in Kansas City. A few days later, the U.S. occupation top brass, reacting to a flood of complaints, pulled the film, saying it gave Germans the wrong image of America.

Mike and Monica were what some would call a "good fit." She liked to talk, and he liked to listen. He would correct her English at times, particularly when she would misuse words that sounded like German ones but had different meanings. "Will," meaning "want" in German, was a common problem for her. So was her old nemesis "sehen", meaning "see." Monica didn't like to be interrupted. But she accepted Mike's help as genuine, not condescending.

She also appreciated his wit, his understanding of German history and culture, and most of all his good manners. He did not play the macho game so many other American men tried, and he avoided war stories unless she asked. Then he would always use the passive voice, describing what happened in a certain combat situation, but not who did what to whom. Usually he'd try tasteful humor, making fun of compatriots who got themselves in harmless but embarrassing situations, such as buddies who, through their own carelessness, suffered minor wounds on their backsides or ran their jeeps into "honey wagons" full of raw sewage. He kept the grim stuff to himself, as so many other veterans did.

Because of Mike's tact and decency, Monica never felt defensive with him. With so much turmoil and depravation around them, she found her time with him tranquil, relaxing and enjoyable.

Their next date was to a club that had just opened and claimed to be a haven for jazz lovers. Mike, whose Kansas City roots put jazz in his blood, thought Monica might like to hear a live performance of the unique American art form. She accepted.

It was awful. The group had just formed and gave the customers little more than an on-stage rehearsal. After a brutal half hour, Mike and Monica relocated to a quiet kneipe in their neighborhood and just talked. About the occupation. About the tighter rations. About the black market. About American and German film stars. About classical music. And even a little about Monica's wartime experiences. Mike railed at the officer who had abandoned her group in Vienna. He tried to explain the fighter pilot's reason for strafing the farmer the day almost a year earlier when she cycled to Gmuend. But he sensed danger and quickly changed that subject.

Their third date was to a reception hosted by one of the officers in charge of OMGUS in Baden state. This required a new outfit for Monica to match Mike's dress uniform. Gisela found a seamstress in need of cloth and traded some old curtains for a dress that Edith Head would have envied.

Mike stood by Monica like a prop most of the evening as one officer after another chatted up the attractive German redhead who spoke near perfect English. Mike's only interaction with his date was for introductions or when Monica struggled for the right word and asked Mike's help. He didn't mind a bit. If she was a star, he was basking in the glow.

A couple of weeks later came Mike's birthday. After consulting with Gisela and contemplating all the possible ramifications, Monica decided to offer Mike a dinner prepared in his apartment as a birthday gift. She also bought him a small pocket knife as a present, but dinner was the main event.

Mike was happy to accept, leaving both of them just short of terrified. Monica had not practiced her cooking skills lately, and Mike had not been the most fastidious housekeeper. So in the days leading up to the dinner, Monica tried several basic dishes on Gisela, using ration goods plus a few things from Ingrid's pantry. Monica knew she could have asked for some PX items from Mike, but that would have been cheating.

The winning menu was a red cabbage and cucumber salad followed by beef rouladen and homemade noodles called spaetzle. Gisela found a suitable German red wine, and Monica capped it with a homemade apple tart.

With Gisela's help, Monica had prepared as much as she could beforehand. So on the night of May 4, Monica and Gisela paraded the ingredients down the street and into Mike's apartment, where he had hired a maid the day before to make the place presentable and get his kitchen in order. All the necessary utensils were on display so that Monica could start her project without the awkward delay of searching through cabinets and drawers for this and that. Mike poured wine for both, which served more as a sedative than intoxicant.

Despite Monica's unfamiliarity with Mike's kitchen and his latent gas phobia, everything went as planned. The salad was fresh and crisp, the rouladen tender and flavorful, the spaetzle (the most labor-intensive dish) firm but not pasty or rubbery, and the apple tart light and refreshing. Mike had set aside some bean coffee for after dinner, and he poured Monica a celebratory sherry to toast her culinary success. Mike would deal with the dishes later.

The conversation throughout dinner had been almost entirely about dinner. Where things were bought, how they were prepared, this history of the dishes. Now, as they sat on the lumpy sofa in Mike's living room savoring the afterglow of a fine meal and good spirits, each found small talk more and more difficult. So the silent pauses got longer between comments. Each looked at their glass as if it had grown a new life form.

Mike couldn't stand it any longer. He put down his glass, put his arm around Monica and without a word kissed her briefly and lightly on the lips.

"Thank you for the best birthday dinner I've ever had," he whispered, meaning every word.

Monica said nothing. She just leaned toward him and kissed him back, placing her hands gently around the back of his head. This was no patronizing "you're welcome" kiss. Monica had never kissed a man this way, and at that moment she wasn't sure she ever wanted to kiss any other man in her life.

The embrace tightened, the kiss endured and deepened. They savored every second, thinking of nothing other than the gentle pleasure of the moment. No lunging or groping or testing or defensive blocking. Nothing like that was attempted, intended or wanted.

After an unmeasured amount of time, they came up for air, sipping their sherries and just looking at each other with satisfied smiles of people who had just discovered something important about themselves.

Mike, his Midwest shyness kicking in, felt compelled to say something, anything. So he quietly came up with the best he could manage at the moment.

"So how did you learn to make those noodles?"

For Monica, it was like a splash of cold water. She still did not know him well enough to understand is penchant for diversionary conversation when he felt vulnerable.

She laughed, looked at him smiling, and shook her head.

"Is that really what you want to talk about?"

Recognizing the absurdity of his question, he could think of only one way to recover. He leaned toward her and they kissed again, another long, easy, gentle kiss enhanced by a soothing embrace.

The rest of the evening was a mixture of sedating conversation interrupted by intoxicating kisses. Slang would call it making out. But it was more than that. They said nothing about their feelings for each other, the future or anything nearly so deep because they would not have known what to say without sounding insincere or juvenile. Both realized that this first revelation was to be savored but not analyzed. There would be time for that later if something permanent grew from this evening.

Mike knew that how this evening ended would go a long way to determine the course of future evenings. So he made the first move to bring the curtain down.

"It's late, and I have to work on a feature in the morning. I can't thank you enough for this wonderful evening. I would like to see you again, and often."

"I want that too," Monica replied, putting her hand on Mike's cheek as they rose from the sofa. "I also had a wonderful evening. I'm glad you liked my cooking."

With that, Mike escorted her out the door and down the street to her building. He walked her to the door, and they kissed good night.

Mike went back to his apartment and pulled out the Jack Daniels for a nightcap to celebrate his birthday once more and to toast the extraordinary events of the evening. She was an amazing girl. He thought about the first time he had seen her the night of the explosion on her street and traced the course of the relationship since then. He took his time. He liked the feeling.

At the same time, Monica sat curled up in Gisela's overstuffed chair, trying to sort out her feelings about what had just happened. She had feelings for Mike, but she didn't know what they represented. Was she honestly falling in love with Mike? Or was she in love with being loved? Or was she loving the more pragmatic potential of a relationship with an American who could improve the quality of her life in many ways. She rejected the last idea out of hand. Her feelings weren't materialistic opportunism. They were something far more meaningful.

When Gisela came through the door, smelling of cigarette smoke and beer, she was still sober enough to know her roommate was in a quandary. When Monica told her how the evening had ended, Gisela unleashed a schoolgirl squeal and clapped her hands.

"Are you in love with him? Does he love you?"

"I don't know. This is all so new for both of us."

"Did you do anything else but kiss?"

"Gisela! Of course not. And he didn't try."

"Ah ha. That's serious. That means he really cares."

"Maybe. Maybe not. I don't know."

Then, with fatigue freeing her tongue, she added, "I hope so."

Gisela walked over to the chair, patted Monica on the shoulder and said good night. Monica didn't move, and eventually, as she tried to sort out her feelings, she dozed off in the chair.

From then on, their meetings were frequent, and the tone of their voices toward each other was more relaxed, less formal. They talked as close friends, not professional acquaintances or social prowlers. Gisela grew accustomed to making her party rounds without her roommate. Anyone asking about Monica was told she had other things to do. Gisela figured it was nobody's business.

Mike found himself planning his days around Monica, not his job. His reporting and writing were as strong as ever. But George started noticing that requests for off-hour work that once were accepted now were met with excuses or suggestions that someone else get the assignment.

One part of George chafed at this development, expecting a pro like Mike to take any assignment without question. But George also knew Monica and had seen them together in some of the local cafes. He decided Mike had earned some slack, and the bureau had several other good staffers who could cover for Mike.

For Monica, as her relationship with Mike deepened, so did her anxiety over the inevitable challenge both would face – telling her family. Monica knew her father's attitude toward Americans had softened in the canteen kitchen, but it had not reached the level of acceptance. Max thought the GI's that passed through the redeployment center on their way home were undisciplined, wore sloppy uniforms and showed no respect for superior officers or anyone else in authority.

And Max had some impressive company with those ideas. OMGUS commanders and civilian officials had seen a drop in efficiency, discipline and morale as American soldiers eager to go home were delayed by occupation duty or the lack of available transportation. In some areas, crimes by Americans against German civilians were increasing, making the occupation itself more unpopular with the locals, wiping out the positive effects created by CARE packages and other positive innovations of a benevolent conqueror.

Monica had been careful not to meet Mike in the canteen or any other location where her father might see them together. Just looking at them in an unguarded moment would convince anyone that they were getting very serious.

One night in Mike's apartment, Monica worked up the courage to raise the issue.

"You know, we should tell my parents about us," she said, hoping to get quick agreement.

"Yeah, I suppose we're at that point," Mike sighed. "How are we gonna do it?"

Monica wasn't ready for such a rapid move to the next step. So she just shrugged and stared at her glass of wine in her hand.

"Should we tell them together?"

"No way. That has to come from you. After that, if everything is OK, I should formally meet them. Invite me to dinner."

Monica knew that was the proper scenario, but it scared her. She cringed while contemplating the image of her father eyeing Mike across the dinner table, judging every move and every inflection in his voice, wrestling with the notion of his little girl with some overpaid, oversexed, undereducated cowboy from Kansas. Never mind that Mike had never ridden a horse or touched a cow, and had rarely crossed State Line Road into Kansas.

"When?"

"Probably the sooner the better."

He slid closer to her on the sofa, put his arm gently around her shoulders, and said the obvious.

"We've got something here that's going to last awhile. Or at least I hope it does."

She nodded, affirming his assessment of their relationship.

"It's time they should know. We don't want them finding out from someone else. That would be a disaster."

"I'm supposed to have dinner there next Sunday."

"Tell them next Sunday, and we'll take it from there."

GOLDEN TIMES XI

It was Ingrid's Sunday to host the family dinner. The setting had worked for previous big events, so she allowed herself some rare superstition and counted on it one more time.

Monica again rehearsed her lines with Gisela and even a few times with Mike, who did a remarkable job as a stand-in for her father. She chose the same dress she had worn for the moving out pitch and rode her bicycle to the house in splendid early summer weather.

A major complication confronted Monica when she walked into dining room. In the adjacent sitting room, Fritz was having a political debate with Axel. They weren't arguing yet, but fuses were lit.

She greeted her brother with a kiss on his forehead and hurried to the kitchen.

"You didn't tell me Axel would be here," Monica moaned to Ingrid as she pulled a roast from the oven. Monica was so upset she didn't even think to ask where Ingrid had found such a fine piece of pork.

"Since when do I have to get approval for my guest list from you?" Ingrid said. "He's been doing pretty well, from what I hear, so I thought we could invite him to dinner without fear of being asked for money. It's been a long time since father and Axel have spoken."

"Did father agree to this?"

"Only after a long talk with me and mother. He eventually said yes when we promised him the dinner would be peaceful and free of controversy."

Monica had to sit down. Ingrid saw her sister was upset but had no patience or sympathy, now that the meal was nearly ready.

At Ingrid's request, Monica called Fritz, Axel and her parents to the table. Fritz and Axel kept up a running discussion as they sat down. It stopped abruptly when Max and Emma walked in, both dressed as if they were attending a funeral.

Max sat at the head of the table, with Emma to his right and Monica to his left. Axel was next to Monica, leaving his good left arm free for eating. Ingrid was next to Emma with easy access to the kitchen or Elisabeth, and Fritz was at the far end of the table opposite Max. Everyone sat stiffly silent for a moment, as if waiting for some signal to start.

Max sounded it.

"How are you Axel? I understand your antique restoration business is picking up."

"It's not bad," Axel said, raising a glass of white wine as he spoke. "As bad as the economy is, there always seems to be a market for antiques. The rich might as well enjoy them while they can."

Max flinched and Fritz was ready to answer the slur on capitalism when Ingrid shut off further debate.

"Take some roast before it gets cold, and pass the sauce please, Monica."

It was a simple dinner comprised of easily obtained items, either with ration cards or on the black market. The roast had come from a butcher in Gmuend who wanted fruit preserves. Noodles were easy to find, and the salad was a mixture of vegetables from street vendors and Emma's garden. It was a rare feast for the times and good enough to stop all talking.

They ate in silence for several minutes until Max turned to Monica to try small talk.

"How are things at the call center? I don't see you in the canteen very much anymore."

Max still forbade contact, but he would often see his daughter from his post at the kitchen sink.

"We are very busy, father. I sometimes have to work extra hours and even extra days. But I don't mind."

"They ought to put you in charge," Axel injected, happy to toss his little sister a compliment. "The only Americans left here for the occupation are lazy or stupid."

Axel never saw it coming.

"They are not," Monica shot back. "They are fine, generous people. Look how they are treating us. We started a war and killed the Jews and destroyed most of Europe and they give us order and safety and work and CARE packages. What do you know about Americans?"

Axel didn't speak quick enough.

"I see them every day," Max said, "and I'm not impressed. They are not disciplined. Their uniforms are a mess. Some look like refugees. Sometimes I wonder how they won."

Ingrid and Emma kept busy with their pork and noodles, going slowly to give them an excuse to stay out of the growing debate.

"They were good fighters," Fritz said. "They surprised us. We were told they would be no match for us. Look what happened."

"They're nothing compared to the Russians," Axel jumped in, seeing a propaganda opening. "The Russians beat us, not the Americans. And they did it because they have a superior political system."

"Just a moment." It was Max's turn. "Their system is brutal. Stalin kills as many of his own people as Hitler did. Communism is a charade. Stalin uses it to camouflage his totalitarian regime."

Axel squirmed in his chair, trying to decide whether to pursue an unwinnable argument or just let it slide.

Monica came to his rescue.

"I don't know about the Russians. All I know is that the Americans here are good people and they have been very nice to me and to father."

Axel munched a piece of bread and Max nodded in silent agreement, bringing the eruption to an end before it reached its full furry.

As Emma and Ingrid rose to clear the table, Monica decided the moment was as good as any, and seized it.

"In fact, there's one American who has been especially nice to me."

Emma and Ingrid froze. Max, Fritz and Axel snapped their gazes toward Monica, and she knew there was no turning back.

"Who?" Max said it, but everyone wanted to.

"His name is Michael Falwell. He is a journalist with the Military News Service here in Karlsruhe. We met when I worked for a couple of weeks at the bureau."

"An American AND a journalist," Max said almost to himself, shaking his head in disbelief. "What is your relationship with this man?"

"We have been seeing each other quite a lot. We really get along well. He is kind, polite, gentle, serious, respectful…"

"A real Boy Scout," Fritz said to himself with a sardonic smile.

"A gentleman," Monica fired back. "He is respected in his profession and he has real writing talent."

"So he's a civilian?" Axel asked, knowing that combat journalists were being phased out of occupation media jobs.

"No, he is still in the army. He is a sergeant."

"Was he in combat?" Axel asked, suddenly aware that his sister was serious.

"Yes, from Normandy to here. He wrote news articles about the fighting."

Axel: "Did he fight?"

"I think so, but we don't talk much about that."

Max: "What do you talk about?"

"Lots of things. Politics, music, work mostly."

Max: "Does he speak German?"

"Yes, very well. Almost fluent."

Fritz: "Where is his family home?"

"Kansas City. It's in the middle of the country. He doesn't like it much."

The machine-gun questioning was starting to annoy Monica. But she held her temper and her ground, knowing that she might otherwise jeopardize her main objective.

Max: "Have I seen this young man?"

"I don't know, father. But I didn't think that was the place you wanted to meet him."

Max: "Thank you for that at least. How serious are you about this American?"

"I don't know how to answer that yet. But I do know I think you should meet him. Here. We should invite him for dinner."

Everyone looked to Max for their cues. He was quick to respond.

"Out of the question. I won't have an American here. What would people say?"

That was Emma's cue.

"Since when do we worry about what people say?" she said, casting a challenging glance at her husband. "If Monica likes this man, we should meet him."

Max was starting to weaken. Ingrid nodded in silent agreement. Fritz remained noncommittal. Axel misread the table.

"I wouldn't sit at the same table as an American GI," he growled, "especially in this house."

Max took the floor.

"This is not your house. You left, so you lost any right to say who comes here."

Axel reddened but said nothing.

Max turned to his youngest child and just looked at her for a moment.

"Is this really important to you?"

"Yes father. It is very important."

More silence. Everyone looked down at the empty table in front of them, except Emma, who gave Max a long-ago perfected look of anticipation mixed with defiance.

Max sighed, looked at Emma and then turned to Monica.

"It probably would do no harm to meet the man. Invite him to dinner next Sunday."

The suspense around the table eased, except for Axel's stunned realization that an American would be sitting in his seat next Sunday. Axel rose, said he had work to do, and left.

Max's sad eyes watched his son walk out. Typical, he thought.

Then Max turned to Fritz, and in a rare concession asked his son-in-law for his opinion.

"Well," Fritz said with a wry grin, "I think it will be all right. But just to be safe, I'll count the silverware after he leaves."

That line got a bigger laugh than it deserved because of the tension it released. Monica yelped and gently punched her brother-in-law on the shoulder and then skipped into the kitchen to help with dessert, celebrate her latest triumph and start planning the next pivotal day in her life.

The next six evenings were filled with long, intense rehearsals, but this time only Mike and Monica were the players.

For Mike, it was like cramming for finals. Monica tried to teach him all about her relatives, their likes, dislikes, quirks and conversation mine fields to avoid. She gave him a primer on her father's life and career, his military service and even his denazification troubles. He learned that Emma and Ingrid would not be major players in the table talk, and Fritz could be alternately political and frivolous, depending on his mood and motivation.

Mike knew enough about German culture to know Monica's father was the key, as in most societies. So he concentrated on Max facts while breaking out his German grammar book just to refresh his memory on some of the more confounding rules of the language, such as case endings and noun genders.

After checking regulations just to be sure, he had his dress uniform cleaned and pressed. He arranged to borrow George's Volkswagen so he would spare his hosts the embarrassment of a jeep parked out front. He brushed up on his World War I military history as well as the saga of the Weimar Republic and the inflation times. He found some classical recordings and refreshed his memory on Beethoven and Schubert. He tried to read Goethe, but just like in school he gave up. He visited a neighborhood wine shop for a crash course on regional brands and vintages. In the American library, he found a book on German art and tried to memorize trivia about the masters.

Monica mercifully stifled giggles when every evening she would knock on Mike's door and he would greet her with a torrent of new minutia he had packed into his overworking mind that day. She loved how serious he was taking this. She loved how hard he was working to impress her family. She was increasingly sure that she just plain loved him.

They decided they should go to the house separately on Sunday to assuage any suspicions about cohabitation or anything close to that. H-hour was 1300. So late that morning, after seeing Mike once more and giving him all the emotional encouragement she could, Monica rode her bicycle to her family home, and there she got dressed in her former attic room that still held some of her clothes.

Monica again let superstition creep into the process. She insisted on a menu featuring rouladen and spaetzle. Ingrid prepared the meat, but Monica asked her mother, a spaetzle specialist, to handle that dish.

As the hour approached, Max and Fritz retired to the ground floor sitting room while the women put the final touches on the midday feast. Everyone was dressed for a wedding, an irony not lost on Fritz. But he wisely decided now was not the time for a wisecrack, particularly on that subject.

Promptly at 1 p.m., a blue Volkswagen drove up the street and came to a screeching halt in front of the house. Wonderful, Monica thought, a fine first impression.

The door bell rang, and Monica answered.

"Sorry about the stop," Mike whispered as he kissed her. "Bad brakes."

Monica was past that. She just wanted to stare at Mike for a second. His dress uniform was perfectly ironed, his tie knotted according to regulations, his service hardware impressive but not ostentatious like the Russians did it. He looked gorgeous.

She walked him into the foyer, where something of a receiving line had formed. Elisabeth had been banished to a neighbor's house for the afternoon to prevent any unfortunate distractions. So that just left the four adults.

Monica first introduced her mother and sister, who shook his hand and, in a reflex action that annoyed Max, curtsied. According to protocol, Ingrid was the official hostess, so she received Mike's bouquet of white and yellow flowers. Next came Fritz, who instantly felt some kind of comradeship with Mike and greeted him warmly but within the bounds of propriety. Last, Mike stepped toward Max and before the dour father could say anything, Mike said in perfect German, "It's an honor to meet

Monica's father and her family. Thank you very much for this invitation."

Max was nonplussed by Mike's assertive greeting, so he simply welcomed him and gestured toward the sitting room. Mike heeded Max's gesture to sit and accepted a beer that was poured by Fritz. Max opened the small talk by asking Mike how he liked Germany.

"I have always liked this country," Mike said. He had decided early on to tell the truth instead of guessing what his hosts might want to hear. "I am sorry for the people who are suffering now, but unfortunately those are the consequences of war."

No blame assigned. No judgment made. So far so good.

"Yes, these are very difficult times for us," Max said. "But we are industrious people, and if the occupiers allow us, I think we will emerge as a strong, decent country."

The concept of collective guilt was fermenting in Germany, and Max was not ready for that topic yet.

Fritz couldn't help himself and asked Mike which unit he had served with during the war. Max shot him a disapproving glance, a reminder that they had agreed not to discuss such things today. When Mike named his unit, Fritz just nodded as if he recognized it and let it drop.

Mike sensed an opening to use some of Monica's indoctrination about her father's past.

"We went through a part of France that I believe you saw during the first war, Herr Baumann," Mike said evenly. "Monica tells me you were in the Bavarian Army. From what I've read, they held the German left flank with tenacity and honor during the war."

Max did not often talk about his war years. But he was flattered that Mike knew the military history so well, and he appreciated the compliment.

"Yes, we were not tested as much as the others, but those were difficult times. Was your father in the war?"

"Yes, in the Argonne area. I don't think that was your part of the front."

"No, we were farther east," Max said, relieved that he had not been shooting at Mike's father.

Deciding to get off war talk, Max abruptly lurched toward politics.

"What do the American people think of Germany and the occupation now?"

Mike took a second. This could be trouble.

"We're eager for all our troops to return home, but I am not sure when that can happen. Germany will need time to rebuild. We don't know what the Soviets intend to do, but we're growing more worried every day. We may need Germany's help to keep order in Europe."

Max noted the unintended irony of Mike's words about Germany keeping order in Europe. That was Hitler's line too.

"But Russia was your ally," Fritz injected. "Didn't you sort all this out at Yalta and Potsdam?"

"Yes, we came to some agreements with Stalin," Mike said, tempted to give his hosts a peek at his personal political ideas. "But Stalin had an agreement with Germany too. I'm not sure Stalin puts much stock in agreements anymore."

Mike meant no harm, but as the words came out of his mouth he realized he was reminding his hosts of how Hitler had broken his peace deal with Stalin and invaded the Soviet Union in 1941. It was historically accurate, but Mike wasn't sure how it would be taken.

Max and Fritz gave it a pass. They could have accused Mike of blaming Germany for making Stalin an unreliable ally. But neither took it that way.

Nevertheless, Mike was relieved when Max changed the subject again while looking past his guest to see if dinner was on the table.

"Tell me about your home," Max said, honestly interested in learning something about America. "Monica says it is in Kansas."

"Not exactly, sir. It is in Missouri, but it's called Kansas City."

"But there is a state called Kansas, I believe."

"Yes, it is next to Missouri. Kansas City is on the border."

"But if it is so close to Kansas, and it is called Kansas City, why is it in Missouri?"

Mike was not about to get into the Civil War, slavery, the Kansas-Nebraska Act, the Missouri Compromise or any other part of that chapter in American history. He wasn't sure of his facts, but he was sure he lacked the necessary German to do it justice.

"It's just one of those accidents of history, Herr Baumann, something like South Tyrol and Austria."

The two Germans gave sage nods of comprehension. That is complicated, Fritz thought. He doesn't know, Max the teacher thought. So they moved on.

"Do you have family there?"

"My parents and a brother."

"And what does your father do."

Another warning light went on.

"He owns some factories."

"And what do they make?"

"Steel products. Pipes, bars, rods, that sort of thing. Mostly for construction. He has a lot of government contracts."

"And did he prosper during the war?"

"Yes sir."

"What did his factories make for the war?"

Here goes, Mike thought.

"Casings for bombs and artillery shells."

"Ah, I see," Max said, somewhat embarrassed by the turn the conversation had just taken.

Ingrid saved everyone by announcing dinner was ready.

The seating arrangement matched the previous Sunday, except Mike was in the place occupied the previous week by Axel. He kept up with the table talk while stealing glances at Monica. She kept glancing back at him but stayed out of the conversation, waiting for a moment where she might need to jump in to head off a problem.

Mike saw the rouladen and smiled.

"You like rouladen and spaetzle?" Emma asked, pleased with his reaction to the main course.

"Yes, it's one of my favorites. What a nice coincidence."

He risked a sardonic look at Monica, who worked hard to stifle a giggle.

Mike also praised the German red wine that Max had poured, noting how rare it was outside Germany. Max was impressed with

Mike's wine savvy, although he was starting to suspect his daughter might have had something to do with his expertise.

The dinner progressed with more talk about jazz, journalism, German culture and other benign topics. Journalism strayed closest to controversy when Max shared his low opinion of German journalists. Mike had seen some prewar evidence to support Max's opinion, but he thought better of prolonging that subject and instead talked about American journalism standards of accuracy and balance. They sounded utopian to Max, and Mike didn't mention that those standards were goals not always achieved.

Monica helped Ingrid and Emma clear the table, flashing Mike a quick, encouraging smile as she passed by him. Max poured the last of the wine, and then Ingrid crowned the occasion with her unrivaled Black Forest cherry torte, a regional specialty and a Mike Falwell weakness. Monica had worked a deal for some real coffee to punctuate a marvelous meal.

As Mike finished his second piece of torte and washed it down with the last drops of his coffee, he allowed himself a brief moment of levity and sighed, in English, "Shoot me. This is how I want to die."

The others turned to Monica for a translation. She did her best, but the sarcasm was lost in her first attempt, and Emma and Ingrid wondered whether he really wanted to kill himself. The alarm faded from their faces as Monica carefully explained the true intent of the phrase as a compliment.

Mike saw the perplexed looks on his hosts' faces, and heard Monica's tortured attempt at translation, and decided never to try that again.

As the women cleared the table a final time, Max motioned Fritz and Mike back into the sitting room. But Mike asked to be excused briefly, and the other men assumed he needed a washroom break. Instead, through the picture window they saw him approach his VW, reach inside and retrieve a round brown paper bag. He returned to the room moments later, and out of the bag came a bottle of fine French cognac, a treasure worth its weight in gold on the black market and not seen in the Baumann home since the war started.

"I hope you don't mind, but I thought you might enjoy this," Mike said.

He didn't have to wait for an answer. Max barked an order for cognac glasses, but Fritz was already on his way to the china cabinet. Max called to the women to come see what the American had brought. Ingrid insisted on her share. Monica stood behind Mike and smiled, knowing he had, as the Americans would say, hit a home run.

But Emma politely but firmly declined a glass offered by Fritz, saying only, "It's French."

Max rolled his eyes and shook his head in momentary annoyance before returning to the precious ambrosia. Fritz and Ingrid just shrugged. Mike let it slide, but Monica glowered at her mother.

After more parlor talk about emerging postwar German culture and other safe topics, Mike waited for the proper lull to say goodbye. He thanked each one with a personal compliment for their contribution to the meal or the conversation, saving Max for last.

"Herr Baumann, this has been the nicest Sunday afternoon I have spent in Germany. Thank you for your generous and warm hospitality. I know this sort of thing is not easy for a German family. I hope to somehow return the favor some day. I have known for some time that you have a remarkable daughter. Now I know why. She comes from a remarkable family. Good evening to you all."

He shook everyone's hand and then let Monica take his arm as he walked out to his car. Fearing surveillance from her family, they did not kiss. But she whispered to him that he had been marvelous and she wanted to see him later.

Mike got into the VW and as he pulled away, he waved to Monica and anyone else who might be watching. Normally the whole family would have been waving from the sidewalk. But in this case they let Monica see Mike off alone.

When he had turned the corner and was out of the Baumann's sight, he pulled over, undid his tie, unbuttoned his shirt and let out the longest sigh of his life. He had been on stage for four of the most grueling hours of his life. As he rolled away toward home, he started replaying the entire afternoon in his mind, searching for moments that may have somehow scuttled his chances with Monica. As he wracked his brain, a revelation festering there for weeks finally popped out. He really wanted their approval. Because he loved her.

At the Baumann house, the post mortem was clinical and subdued. Max agreed that he seemed like a nice man, for an American. He was impressed with his German and his familiarity with German culture and history. And he convinced himself that any man who puts himself through that kind of stress has to be serious about his daughter.

Fritz liked Mike and admired how he handled Max. As he applied ointment to his healing back, he thought about where that relationship might go. He had watched Monica. And based on what he had seen in her expressions, he was happy for her.

Ingrid rattled on and on in the kitchen about what a fine, handsome man Mike was and how smart he seemed to be. Monica, herself drained from the stress, just let her sister prattle to her mother, who said nothing. After repeated prompting by both daughters, Emma offered bland acceptance that fell short of Monica's hopes. When pressed for more, Emma said nothing and went upstairs for the night.

Max was savoring one more sip of Mike's cognac and reading the label on the bottle he had so generously left behind when Monica walked into the sitting room. Ostensibly she wanted to say goodbye and thank her father for the hospitality he had shown Mike.

"He's a nice young man," Max offered. "But he's American. He will leave some day. And when that time comes, I'm not sure what he will say to you. Until that time comes, I will have concerns."

Monica had never thought that far into the future. While glad to hear her father's provisional endorsement, his cautious skepticism gave her a chill. She knew now she was very much in love with him, but the relationship had been day-to-day. Maybe it was time to look farther ahead. The uncertainty of that next step scared her, so she set it aside for the moment.

She changed into casual clothes, rode her bicycle back to the apartment and trotted over to Mike's place. When she knocked on the door, it had hardly opened when Mike was kissing her as hard as he ever had. And she kissed him right back as long as he wanted.

People walking up the stairs were the only reason they stopped. Once inside, he poured both of them a drink and they then went over every moment of the afternoon. They jointly declared the day a complete success, and at that moment Mike walked over to Monica, leaned over her on the couch, gave her a long, passionate kiss that was returned in full, picked her up and carried her into his bedroom.

She was at first surprised, then momentarily scared, then totally committed to what was happening between them. So she let it happen, then helped it happen, then made it happen.

She spent the night with Mike, and it was not restful. In the morning, he got up first and made coffee. She took a quick bath and put on his robe before joining him in his small kitchen nook. She hugged him from behind while he was pouring coffee, almost causing a painful accident. He put the pot down, turned, and they kissed.

"Did I tell you I love you?" Mike asked, knowing the question was silly.

"You didn't have to," Monica replied. "But I still want to hear it. A lot."

"I love you."

"I love you too."

A hug. A pause. Then Monica gave Mike a quizzical look.

"Last night, was that fraternization?"

Mike's burst of laughter approached a guffaw, drawing another quizzical look. He kissed her on the cheek, nodded and handed her a cup of coffee.

"You bet it was. By the book."

GOLDEN TIMES XII

As spring passed through the first anniversary of VE day and into summer, Mike and Monica were as inseparable as two people with separate jobs and separate apartments could be. They observed the standards of that time and did not live together. They also tried to keep sex out of the relationship for the obvious reasons, with glorious relapses every so often.

Monica preferred spending time in Mike's apartment, with its superior radio, appliances, furnishings and privacy compared to the one she shared with Gisela. They were still best friends, but Monica would only see her in the evening just before both went to bed. And their chatter became noticeably one dimensional. Monica would talk about Mike, and Gisela would ask about Mike, but Gisela grew increasingly silent about her own social life. No tales of night club revelry or new friends or new cocktails or any of the other frivolous but fun things Gisela had regaled Monica with before she got serious with Mike. Monica didn't pry, but she started to wonder.

One weekend, Monica went to Pforzheim to visit a former classmate who had just had a baby. That left Mike with time on his hands for errands, and at the PX he found a coffee brand that he knew Gisela liked. He had enough at home to last a while, so he bought a pound for her.

After putting away his own PX purchases, he walked down the street, up the stairs to Gisela's and Monica's apartment and rang the bell, half expecting her to be out. He was ready to leave it with a note when Gisela opened the door wide enough so that Mike could see inside. He started to hand her the coffee and say something when he stopped in mid-sentence.

Sitting on the sofa was a handsome young man with curly black hair, a thin moustache, smoking a cigarette and staring past Gisela at the stranger who had interrupted them.

"I thought you'd like this, so I picked it up at the PX," Mike said, staring at the man while handing the coffee to Gisela. "I'm sorry to disturb you. I'll see you later."

Gisela gently pulled at his arm as he turned to leave.

"Mike, please come in. I want you to meet someone."

Mike stepped through the door as the other man struggled to stand up. Only then did Mike notice the chrome hook. The man stepped toward Mike with a jerking gait caused by his prosthetic leg.

"Mike, I don't think you've met Axel. This is Monica's brother."

Mike's profession required stoicism whenever humanely possible for the sake of objective reporting. At that moment, he called on that mental conditioning to mask his surprise with an air of cordial familiarity as he put out his right hand and adroitly shook Axel's good left hand.

"I wondered when we would meet," Mike said, genuinely glad to finally meet the brother Monica adored but rarely mentioned. "But I sure didn't expect this."

"I have heard fine things about you," Axel said, somewhat stifly as he sized up his sister's American boyfriend. Mike was fortunate to be in civilian clothes; a uniform would have started things very badly.

"Monica says great things about you too. She's very fond of her big brother."

Axel allowed himself a rare smile. "I am fond of her too. We are very close."

There was no hint of menace in Axel's voice, but Mike got the message.

Gisela told Mike and Axel to sit down while she went to the kitchen for two beers. Axel flopped awkwardly back onto the sofa, while Mike settled into the overstuffed chair. Gisela poured the beers into glasses and then sat on the floor close to Axel. Very close.

Mike didn't know what to say. He was slightly intimidated by Monica's brother, the former journalist, critic, musician and artist – a towering talent maimed by a Soviet artillery shell. Here was no frivolous man. Say the wrong thing, and he could shred you in seconds with a withering rebuttal.

Axel had been banished from the Baumann house long before Mike showed up for dinner. Monica had explained why to Mike in the barest of details, giving Axel a roguish aura and piquing Mike's curiosity. Mike wanted to meet him very much, but he had hoped the circumstances would be more conventional than the ones he had walked into.

Axel sensed Mike's unease and was mildly amused. He was tempted to test Mike's mettle, but Gisela intervened.

"I'm sure you are wondering what's going on," Gisela said.

"No, it's not really any of my business." Diplomatic, and dishonest. Axel saw through it, and Mike knew he did.

"Monica hasn't been here much except to sleep" Thank you Gisela! "but neither have I. Axel and I have been seeing each other for a few months now."

"Does Monica know?"

"I've been trying to find the right time and place to tell her," Gisela said, stroking Axel's good arm.

"Don't worry about me," Mike said. "I can keep a secret."

"You shouldn't have to," Axel said. "It's not fair and Monica should know anyway."

Always the reporter, Mike was dying for the whole story.

"How did you two get together?"

While Axel sipped his beer and lit a cigarette, Gisela told how they had met one day when she was having coffee with Monica at a café not far from Axel's home and workshop. When Axel happened to walk by, Monica raced out to invite him to meet her roommate.

The attraction was instant and intellectual. After brief small talk, Axel and Gisela delved deeper into philosophy, art, theater, music and other esoteric topics that demoted Monica to the role of silent spectator occasionally waving to a waiter for more refreshments.

After that meeting, Gisela never spoke about Axel to Monica. But she found his workshop and started showing up on a regular basis, sharing conversation and the handwork of antique repair and restoration. Gisela would never inject herself in his work but would happily help if asked. Usually the task required more than one hand or some other action that Axel's disability complicated.

Axel enjoyed Gisela's companionship. He relished her sunny personality and admired her intellectual depth. At first, she tolerated his political soliloquies and even tried to rebut some of his theories. But his force of intellect and command of supporting details caused her own political opinions to start drifting even farther left toward his.

By the time Mike came to the door, they had been together frequently for weeks. Axel found her relaxing and she found him exciting.

As Mike drained his glass, he felt duty bound to ask the obvious.

"Who's going to tell Monica?"

"We will do that soon," Axel said, putting out his cigarette. "Please don't say anything."

He didn't have to. Monica had cut short her visit to Pforzheim because the baby was ill and the new parents were distracted. Mike was planning to pick her up at the station later that evening. But she got back to Karlsruhe hours ahead of schedule and hitched a ride home.

So as Mike was rising to leave, the door opened without warning and Monica strolled in, starting to talk to Gisela before she could even take in what was in front of her.

All three abruptly stood up, even Axel, as Monica stopped in mid-word, her mouth formed to continue but with nothing coming out.

"Axel? Mike?" She didn't know who to hug first, so she froze.

Then her brow furrowed, her face tightened and her teeth slowly started clinching.

"What's going on here? Mike, when did you meet Axel? I wanted to introduce you. Gisela, what is Axel doing here? Did he come to see me? Does he need money? Is he bothering you? Axel? What are you doing here? Are you in trouble? Do you have a problem with Mike?

The other three tried alternately to answer but were cut off by the next question in the torrent spilling from Monica. She was confused, concerned and a little hurt. She started thinking she had been the victim of some conspiracy or subterfuge involving her friend, her brother and the man she loved.

Of course, none of that was true, but it took a long round-table discussion that evening and into the night to sort it all out. Monica heard how the café encounter had blossomed into much more. Gisela let Mike off the hook by telling how he had blundered onto their secret. Axel gave a rather clinical account of their relationship, but Monica learned far more by watching Gisela look at Axel. Mike knew his role – he kept his mouth shut.

When all the blanks had been filled in, Monica decided it was too much to digest at one time. It was getting late, and she politely asked both men to leave. There was an awkward final act when Axel kissed Gisela good night and Mike did the same to Monica. Nobody was looking where they should. Monica and Mike both glanced sideways to gauge Axel's reaction. Gisela and Axel cast sideways glances at Monica. All told, there was no passion in those kisses that night.

Mike walked out with Axel, first offering him a nightcap and then a ride. Axel politely declined both but said he hoped to see Mike again soon. And he meant it. Mike was relieved, promised they would, and left the famous Axel to find his way home across town. They would rarely meet again, but they would always ask for updates about the other from Monica or Gisela. They had found several reasons for bonding. War, writing and most of all, Monica.

Mike refrained from talking much about Axel with Monica. He knew it was a difficult subject because of the estrangement between her father and brother. But he contemplated their meeting often in the days following that intense Sunday afternoon.

Until Friday, when news reached the bureau that snapped him into another frame of mind.

Mike was working on a routine story about how denazified Germans were steadily moving into key positions such as utilities, banking, heavy industry and civil administration. In covering tribunal hearings, he discovered that Germans and Americans had different definitions for denazification. Americans saw it as relegating anyone who profited from Nazi Party membership or connections to common laborer status as punishment for their support of the regime. Germans, however, considered low-level Nazi party members and functionaries denazified if they renounced their past, seemed contrite and appeared ready to contribute responsibly to German society.

American public opinion did not appreciate the German version, seeing it as a way for Nazis to escape punishment. Germans, however, saw the American approach as vindictive and unrealistic. With some backing from American occupation managers in Germany, they argued that the American approach would deny Germany the skills it needed to recover from the war and get its economy and infrastructure functioning again. So Max Baumann's case languished because educators had a lower priority in denazification than just about any other profession. Utilities, banks and businesses had to get up and running. Teachers could wait.

Mike was searching for a way to explain all this for the proverbial Kansas City milkman when he was interrupted by a ringing phone. He looked around and saw nobody to answer it, so he picked up. It was the boss in Frankfurt calling urgently for George Martin.

Mike yelled for George to take the call and then watched his boss through the the glass of his office wall. George listened for a minute, jerked his head back as if thumped by Joe Louis, and then sat down for the rest of the conversation, which mostly involved George listening and nodding.

When the call ended, George put down the phone and stared out his window for several minutes. Mike's nosy nature got the better of him and he crossed the room to George's office. He had to knock to get his attention.

George waved Mike in, told him to close the door, and didn't immediately answer when Mike asked if everything was OK.

"Nope, things are not OK. I just got a call from Sampson in Frankfurt." Mike knew that but kept quiet. "He told me what I have been afraid of. By the end of the year, there won't be a Military News Service. They're shutting us down."

Mike thought his mind would explode. How soon? What'll I do? Where will I get a job? Will I have to go home? And then the $64 question hit him – What about Monica?

"We still have until January," George continued. "Sampson said they'd help us find jobs as best they could, but they'll probably be in the states. It looks like our days here are numbered."

Mike didn't hear much after that. He had established a solid reputation, and he had plenty of contacts with wire services in the states. AP and UP guys had even told him he could count on something in Washington when he was done in Europe.

All the professional concerns quickly yielded to one issue – Monica. He needed to think. He needed time. He needed a drink.

George was no sentimental softy, but he knew what Mike's chief worry would be. He told Mike to finish his piece, take the rest of the day off and go home. Mike threw some words on paper to get the story off his hands, handed it to George and left before it had been edited. Just this once, George tolerated this breach of reporting etiquette. He rewrote the final four graphs and punched the story onto the wire himself. He knew Mike would be worthless for the rest of the day, and maybe longer.

Mike walked across the street to his apartment, ate a stale roll to put something on his stomach, and broke out the Jack Daniels. He didn't even bother to get ice. He wiped out a glass that had been left on the kitchen counter, filled it halfway, sat down in his upholstered chair, and started drinking and thinking.

Before the first sip was down the hatch, he knew what he would have to do. He had been thinking about it – sometimes fixating on it – plenty in the past few weeks. He loved Monica. It was no infatuation, no port in the storm relationship stoked by being lonely or homesick. All the corny phrases in the big band love songs applied. He could not imagine life without her. Ever. He wanted to marry her. Until now, it had been an abstract concept. Now reality loomed.

As he sipped the whiskey, he tried to be analytical about a future with Monica. The best job opportunities were in the states. That's where he would have to build his journalism career. Most of the contacts who could help him had been in Germany but were now back home. Maybe George or Sampson could put in a good word for him so he could hook up with a wire service. Washington would be great, but he'd take just about any good news town to start.

Monica. She'd have to leave home, her family, her friends, her country, everything. She'd have to bet her life on him. He was sure he could offer a better life than she would have in occupied, war-ravaged Germany. It would take years for some semblance of normalcy return, if then. But she'd have to leave everything and everyone she knew. Getting settled in a strange land would be tough, even for someone who went through what she's gone through. What if she didn't like it? What if she decided she couldn't stand it there? Then what would he do?

More Jack Daniels, and the thought process started to lose its precision.

Other German gals married GI's and went home with them. You don't hear much about them having trouble. (Some did, but not enough to call it a trend.) Monica is a wonderful person. She gets along with anyone. She would be fine. Americans like Germans. Well, most of them do, now that the war is over. America is full of people with Germans in their family trees. She'll find plenty of her own people there. She'll feel right at home.

That's when he turned morose. He was gonna lose her. He was gonna go home without her. Her family won't let her go. Her father hates America. Her brother hates Americans. Why did I ever get involved with her? I should have seen this coming. I should have known it would end like this. She can't love me enough to leave everything in her life behind her. I can't be that lucky. I can't expect that.

When Monica walked in, she was confronted with a first – Mike drunk. Mumbling, babbling, head-hanging blasted. He could barely focus on her as she stood there, hands on hips, wondering what had brought all this on. He tried to pull himself together enough to speak an intelligible sentence to explain his condition. He failed pathetically.

Monica was not amused or angry, just concerned. Something caused this, and she couldn't wait to hear what it was. She sensed it might be bad, but she'd have to be patient. Mike couldn't tell her tonight if he wanted to. So she helped him up out of his chair, guided him to his bed, let him flop into it fully clothed and covered him with a blanket. He was out before his head sunk into his pillow. Monica fought through the smell of liquor on his breath, kissed him on the forehead and went home. Mike slept 12 straight hours. Monica hardly slept a wink.

Mercifully for Mike, the next morning was a Saturday. He could sleep it off and then nurse a ferocious hangover on his day off. Monica had promised to look after Elisabeth while Fritz and Ingrid made a produce run to Gmuend, so Mike was on his own.

First, coffee. He had no idea a percolator could clatter, puff and wheeze so loud. Then bread. He didn't dare try to slice a loaf he had in the icebox. So he tore off a chunk and bit into it. Cotton mouth stopped that process cold. So he swished some orange juice into his mouth to dislodge the bread and then forced himself to swallow the ungodly breakfast concoction in his mouth. Coffee with aspirins started the recuperation in earnest. He lounged on his sofa, waiting for his head to stop hurting. What was he thinking? Why did he let that happen?

He thought Monica had appeared at some point during his journey to stupefaction, but he wasn't sure. Maybe that's how he got to bed. He knew she'd be at Ingrid's for the day, so answers would come later.

Then the reason for his binge forced its way back into his brain. MNS going out of business. Going home. Monica. And he started all over again, this time without Jack's help. He thought about making a list but dismissed that idea as silly. He wasn't buying a car, he was planning the rest of his life. He found a picture of them at a city park picnic, and he just stared at her. He couldn't leave her. No way. He knew what he had to do, but he kept forcing it to the side of his mind, trying to study other angles, worried that he might be jumping to the wrong conclusion because it was the one he liked best. No matter what he tried, he always came back to the same train of thought. He savored it, but it scared him. Rejection, failure, unfulfilled promises, unmet expectations. Any of those could scuttle his life plan if they cost him Monica.

His ebbing headache made one brief comeback when the door bell rang. Monica had locked the door when she left, so Mike had to struggle up off the sofa to answer it. He opened the door just enough to recognized George's round, weathered face.

"Boy, you sure look like you fell in a thicket of whiz-bangs last night," George said as he walked in past Mike and sat himself on the couch. "Party with Monica?"

"Nope, 'fraid not. This was a solo job." Mike poured himself another cup of coffee and offered one to George, who took it.

"I thought so," George said after a loud slurp from the cup. "The news hit us all pretty hard. But you have a special problem. Figure out what you're going to do yet?"

"I just don't know," Mike said, not wanting to show all his cards. He needed career advice, and George was as good a source as any. "What do you think I should do?"

"Marry her," George snapped back, smiling. Mike always liked George's aversion to bullshit. It made him a great editor.

"I meant my career," Mike said, again shading the truth.

"That should take care of itself. I know plenty of guys who will hire you the minute you apply. You may not know it, but you're reputation is pretty solid. Good editing does that for a guy."

Mike and George both smiled at the sarcasm, knowing it was also true.

"Mike, maybe this is none of my business, but I think you need to hear this from a friend. I've seen you and Monica together for months now. I saw you two the first day you met. I have never seen two people who are a better fit. You two are naturals for each other. She's one hell of a lady, even if she can't file the wire worth a damn."

George could never stay serious for long. But he got back on track before Mike could interrupt.

"I don't pretend to understand women, but I'd bet anything that she'd follow you anywhere. I see her looking at you. I see her talking to you. That gal is no-doubt-about-it head over heels in love with you. And she likes you too. She's not just a girlfriend. She's a friend. My dad always said that you probably won't have more than two real friends in your life. And if you're lucky, one of 'em will be your wife."

Mike was liking this. George was reinforcing everything Mike hoped was true but was afraid to really believe by himself. George was the second source, the confirmation he needed to validate his feelings about Monica and the future.

George sensed it was time to shut up. He sat on the sofa, taking periodic slurps of coffee, watching Mike think.

"I guess it's pretty obvious what has to happen," Mike said after a long silent interval. "I really do love her more than anything. I'll have to go home, and I can't leave without her."

"Do I hear wedding bells?" George asked.

"Yeah, I guess you do. So now what?"

"Propose to her, you moron. And as far as the job thing is concerned, let me make some calls Monday. I have to check out some things for myself, so I'll ask around for you too."

"Thanks, George, I really appreciate all this, " Mike said as he walked George to the door. "And I promise my work won't suffer from all these distractions. I'll give the job everything I've got until the last day."

"Damn right you will," George said, shaking Mike's hand as he left. "I'll make sure of that."

As the whiskey fog lifted and he struggled back to full status as a functioning human, Mike started thinking about the question – daydreaming really. What setting or circumstance would be best? He decided silence was no longer the proper environment, so he turned on the radio to hear the news.

One scenario after another floated into his mind and was thrown out as unrealistic, not romantic enough or too bombastic. No setting seemed just right. Restaurant, park, apartment, Black Forest walk, Rhine river cruise – nothing. He took a mental detour to the meeting he would have to arrange with her father. He would want Max's blessing. He was sure he would get it.

As he sought the perfect Monica script, the radio broke into his thoughts with a news bulletin about a train wreck in Italy. Glad I don't have to cover that, he thought. Then the seed sprouted, popping him to his feet and getting him pacing around the room, talking to himself.

That would be perfect. If he could get help from George and Frankfurt, it might work. But it would have risks. If it backfired, he would have no choice. He'd have to join a monastery. Or maybe the Foreign Legion.

GOLDEN TIMES XIII

After further consultation with George, Mike decided he had to tell Monica about the limited life expectancy of MNS. Then he would let her dictate where the conversation headed.

He was surprised at how accurately he anticipated her reaction. She had seen the stream of servicemen dwindle as the occupation evolved from military to civilian management. More than 100,000 U.S. troops were still in the American zone, but they were mostly there to ensure stability and prevent any major unrest. Germans had long ago accepted defeat and occupation, viewing National Socialism as a virulent, self-inflicted plague that had left terrible scars that no amount of corrective surgery or cosmetics could ever erase completely. Now, having been cured by force of arms, they preferred to concentrate on survival and building a new nation.

So over dinner at their favorite restaurant a week after he got the news from George, Mike gently and gradually broke it to Monica.

She struggled to hold off tears as the same barrage of thoughts that had afflicted Mike rattled through her mind. She was upset, but did not panic. She knew she couldn't fly off the handle. What would Mike think? And it wasn't her style anyway.

Gaining her composure, she set out to peel back the many layers of issues confronting both of them, starting with the easy stuff.

"Where will you find work?"

"I suppose I can look around here," Mike said, priming the charge, "but I think I'll probably have to go back to the states. Washington, maybe."

"That would be good for you," Monica said, not really giving a damn about his career prospects at that moment.

She couldn't hold back another second.

"And what about us?"

"That's what we have to figure out," Mike said, almost whispering as he looked down at his sauerbraten as it got cold. "Together. You have to be honest with me and I'll be honest with you. We have to talk this over very carefully."

Monica wasn't sure where the conversation was going, and anger was spreading over her softly lit face.

"How's this for honesty," she said with more edge in her voice than she wanted. "I love you more than anything. I don't ever want to be without you. I will do anything to be with you. Anything."

Mike wanted to leap out of his chair and hug her, but he knew that restraint was required for the sake of the discussion.

"Monica, I feel exactly the same way you do. I love you so much. But I don't want to lead you into a life you don't like. If I stay here, I may not be able to make much money. If you go back to the states with me, you would have to leave everyone and everything you have ever known and loved. It would be a huge change for you. You'd be the one to suffer. I'd just be going home. I'm not sure I want to risk making you unhappy."

Monica was fairly confident he was being noble. She couldn't imagine he was trying to set her up for a split. She trusted him, and she appreciated his concern for her. But if he truly understood how much she loved him, he would understand how none of those other things really mattered. She wanted to be with him, that's all.

Oddly, or maybe fortunately, the "m" word never came up that night. It hovered over the table, and both knew it was there.

But neither had the nerve to drag it into the conversation. All the issues were being covered. No need to introduce a loaded and potentially dangerous word at that point.

As Mike and Monica walked out of the restaurant, he put his arm around her shoulders to ward off an early fall chill. She loved how he touched her, and it took the edge off the difficult dinner discussion. They rode home in Mike's borrowed VW in silence.

He parked, walked her to her door, kissed her gently for a long time, and said good night. He left not knowing how she would deal with the crisis. He was fairly certain they both knew the ultimate answer. But now there was no turning back. He had to put his plan in motion.

On Monday, Mike told George what he had in mind. George, a sentimental softy at heart, loved it and immediately got on the phone with Sampson, who initially balked on procedural grounds but caved when George knocked down all his objections. The Frankfurt manager had wanted to say yes anyway.

Mike then set Wednesday as D-day. It gave them just enough time to send out all the proper notices and perfect their timetable, while limiting the chance of a leak ruining the plan.

Mike saw Monica briefly Monday night but made some excuse for heading home early. Tuesday he said he had to stay late to cover the evening shift, and then did, giving Jimmy the night off to cover the deception.

Wednesday, the wheels almost came off. Mike and his co-conspirators had set 5:15 p.m. as H-hour. That would give Monica time to wrap up her call center work, come up stairs and drop by the bureau to see Mike before heading home. But around 3:30 p.m., Gisela stopped Mike in the hallway and invited him to an impromptu birthday party for a new girl in the call center. It would start at 5.

Mike said yes, but his mind was racing. Now what? He ran upstairs to the bureau and into George's office.

"We're screwed," Mike said, out of breath. "Monica has to be at a birthday party downstairs. It starts at 5. She'll never get up here on time."

George thought for just a moment and had the solution.

"I'll set it up by phone. When she's here, I'll give the signal. If we're a little late, I don't think anyone will mind."

That was good enough for Mike. He went back to his desk and endured the longest 90 minutes of his life.

Finally, 5 p.m. Getting a final thumbs up from George in his office, Mike strolled as nonchalantly as humanly possible for a nervous wreck down the stairs and into the call center, where Monica, Gisela and about a dozen coworkers were just presenting a cake to the birthday girl.

Mike sauntered over to Monica and locked onto her for the next 10 minutes, faking interest in what everyone was saying and making gestures to Monica indicating he was eager to leave.

She was at first amused and then a little annoyed by his antsy behavior. It was not like him, and she didn't want to hurt the honoree's feelings. But when the cake was cut, served and Happy Birthday was sung, Monica felt she could extricate herself gracefully. She said goodbye to the group, took Mike's hand and walked him out the door toward the stairs. As they walked up the stairs, she wanted an explanation.

"What is wrong with you? Couldn't you give up just a few precious minutes for that girl's party? She's had a rough time. This was the first nice time she's had for a long time."

"I'm sorry," Mike said impatiently, steering Monica toward the bureau front door. "Something else was on my mind. I wasn't thinking."

Abruptly the subject changed.

"Before I left," Mike said, "a hell of a story was brewing. Let's just stop in for a minute to see if we get any details."

"What kind of story?" Monica normally wouldn't have cared, but Mike's behavior put her antennae up.

"Don't know yet," Mike said, placing Monica in a chair near the bank of wire machines. She hated sitting near those things, but she didn't expect to stay long.

She didn't see Mike give wave to George, who was on the phone in his office. George gave a thumbs-up, said something and then turned to look into the newsroom.

Mike was standing by the regional wire, which was strangely quiet for a Wednesday evening. Monica didn't notice that, but 10 seconds later the conspiracy hatched.

Wire services used a system of bells to signal items of significance to customers and bureaus. Three bells announced an advisory. Four heralded an urgent, the first few paragraphs of a breaking story. Five bells preceded a bulletin, the adrenalin-pumping one-paragraph announcement of major headline-making news.

The most electrifying news a wire could offer was the flash – 10 bells then one line announcing something historic. The election or death of a president, the end of a war – usually the top story of the year. If bulletins got people walking to a wire machine, flashes got them running.

In the bureau, the regional wire suddenly erupted with bells. Monica had learned enough to count the bells, and when they passed five she jumped up and raced to the wire where Mike was standing. She failed to notice that nobody else in the bureau moved.

She stared at the wire as the keys came to life.

MONICA, WILL YOU MARRY ME? MIKE

Monica's stared at the wire for a split second before her jaw dropped, her right hand flipped up to cover her mouth, and then she leapt into Mike's embrace, almost knocking them both off their feet.

"Yes!"

That was all she could get out. She held tight and cried as Mike kissed her neck and squeezed her in his arms. He didn't say anything. He had heard what he wanted to hear.

She looked at him, half laughing and half crying, and they kissed longer and harder than they ever had. They didn't care that George had come out of his office to congratulate them and that Morton and Jimmy were standing by to do the same. They hugged for a few minutes before separating to accept congratulations.

Then they had to turn back to the wire, where more bells were ringing and one message had already appeared three times.

ANSWER PLS???

Monica had to do it. She hit the break key to take control of the circuit, and typing directly onto the wire, avoiding the hated tape, she typed two letters:

II

Wirese for yes.

A torrent of congratulatory messages followed, a few touching but most sarcastic in the true wire service tradition. A few minutes later the wire returned to its normal duty, clacking out stories that had backed up to make room for Mike's proposal.

The newly engaged couple quickly left to celebrate privately. In his apartment, as they sipped champagne he had found from a source he would not name, he told her how he had set up the flash with George and the Frankfurt office and how they had received permission from clients to disrupt their service at a busy time of day.

Monica was awash with emotions. She wanted to hold Mike and kiss him and never let go. She loved him for his resourceful proposal. She was relieved that there was no doubt their future was together. She couldn't wait to go home and tell Gisela, although she would have to promise to keep Axel in the dark until the rest of her family knew.

Her family. Her parents. Her father.

"How are we going to tell everyone," she said, ducking the precise question she really wanted to ask.

"First, we have to tell your parents. I have to get your father's approval."

Monica was touched by Mike's respect for tradition.

"What if he says no," she asked playfully, hiding just a bit of dread embedded in the question.

"He won't," Mike said, showing a bravado that was genuine.

The plan was to announced their engagement a week from Sunday, when Mike had already been invited to dinner. He would first ask to meet privately with Max, and then they would reveal their intentions. At least that was the plan. They were sure they could keep the secret until then.

They rehearsed a number of scenes they could anticipate at the Baumann home, some pleasant and some awkward. Monica thoroughly coached Mike on how her family would expect him to react to any of the imagined situations.

It started serious, but they were both so happy they couldn't resist letting it slip into silliness. In one scenario, Mike reacted to rejection by feigning a heart attack.

"Doctor, doctor," he rasped as he collapsed, dragging a laughing Monica to the floor with him for more hugs and kisses.

"As long as it isn't Dr. Huber," she said, helping her future husband off the floor.

"Who's he?"

"He's this awful man in our neighborhood who has been charging for his services by forcing people to give him things worth far more than his fee."

"What a scam," Mike said, sensing a story.

"When Elisabeth was sick, he came to give her some medicine and wouldn't take Reichsmarks. He coerced my mother into giving him a Majolica figurine that was my parents' most cherished treasure. It broke my mother's heart. That son of a bitch."

Mike, admiring his future bride's growing mastery of American obscenity, wanted to know more. Relying on gossip from Ingrid, Monica described how other families in the area were victimized by Huber, who openly bragged about his collection of fine art work without saying he had extorted the dozen or so pieces from defenseless families.

Then, for the first and last time in his career, Mike put personal interests ahead of his professional responsibilities. He was sure the Huber story would get good play, but he hatched another plot that he liked even better.

With Monica's help, Mike found some of Huber's other victims to make sure his premise was solid. Then he made an appointment to visit the doctor, claiming he wanted to do a story on his collection.

Huber let his vanity override his good sense and welcomed the American journalist into his home without hesitation. He offered Mike a glass of wine and then led him directly to the dining room that featured a curio cabinet with Huber's treasures.

Mike let Huber explain the origin and significance of each piece, dutifully taking notes, interrupting periodically for correct spellings, and snapping a few photos with his Leica.

When Huber was gushed out, Mike went into action.

"So, Dr. Huber, just where did you get all these fine pieces?"

"I acquired them locally in the past year or so."

"Since the end of the war?"

"Yes."

"From dealers?"

"No, not exactly."

"I hope you won't tell me these came from the black market."

Huber got defensive.

"O no, nothing like that. They came from people I know."

"Friends?"

"Yes, some."

"Patients?"

Huber stiffened.

"Yes, as payment for my services. It was all quite legitimate."

"I'm sure. How much are these pieces worth?"

Sensing danger, Huber tried to duck.

"I'm not really sure. And their value is not important to me. In my mind, they are priceless."

"I'm sure I could get estimates from experts if I showed them these pictures," Mike said, gesturing to his camera hanging from his neck. "But I'd much rather get that information from you. It would be far more authoritative."

Huber let down his guard.

"I suppose, if they were sold to a museum or art gallery, they might fetch several hundred dollars each, maybe more. But that's just a rough estimate."

"That's amazing," Mike said, patronizing the ruddy doctor who was starting to perspire. "Then the people who paid their bills with these things must have really been sick."

"No, just the usual things. Fevers, minor injuries."

The trap snapped shut.

"Well," Mike said, looking directly at Huber, "how can you justify letting patients pay for routine treatment with such valuable artwork? It looks like they paid far more than the usual fee for such things."

Huber's look and tone turned icy.

"They didn't have the money to pay, so they offered these instead."

"Dr. Huber, that's not what I've heard. Several families around here say you refused to take cash or give them credit and demanded these things as payment. They say you threatened them with legal action or other retribution if they did not agree."

"That's absurd. Who would say such a thing?"

Mike then flipped to a page in his notebook that listed six families, what they had given to Huber and the approximate value in dollars.

"These people have all talked to me on the record, and I'm sure the authorities would be very interested in what they have to say. Profiteering is a crime, Dr. Huber. A very serious crime."

"How dare you accuse me of illegal activity," Huber blustered. "Who do you think you are? You Americans think you can do anything you like and get away with it. There are libel laws too, you know."

"Yes sir," Mike said, ready for this attack. "But truth is a defense in libel, even here in occupied Germany. If I write this story, I bet even more families come forward with similar stories about your unusual billing methods."

Huber sat down in a dining room chair and wiped his forehead with a napkin. He was firmly snagged on Mike's hook. Mike gave him time to think of a way to wiggle free.

Huber took a long look at his prized art collection, then sighed.

"I think there has been a terrible misunderstanding," Huber said. "I only accepted these things from those families as collateral. I thought they understood that when they had the cash to pay the bill, I would happily take the money and return their sculpture."

Mike didn't flinch.

"I think I can understand how that might happen," he deadpanned. "In times of duress, communication is not always clear.

So are you saying that you would return these things to those families if they paid your fee in Reichsmarks?"

"No, dollars or pounds," Huber said.

Mike shot him a frown, and Huber gave up.

"Yes, Reichsmarks."

"Well," Mike said, putting away his notepad, "with no collection, I guess there's no story. I hope I haven't taken up too much of your time. But I've enjoyed our conversation very much."

"Not at all," growled Huber, staring at his adversary before looking at the soon to be empty cabinet.

"O, one other thing," Mike said. "I think I can help you return at least one of these."

He pointed to the Majolica figurine of a reclining horse, the most prominent item in Huber's collection.

"The Baumanns are good friends of mine. Nice people. I'd appreciate the opportunity to return this to them. How much did they owe?"

Huber could barely remember the case, so Mike reminded him about the treatment for Elisabeth.

"I think, maybe, 200 Reichsmarks?" Huber said as a question, as if Mike knew.

"Fine, here's the money. I'll get it from them later."

Mike put a wad of Reichsmarks in Huber's sweaty palm and then let Huber take the figurine out of the curio cabinet, wrap it in plain paper, slide it carefully into a sturdy shopping bag and hand it to Mike, holding the handles and the bottom of the bag.

Mike thanked Huber, briefly freed his right hand to shake Huber's, and then let himself out. He gently put the bag on the floor of his jeep, surrounded it with a blanket he kept in the back, and carefully drove home, where he hid it in his closet.

Three days later, Monica and Mike acted out their charade one last time at the Baumann home. Monica went in the morning, changed clothes and greeted Mike at the door as always. This time she was radiant and nervous as hell. So was he.

The ritual played out as always, with Max and Fritz hosting Mike in the sitting room with a glass of beer as the final preparations for dinner were made.

But this time, Mike surprised his hosts.

"Herr Baumann, may I speak with you alone?"

Fritz and Max both were startled by this departure from routine. But Mike looked serious, so Max invited him upstairs into his living room. Max sat down in his leather chair behind his imposing oak desk, and Mike sat in a leather arm chair on the other side.

Max started.

"What can I do for you, Michael?"

"Herr Baumann, I have known Monica now for a long time."

"Not that long, Michael. It has not even been a year."

"Yes sir," Mike said, slipping into English in his nervousness before returning to German.

"It may not seem long to you, sir, but we have gotten to know each other very well. As well as any two people can know each other."

Max actually felt sorry for the uniformed young man squirming and sweating on the other side of the desk. He thought he knew what was coming, but he wanted to savor the drama.

"What are you trying to tell me, Michael?"

Mike saw no reason to continue the preliminaries.

"Well, sir, Monica and I love each other very much. And I would be honored if you would consent to let me marry your wonderful, beautiful daughter."

Max wasn't surprised by the request. But its effect on him was a surprise. He got defensive about his daughter. How could this American make her happy? What does he know about living in Germany? What kind of future would he have here as a journalist?

Max kept his composure.

"I think it's nice that you feel that way about my daughter. It has been clear for some time how she feels about you. But I am her father, and I have to ask some very difficult questions."

Mike sat up straight, ready for the grilling.

"How would you support my daughter? How would you earn a living? Do you think an American journalist working in Germany can earn enough to support a wife, and later a family?"

Mike loaded for the second salvo.

"No, Herr Baumann. Not here. But in the United States. Monica and I would make our lives together there. I have a future there. I have a good reputation there and already have good offers for reporting jobs in Washington."

This was true. AP had just offered him a general assignment reporting job, hinting that beat work would not be far behind. His career path was set. But Max did not comprehend the workings of American media, and all he saw was the loss of his favorite child.

"You would take Monica from us? You would take her to a strange place where she has no family, no friends? We might never see her again. We would never see our grandchildren."

Mike thought Max was getting a little ahead of things, but he was ready for the separation issue.

"I have promised Monica that she can come home to visit every year, if that's what she wants. We'll be able to afford that. (Somehow, he thought to himself.) It is true that she will not be here with you. But she will have a better life than she can hope for here, at least in the near future. Germany is still trying to recover from the war. That will take years. The quality of life is much better in the United States. Besides, lots of German women have gone there with American husbands and are doing fine."

Mike was grateful that Max did not demand proof of this claim. So he moved to the finale.

"Herr Baumann, I have the greatest respect for you and your family. And I deeply love Monica. I want to make her happy and protect her and give her the best life possible. I think I can do that, and I think the best place for that right now is America."

Then Mike took a chance.

"Sir, if Monica was my wife and she decided that America was unbearable for her and she wanted to come back, we would come back. I would find something to do. Foreign correspondents make good salaries. (Never mind that those postings are the crown jewels of journalism.) Some have become famous authors. I just want to assure you that I will spend the rest of my life doing anything in my power to make Monica the happiest woman on earth."

A bit of hyperbole, but not bad. Mike rested his case.

Max sat silent for a minute or so, looking down at his hands folded on his desk.

He sighed, looked up at Mike, and surrendered to the inevitable, as he always knew he would.

"Like I said, Michael, you are a fine young man. Some Americans I don't like. But you are different. I can tell you are serious, you have ambition, a good thing. I hear you are a talented writer and respected in your profession. Most of all, I am convinced you deeply love my daughter, and she feels the same way about you.

"If you mean everything you have promised me here, and if you truly intend to do anything you can to make my daughter safe and happy for the rest of her life, then I will agree to your marriage."

Mike took a minute to replay the last part in his translating mind. Then he forced himself to stay seated and quiet for just a split second before smiling, standing, reaching across the desk and fervently but not too deferentially thanking his future father-in-law. Max saw the smile grow wider across Mike's face, even as the tension faded, and he could not help smiling as well. A small lump started growing in his throat as he realized he had just given his darling Monica away. Ingrid's marriage to Fritz was a welcome relief because her parents were not sure she would ever try to meet someone to marry. Monica was another matter. They knew she would be popular and outgoing and might even break their hearts when she chose her husband. In a way, she had done exactly that. But it could have been worse. And Max was to learn it could not have been much better either.

Max rose from his desk escort Mike down to dinner, but Mike stopped him.

"Sir, please wait here. I have something for you."

Another bottle of cognac, Max thought. A little early in the day, but this is a special day.

Mike raced downstairs and out to his VW, where he carefully retrieved a shopping bag and carried it with deliberate steps up to Max, who was still sitting behind his desk.

"I thought you might like this."

By the way Mike handed him the bag, Max could tell the contents were fragile. Max set the bag on the desk, laid it carefully on its side, and slid the paper-wrapped object out onto the desk. He then slowly removed the wrapping paper until the head of a horse appeared. Max gasped and tossed the rest of the paper aside, revealing the Majolica figurine that once sat on the cabinet across the room.

He gave Mike an astonished look and yelled "Emma!" so loud that the neighbors heard him. A few tears had already dampened his eyes when Emma hurried into the room, followed closely by the others.

Max said nothing as Emma spotted the figurine on his desk. A shocked shriek startled the others, who could not see the figurine yet. Then they looked past Emma and saw the cause. Mike was standing to the side of the desk, and Monica hurried to his side. Emma slowly picked up the little horse and walked it across the room, placing it on the exact spot it had owned for most of their lives together.

She then turned to Max with one word. "How?"

Max turned to Mike. "Ask your future son-in-law."

More shrieks. The neighbors stared at the house, wondering what had gotten into the Baumanns.

Monica hugged Mike and kissed him just before Ingrid rushed over to hug them both. Fritz shook both Monica's and Mike's hands more violently than normal, but nobody minded. Emma, in tears, was the last to hug her daughter. Then she looked at Mike.

"I am very happy you are marrying Monica. You are perfect for her."

Mike teared up at that and had to think about baseball and cars and other guy stuff to pull himself back together.

Elisabeth was making a fuss downstairs, reminding everybody that dinner was waiting.

As they filed out of the room, Monica and Mike lingered for a celebratory kiss, even though Max was still there. As they headed for the door, Max touched Mike's arm.

"Tell me something," Max said. "Why did you wait until after I said yes to bring us your wonderful gift."

"I didn't want you to think of it as a bribe or an offer to buy your daughter. I wanted your blessing on its own merits."

Max looked at Mike with even more admiration.

"And what would you have done if I had said no?"

"I don't know," Mike said with a wink to Monica. "I never thought about it."

"Hmph," Max said as he pushed the couple in front of him. "Americans."

GOLDEN TIMES XIV

Life in occupied Germany never allowed anyone much time for unbridled joy. Some crisis or disaster would always intervene. A POW would return home to his happy family but then squeeze into already overcrowded living space and add one more mouth to feed. A home or flat would be restored enough to withstand human habitation, and the owners would find themselves forced to accept a displaced family as boarders. Luxuries, no matter how they were acquired, could rarely be savored. They were hidden away for the day they could be traded for some necessity.

And so it was for the Baumann family. Word spread quickly through the neighorhood about Monica and Mike, and Emma found unusual joy in accepting the warm good wishes of friends dropping by. The first person Monica told outside the family was Gisela, who seized the moment to reveal her relationship with Axel was cooling.

Monica wasn't sure how to react.

"He's a wonderful, fascinating man," Gisela said. "But it is difficult."

"You mean because of his…condition?"

"No, not so much that. He can be a very complicated man. Sometimes his mind is at full speed, and those are the moments I love with him. But other times, the darker times, like when he has been drinking, his whole personality turns dark, ominous.

He never causes any trouble, but it worries me. I don't know which man I am with sometimes."

Monica nodded but said nothing. She knew her brother well enough to understand Gisela full well. And she had no advice or solace for her friend.

She was more eager to talk about Mike. But the lilt had gone out of the banter, so Monica truthfully told her roommate the events of the day had exhausted her, and both went to their rooms.

Down the street, Mike sat alone in his apartment, sipping a celebratory whiskey and replaying the day's events in his mind. He also took a first stab at a chronology for the wedding and his return home with his bride. But he needed more time. It was too soon. One task was unavoidable, however. He had to tell his parents. He daydreamed a bit about how they would react, maybe throw a party welcoming the newlyweds in Kansas City, and what kind of faux high society spectacle that might be. Poor Monica. She had no idea what was coming. At least she'd have distance to protect her.

At the Baumann home, Max let the women in the house babble and buzz about the upcoming wedding. So did Fritz, whose back was almost healed. But he was finding something better to do than lift rubble. As he had convalesced, friends and friends of friends started bringing him small accounting jobs he could do at home. Their businesses were starting to take hold, but true to the good news-bad news spirit of the times, they needed to make sure their books were in order for new tax and licensing laws. Fritz was being paid with both cash and, ironically, undocumented barter goods. All he cared about was functioning again as a breadwinner for his wife and increasingly active child.

Max found himself admiring Fritz's initiative and even envied him. At least Fritz was practicing his profession, not washing dishes.

Both men had an unspoken pact – they would stay out of the wedding planning circus. They knew that even if they did try to get involved, the women wouldn't listen. So they went about their business, each wondering how long the glow would last.

They got their answer 10 days later.

On the last day of July, Max received formal notice that a denazification tribunal had moved up his case and was ready to set a hearing date. It had come in a simple letter listing his rights and suggesting how he could prepare his case. Some friends and former students had collected a small fund to hire a respected neighborhood lawyer, Albrecht Schumacher, who had helped other professionals survive their ordeals. Schumacher agreed without hesitation, even though the donation would hardly cover the time he would put into the case. Max had educated Schumacher's two sons, both of whom had gone on to outstanding academic careers in Munich.

So the next day, after Max came home from the canteen kitchen, the two men started collaborating on how Max could explain his actions of six years earlier and resume his career.

They started with Max's answers on the infamous 131-question Fragebogen (questionnaire). The U.S. screener had reached for his memo pad when he got to Line 40 under Section E, "Membership in Organizations." The form demanded an accounting of membership dates and offices held for more than 50 organizations, associations and groups deemed to have had ties to or the endorsement of the Nazi Party. Line 41 named the NSDAP, the party itself. Max had written an addendum noting how all public employees had been required to join in 1937, and he considered himself covered by that order. Nothing else applied until Line 60, the NS Teachers Federation. Max had to answer yes again and wrote another addendum explaining how that was also mandatory.

Unfortunately for Max, someone else had come forward with another story. His name was Bodo Fenslinger, a former student of Max's who had shown no special qualities in school but had a special knack for self-promotion during the war and self-preservation after. He had held a minor party job in Karlsruhe, but it had given him access to records of all sorts of activities that could prove incriminating if presented with a twist.

He had exposed several local officials who had tried to hide their Nazi-affiliated activities, and thereby spared himself immediate incarceration for his own party record. One of his targets was Herr Max Baumann, whose stern standards and honest grading had caused Fenslinger grief, physical and emotional, every time he took his report card home. Fenslinger knew something about Max that might help him gain a nice measure of revenge and further ingratiate himself with the occupiers.

Early in the discovery stage of their preparations, Max and Schumacher uncovered Fenslinger's role in the case. Max exploded at the news, which the lawyer anticipated. But he did not expect an even greater eruption from Emma. The lawyer was ready to excuse a loyal spouse's outrage until Emma told her story – which neither man had ever heard.

"It was some time in the fall of '43. An air raid was coming. Ingrid was away somewhere, and Max always insisted on staying with the house. So Monica and I ran to the air raid bunker at the end of the street. We were there with several other people, and the only light was someone's flashlight. We were all very quiet, listening for the bombs to see how close they would come. First we heard the thump-thump of the antiaircraft guns, then another kind of thump as the bombs started falling. We knew right away that they were not close, and as it turned out we weren't in the bombing zone that night.

"So we started talking, mostly whispering in the dark. First it was about relatives in the war, then about problems the war was causing at home, the usual things but nothing too critical because you never knew what might cause trouble. Then I said I'd be glad when the war was over and we could live normal lives again. I thought it was a perfectly innocent thing to say.

"But the flashlight came on and shined in my face. A voice of the person holding it said, 'Be very careful, Frau Baumann. You never know who is listening.'

"I couldn't see his face in the dark, but I recognized his voice. It was Bodo Fenslinger. At that time you didn't argue with anyone like him, so I kept quiet.

"Then Fenslinger started talking about how well things were going and how we weren't seeing the full picture. He said his superiors had arranged a holiday for him earlier in the summer. That's what he called it. A holiday. Do you know where he went? Dachau! He spent a holiday in a concentration camp playing guard or administrator or whatever. And he liked it!"

Emma took a breath and slowly shook her head.

"The man is a pig. Why would anyone listen to him?"

Schumacher took notes as Emma talked, but he doubted he could use it against Fenslinger. He needed hard evidence to clear Max.

Two nights later, that quest took their conversation to the difficult issue of Strasbourg. Max knew the subject was inevitable. He dreaded it for himself, but most of all for his wife. He had hoped those days would be buried forever in their past. But if Max had any chance of surviving his denazification process, Schumacher would have to know everything.

After German forces humiliated France in 1940, Berlin ordered French schools in what it considered German regions to switch to German curricula, administrative structures and teaching methods. One of the largest school systems targeted for the changes was Strasbourg. Max was assigned to handle the administrative changes. He didn't volunteer or even hint at wanting the job. Someone who had admired his management of his school had submitted his name, and he got the job.

He spent his working week there and then came home on weekends. It was only a two-hour train ride, but to Emma it was the other side of the world. He would leave early Monday morning, and she would have to fend with three children with only occasional help from an aunt or cousin. Strasbourg was a jewel of a city, with canals and quiet shopping streets and exquisite restaurants. Try as she would, she could not suppress her resentment. It was just one more reason for her to hate the Nazis.

Max concerned himself only with administrative organization. He stayed away from class subject matter, textbooks and other issues that had political overtones. Nevertheless, the swastika was a common sight in schools throughout the city as Max's changes took hold.

The shuttle work continued for six weeks before Emma decided she had waited long enough for an invitation to join him there for a night or two together. Even though it was wartime, she was sure he was enjoying the evenings in the restaurants or bars near his hotel on the city's historic cathedral square, and she decided she had earned the right to share some of the fun.

She always enjoyed surprising Max, so she decided to spring her visit on him. She arranged for her aunt to stay with the children, and on a Wednesday afternoon she took a taxi to the train station. Two nights with Max and then she'd come home with him on Friday.

Holding her bag in her lap the entire way, she reached the Strasbourg station early in the evening and took a cab to Hotel des Rohan. She walked in, introduced herself to the desk clerk, showed her papers and asked for a key so she could surprise her husband, Herr Baumann. Emma assumed the clerk's hesitation was a sign of prudent suspicion, but he said nothing and gave her the key. She carried her small bag up the one flight of stairs to Room 104, slipped the key in the lock and opened the door. She recognized Max's muffled voice and was instantly delighted that she had surprised him.

Then she heard the woman's voice. Equally muffled. Equally surprised. Max and the woman sat up in the bed, gaping at Emma, who was herself frozen with shock, then embarrassment, then rage. Still clutching her bag, she slammed the door, ran down the stairs past the poker-faced clerk and was half way across the square when Max came running out of the hotel, yelling her name twice before realizing that wasn't helping the situation. He was wearing a half buttoned shirt, pants without braces and shoes without socks. Strangers in the square discretely pretended to go about their business, although the French witnesses savored the public anguish of the two Germans.

Max had to tug her arm to get her to stop. She was crying and wanted nothing to do with him. Cliches poured out of his mouth – the dumb things a man says when he is caught red-handed. She pulled away from him, hurried to the nearest taxi stand and rode off to the station, leaving Max standing in the square, red-faced and seething.

Aunt Mina was surprised when Emma arrived late that night after a miserable train ride and a long wait for a cab. When Mina saw her niece's face, she knew it was bad and didn't ask questions. She got dressed, hooked her small bag on the back of her bicycle and pedaled off into the night.

The children were equally surprised the next morning when they found their mother making breakfast. The teens warbled questions, but they got no answers. Ingrid was the first to notice the red, wet eyes. She motioned to Axel and Monica. Axel got it, but Monica had to be kicked under the table before she realized something was wrong. They finished breakfast and went to school, leaving Emma alone the entire day to sort out her feelings and what to do about them.

That evening, after the children had endured a mediocre dinner and were sent to bed early, Emma heard a car pull up outside. She pulled the curtain back and saw Max paying the driver. She wanted to run, but she had nowhere to go. Besides, she thought, maybe she should unload her feelings on Max while they were still raw and honest.

He walked through the door, and Emma confronted him in the foyer. Without saying anything, he walked past her and upstairs, where he said hello to his confounded children and told them to stay in their rooms and go to sleep.

After that preemptive move, he returned downstairs, walked past the stone faced and unmoving Emma and into the living room, where he poured himself a brandy. He sat down in is favorite chair and waited. Emma walked in a few minutes later and just stood there, staring at him and saying nothing.

He couldn't stand the silence, so he started talking. He apologized. He said he never wanted to hurt her. More cliches, and then the explanation. He had met her at his office. She was a young French widow, attractive, pleasant and lonely. So was he. They became friends, and a week before Emma's untimely arrival, they consummated that friendship. Only once, he said. Emma had caught them in their second tryst. She meant nothing to him. He was going to end it right after that. Blah blah blah. Emma just stood there, skewering him with icicle eyes.

Max had told his supervisor he needed Friday off to attend a personal crisis, so he spent the long weekend trying to get Emma to respond or react. Yell, cry, scream, threaten, anything. All he got was silence. The children noticed, but they knew not to intervene or even draw attention. They spent time at friends' homes, ate meals in silence and went to their rooms as soon as possible when chores and homework were completed.

It was Sunday before Emma said anything to Max. And only after he had sent the children to the cinema and raged at his wife for saying nothing since that terrible moment at the Des Rohan. He had to return the next morning, but he would not go without some resolution the crisis he took full responsibility for.

"I will not leave until you say something, anything!" Max raged as she put dishes away in the kitchen. Neighbors heard the ruckus, if not the content.

She was ready. She sat down at the table, and without looking at him, said just one word.

"Why?"

Max was astonished at the babble that poured out his mouth. The truth was, he had no answer other than the opportunity had presented itself. He tried several answers, then gave up.

"Emma, I made a mistake. I will deeply regret it the rest of my life."

That's for sure, she thought.

"What should I do now? Move out? Leave you? Leave the children?"

"Is that what you want?" Emma asked, still not looking at him.

"No, never. I want to keep you, keep my family. You are my life. I promise you I will never do anything like that again. The shame is too much for me. I can't take it. Please don't leave. Please don't take my family from me. I know I deserve anything you do to me. All I can say is I will spend the rest of my life trying to make up for this."

Emma still said nothing. She knew they had to stay together. And she wanted them to. The wound in their marriage was deep, but not fatal. She believed Max was sorry. She didn't know if she could trust him, but she had no viable alternative. What else would she do?

"How much longer must you work in Strasbourg?" she asked, finally breaking her silence.

"Two, maybe three weeks."

"Tell your supervisors you're needed at home. Ask them for permission to end your work there Friday. Make this your last week in Strasbourg."

"I'm not sure they will...."

"Ask them!" Emma snapped, glaring at her husband. "And if you mean what you say, ask them so that they will be sure to say yes. I want you home. I want our lives back to normal. That will take time. It may never happen. I'm willing to try. But we can only start if you're here with your family."

Max nodded and saw he had nothing more to say. It was the best he could hope for under the circumstances. On Monday, he returned to Strasbourg and went straight to his office. He pleaded with his supervisor for a release from his assignment so he could return in time for the start of his school's academic year. Without offering details, he added that a crisis at home required his presence there. With the administrative structure mostly in place because of Max's capable and efficient management, the supervisor was able to grant his wish.

Friday evening, Max was home, and the following week he was back to his school routine. The thaw between Max and Emma was long, slow and difficult. They tried to shield the strain between them from the children. They noticed and were old enough to suspect but too timid to ask. Neighbors had also seen Max's unscheduled arrival and had heard the shouting, so they made up their own stories and gladly shared them in neighborhood gossip sessions. Emma knew it, and it gnawed at her forever.

As far as the Baumanns were concerned, Strasbourg ceased to exist. The parents never mentioned it. Before the war stopped such things, friends would plan outings there only to get a polite but firm rebuff from the Baumanns. The children were kept home from several school trips to the historic city. They were never told why and never asked, but they were sure something awful had happened. They never forget their mother's face that Thursday morning in 1940.

Emma gradually came to terms with the deep wound Max had inflicted. She never completely forgave him, but she reconciled with him and forced herself not to think about it. The war provided an unwanted but effective distraction. Every so often, they would disagree on some issue involving the children or the household, just like any family. But if Emma was determined to get her way, all she had to do was drop a hint or make a cryptic reference. Max always got the message. The debate would end, and Emma would get her way.

It was this deeply private aspect of Max's denazification case that worried Emma. Maybe the Americans wouldn't care, but the process was now in the hands of German neighbors who might find the sordid tale titillating even if it was not germane to the case.

Wrapped in her own personal crisis, Emma was not aware of how controversial the entire process had become and how that could have a bearing on her husband's case.

Germans didn't like judging their fellow countrymen at the behest of the occupation government, and many eligible for tribunal assignments turned them down. This forced authorities to impose a law making refusal to serve on a tribunal illegal.

To get their own handle on the problem after it was thrust upon them, the German civil government required anyone over 18 in the U.S. zone – 13 million – to fill out a Meldebogen, a shorter version of the hated Fragebogen that was the source of Max's case. On May 5, Max had registered and filled his Meldebogen out, but the only changes were rhetorical and procedural. He was listed as having "questionable association" with the Nazi party and would face a tribunal called a Spruchkammer to determine the extent of his guilt. It could range from "major offender" and mandatory jail time to "follower" drawing a small fine. Or he could be exonerated.

No matter how it happened or what it was called, he would still have to answer for his actions in Strasbourg.

Complicating all this were the needs and realities of reconstruction. Denazification had idled thousands of Germans with skills desperately needed to keep basic services running and rebuild the shattered economy. Sexism in the Third Reich had given women a postwar advantage because their records tended to be clean. But there were too few to meet recovery's demands.

So cases against professional men were routinely rushed to lenient conclusions that raised questions and even complaints on both sides of the Atlantic. Adding further pressure against denazification was the growing tension between the western allies and the Soviets. Strategists worried that an alienated populace in western Germany might not relish the role of reliable bulwark against a growing threat from the east.

For Emma, none of this really mattered. She feared Max's hearing before the tribunal might lead to public exposure of their Strasbourg secret. After all that had transpired since then, she wasn't sure she could endure the pain and shame all over again.

Schumacher, tactfully letting the story of Strasbourg pass without comment, tried to assure Emma that the tribunal was only interested in Max's actions as an education administrator, and personal details were immaterial. But the lawyer had enough courtroom experience to know anything could happen, and in the privacy of his own study he prepared a strategy for handling any revelation, no matter how personal.

Lengthy conversations gradually produced a line of defense that might work for Max. He had been involved with administrative matters – staff assignments, class schedules and so on. Nothing political. Others had dealt with classroom matters and textbook content. Also, Max's reluctance to join the party and the teachers federation was implied because his applications came after memberships were required by law. Schumacher speculated that those mitigating factors could be enough to convince a tribunal that Max had been following orders, but not his personal political beliefs, in Strasbourg.

The chief threat to that line of defense was Fenslinger. He claimed that Max had received considerable bonuses and other perks for taking the Strasbourg assignment. As examples, he cited Max's retention of his rector status throughout the war. He insinuated that French forces entering Karlsruhe had been ordered by some unnamed Strasbourg admirer to keep away from the Baumann home. The former student questioned how Fritz had been spared eastern front duty. Finally, he alleged that Axel's defeatist, Marxist rantings in public toward the end of the war had been tolerated because of Max's service to the fatherland in Strasbourg.

Schumacher wanted a case-clincher, an ironclad and dramatic piece of evidence to show Max not only was not active in the party but in some way resisted it.

Monica gave it to him, or at least he thought so. She was listening to her father and his lawyer work on their arguments one Sunday afternoon in Max's book-lined study when Schumacher produced several letters from former students praising Max as an educator and saying he had never spoken in favor of the Nazis. Max was flattered and appreciative, but Schumacher still was not satisfied. Nobody had said Max had spoken against them either.

"Too bad the others aren't here," Monica said.

"What others?" the lawyer asked.

"The ones I used to play with," Monica said with a sarcastic emphasis on "play."

"No use bringing that up," Max said. "That won't help."

"What won't? What's she talking about?" Schumacher did not appreciate being left out of the conversation.

Monica solved the riddle.

"Before the war, when Jews were not allowed in school, the ones thrown out of father's school came here at night, and father tutored them. Basic things, but otherwise they would have had no schooling at all."

Schumacher lurched toward Max.

"Why haven't you told me this?"

"It doesn't matter," Max shrugged. "There were only a few of them, and they all left before the war. Their families were able to emigrate to America. I think they are all still there."

"How many?"

"A dozen or so, that's all."

"They were all Jewish?"

"Yes.

"Do you have any contact with them. Do you know where they are?"

"No. Some American Jewish agency helped the families emigrate, but I never found out where they went."

Schumacher couldn't hide his frustration. Testimony from these children would show that Max risked his own safety and that of his family to help educate Jewish children barred from school by the Nazi race laws of 1935. It was not only an act of generosity. It was an act of defiance.

But without their whereabouts, they were beyond his reach and could not help Max. The story told by anyone else would be dismissed as hearsay.

The lawyer went back to his notes and his collaboration on Max's defense. But he could not stop thinking about those children.

That evening, at Mike's place, Monica told him about the conversation with her father's lawyer and repeated to story of the secret schooling. Mike saw the makings of a story, but he knew too much was missing, and ethically he could never do the story because of his personal involvement. He was not even eligible to cover the hearings. George had already assigned them to Morton and didn't have to tell Mike why.

It was just as well. Mike would have never been able to cover Max's hearing, even if he wanted to. A telegram from home made sure of that.

GOLDEN TIMES XV

Mike was lying on his sofa reading the latest Hemingway novel when the doorbell rang.

A fresh-faced private in an oversized uniform was standing at the door.

"Sergeant Falwell? Telegram."

The messenger turned without waiting for a thank you or anything and raced out of the building to a jeep with the engine running. He must have a lot of deliveries, Mike thought.

Mike looked at the yellow envelope. He hated telegrams. They almost never had good news.

This one was no exception.

> MOTHER VERY ILL STOP RETURN HOME AT ONCE STOP DAD

It was the first communication of any kind he had received from home since the end of the war. Not that he had craved any contact. But he had been disappointed that his letter announcing his engagement a month earlier had not drawn any kind of congratulations or even acknowledgment.

He was surprised by how nervous the news made him. He was not close to his parents, particularly his overbearing, opinionated, snobby mother. She was the most sanctimonious person he had ever known. He could do nothing right. Neither could anyone else for that matter, including her wealthy, hen-pecked husband.

But now he was disturbed, even a little upset. Was his mother dying?

He ran over to the bureau, and with George's okay arranged a transatlantic call home. He went downstairs to the call center, where Monica was working late, and told her what he knew. She made the arrangements for the call and managed the connection to make sure it was done right.

The connection was good, but his father's tone was not. Come home at once. It's her heart. She may not last much longer.

Mike felt a sudden flash of concern for his mother, and he took a moment to wonder why. For years he had loathed his mother, or at least the person she had become. Years later, when someone hit just the right chord at just the right moment, Mike would concede how he had really known two mothers. The first he barely remembered, although the memories were warm and comforting. But he could recite details of the genesis moment for the second mother, the one who had striven to make everyone around her as miserable as she was.

Mike was a baby the day his mother morphed. He barely remembered the details, not sure if they were indeed snippets of his memory or creations of the stories he had heard afterward. Whatever they were, they were memories of pain and trauma for the entire family.

His older brother Sam had loved to play hide-and-seek in the spacious yard and mysterious basement of the family's Victorian-style home on the edge of the pioneering shopping district called the Country Club Plaza. This had become almost a mandatory ritual when neighborhood children came over to play.

On a summer day in 1924, two-year-old Mike was imprisoned in a playpen while seven-year-old Sam went into his disappearing routine. The other kids fell into line and started searching the usual hideouts, including the basement. But Sam had a new strategy based on a cubbyhole he had found just below the gas pipe leading into the kitchen directly above. He figured he was virtually find-proof, so he hunkered down to be as quiet as a seven-year-old could be.

The inevitable squirm and deep breath gave him away, and the other children squealed outside the basement to announce their discovery. Oblivious to the danger of the black pipe just above his head, Sam popped up in hopes of finding a different sanctuary. His shoulder slammed against the pipe, dislodging it from its shoddily installed connection. The metal then scraped against foundation rock, igniting just enough of a spark to turn the pipe into a blowtorch.

The flame spewed onto Sam's back, prompting an unearthly scream the other children would never forget. Doris was there in almost an instant, turning a valve to shut off the gas and then trying with her bare hands to extinguish the human fireball that was her son. She succeeded only with the help of a neighbor who had heard the children screaming and rushed to find the cause.

The family doctor arrived moments later, just ahead of Arthur. Nothing could be done for Sam, but Doris had suffered severe burns on her arms, leaving lifelong scars that compelled Doris to wear long sleeves and gloves whenever possible, even in the worst of the Kansas City summers.

Other, deeper wounds were slow to appear and impossible to cure once they set in. Doris and Arthur tried to cope with the loss as best they could. They even managed to conceive another child a year later, but the first serious rift in the marriage came in the fight over the boy's name. Arthur suggested a variety of names, but Doris insisted on Sam. It was too gruesome for Arthur to bear, but neither did he have the heart to deny the wishes of his latently traumatized wife. So Sam it was, and every day Doris had a living reminder – not of her first son, healthy, bright and mischievous, but of the son she watched, heard and smelled as it was incinerated in her hands and before her eyes. The constant memory of that tragedy drove her true personality deep within her, leaving an angry, cold, heartless shell of a mother for Mike and the younger Sam to endure the rest of her lift.

His own sense of loss and the emergence of the new, loveless woman in his life drove Arthur behind his own wall of emotional protection. Divorce was unthinkable, so he relied on an awkward mix of distance, deference and dalliances to cope with life in another Victorian house beside a woman he hardly knew and liked even less.

For Mike, the story of his older brother Sam was mostly a chapter of family history that he witnessed but could not remember. And yet, something inside remembered. It awoke every time Mike smelled gas or merely confronted its presence, such as when he first walked into his apartment or when he covered the fateful explosion down the street from the Baumann house. First would come the wave of fear and revulsion, then the awareness of why.

So as Mike reacted to the news from home, he let all those emotions play out one more time. After a moment of reflection, he summoned up his toughest version of the unemotional reporter's persona and set to work on the task at hand.

Mike called the local family assistance office, which started the paperwork for emergency transport home. Within 24 hours, he had orders to catch a flight from Frankfurt. He packed as best he could, shared with Monica their first goodbye kiss, and caught a ride with an MNS writer who was in town for a feature and just happened to be heading back home to Frankfurt.

The long C-54 flight to New York linked up with a TWA DC-3 flight to Kansas City, where he called home just after landing at dusk. Less than 72 hours after the telegram arrived, a Yellow Cab carrying an exhausted and starving sergeant pulled up to the two-story Victorian home in the fashionable Brookside area south of downtown where he had grown up. He expected to see his father on the front veranda, but as he paid the driver and turned toward the house, he was staggered by the sight that greeted him in the late twilight of the Midwest summer.

His father, Arthur, was indeed standing there, arms folded, sweat spots darkening each underarm of his blue cotton shirt. To his right, directly at the top the steps was his mother Doris, in her typical blue polka dot dress, looking as cool and healthy as the day he had joined the army five years earlier.

After dropping his bag and shaking is father's hand, he gave his mother a peck on the cheek.

"You look mighty good for someone very ill," Mike said, emphasizing the two words from the telegram.

"Thank you Michael. We need to talk. Please bring your things inside."

Mike was confused, disoriented, tired and above all mystified. Why the telegram? Was she really sick or was this some kind of ruse?

He sank into the overstuffed sofa he had hated for years and accepted a glass of water and a sandwich from his father, who asked perfunctory questions about the flight home while Mike let a floor fan try to cool him off.

Mike said nothing, staring at his mother as she settled into a matching chair across from a coffee table covered with magazines that looked impressive but were never read.

"We felt this was serious enough to get you home as soon as we could," she said, looking directly at him as she always did in their conversations, which were usually more like solo dissertations.

"We got your letter telling us about this Monica girl."

Mike sat up, the moist hairs on the back of his hot neck jumping to attention.

"We were very surprised. Shocked actually. We don't understand how you could let some German girl ruin your life like that."

Mike wanted to throw something. He was so furious he couldn't find words to start a coherent rebuttal. His mother didn't stop.

"We didn't want to discuss this in letters or even on the phone. So we decided to do what was necessary to get you home and talk some sense into you."

Mike glanced at his father, who was looking at the floor. Typical, he thought. Let mother do all the dirty jobs.

"It's obvious this girl is just after you for your money. She thinks she can find the good life here. We've seen this in other families. They get over here and in no time they're stepping out and having a fine old time. It always ends the same way. The American is always the one who gets hurt. We don't want that to happen to you. We think that once you get away from this girl, you'll meet some fine young lady here in the states and forget all about this Monica person. And we're sure she'll be happier with her own kind over there. It will be the best for everyone."

Mike had heard enough.

"The best for you, you mean. You get your fancy wedding, your new connections, your bragging rights to all your pathetic friends. Now you won't be getting any of that crap. You think my marrying Monica is a scandal, an embarassment. You don't know anything about her, and you're already dismissing her as some gold-digging Yank chaser. As usual, mother, you don't have any damn idea what you're talking about."

"No need for language like that," Arthur inserted, lame as ever.

"Fuck my language," Mike said. "Now what are you going to do, spank me? Wash my mouth out? You want language? How's this: I love Monica. I'm crazy about Monica. I'm going to marry Monica. I don't care what you think or say. I haven't since I left home and I won't start now.

"I cannot believe you pulled this kind of a stunt. I hate to admit this, but you scared the hell out of me. I was really worried about you. I should have known. At least I won't fall for that again. I'll have to see a wirephoto of your toes curled before I'll come back here again."

Arthur's face flashed red at the insolence and disrespect. Doris just stared at her son like a sphinx, refusing to give him the satisfaction of seeing the shock and anger she was feeling. Her son had never spoken to her that way. Look what that German woman has done. She's already turned him against his own family.

Like the cavalry riding to the rescue, Mike's younger brother Sam came through the front door just in time to disrupt the donnybrook.

"You look great in uniform," Sam said as Mike rose to shake his hand. "Good to see you home. How long are you staying?"

Only then did Sam stop to look at the body language and facial expressions of his parents and brother.

"I'm leaving here right now," Mike said, grateful for an escape route. "You still have that apartment down by the station?"

"Sure do. Great spot."

"Got room for me?"

"Uh, sure."

Sam tried to figure out what was happening, but he had learned long ago not to pry with his parents. So he followed Mike out the door, grabbed his bag and then led him to his '34 Ford sedan parked at the end of the driveway. Their parents stayed inside, and Mike didn't look back as they drove away.

"What happened in there," Sam pried. The rules with Mike were easier.

"You know about Monica?"

"Yeah. I saw the picture. She's a knockout. Congratulations."

"Thanks. They got me back here with a phony telegram to talk me into dumping her."

Sam let out a slow whistle.

"They've done some nasty stuff, but that's gotta be the worst. And to you of all people. You're their star. They brag about you all the time."

"Well, I guess they have to stop now. I'm going to marry a German."

They pulled up in front of the three-story brick apartment house and went into Sam's first-floor flat. It was typical for a single man trying to make it as a musician. Dingy, cluttered, stuffy, with a worn-out sofa that Mike would sleep on. But Mike was glad to have a sanctuary from his parents. He wanted to get back to Germany as soon as travel could be arranged. But until then, he'd at least have a place to stay, and think.

Sam grabbed two beers from the ice box, handed Mike one and sat down to catch up with his brother. Sam had also seen combat briefly, but he was home on leave when the war ended. They traded war stories and Mike talked about Monica and her family and his work, all the while letting the back of his mind play out the bizarre confrontation in his parents' living room earlier that day.

Sam saw Mike's mind wandering and decided his brother needed more sympathy.

"I still can't believe they did that," Sam said after a lull in the conversation. "I mean, they got you on a plane and everything. I'm wondering if that might even be illegal."

Mike sat up and stared at his brother. Sam thought he had said something wrong and started to apologize, but Mike held up his hand, and Sam stopped talking.

Mike stood up and started pacing, not saying a word. Then he turned, walked over to his brother and started slapping Sam on both shoulders.

"You are really something," Mike said to his bewildered brother. "You just gave me an idea. If it works, not only will I get the parents off my back forever, I might just be able to work a miracle for Monica."

Sam gawked at Mike, waiting for something that made sense.

"Dad really screwed up. I gotta make some phone calls in the morning. If I hear what I think I'm gonna hear, I'll need a ride back out to the house."

"I thought you were never going back there."

"I think I have a good reason to now. You won't want to miss the show."

Early the next morning, Mike walked the three blocks to the hulking Union Station and into the phone center so he could spare his brother the expense of long distance. He called the MNS Washington bureau and asked a friend, Paul Gillespie, to relay a message to the Karlsruhe bureau, addressed to George but intended for Monica. Mike then gave Gillespie his brother's home phone number and asked him to call when he got a reply from Karlsruhe. He promised to cover all the charges, went back to Sam's and waited.

Four hours later, Sam's phone rang. Paul told Mike he had a response from George via the international message wire but it was too long to read on the phone or to put in a telegram. Mike suggested that Paul run down the hall of the War Department press center where MNS was headquartered and ask a common AP acquaintance for a favor. Paul called back 15 minutes later to say the AP had come through, and the message would be waiting for him at the AP bureau in the Kansas City Star building a mile away from Sam's apartment. Despite the late hour, Mike hurried over to the 24-hour bureau, engaged in some small talk to be nice, and then rushed back to Sam's with the wire message containing everything he needed for his grand plan—names and whatever other relevant information Monica could pump out of her perplexed father. Neither of them could guess what Mike was up to, but they trusted him, sensed his urgency and assumed he had a good reason for asking.

Looking at the wire message, Mike knew what he was trying was a long shot. But the effort alone would be worth the trouble. And if it paid off, the results would be priceless.

After a sleepless night, Mike got a ride from Sam back to their parents' house. Without warning, the two sons walked in on Arthur and Doris as they finished their coffee. Sam sat down and started some meaningless chatter with his mother, sealing her off from Arthur as Mike went to his side of the table.

"Dad, something has come up. It's about you and your business. We need to go outside."

"What about the business?" Doris asked, interrupting Sam's monologue about his latest jazz sessions downtown. Sam kept talking, giving Mike enough time and space to grab his father by the arm and drag him out onto the back porch.

"You've got a problem, Dad."

"I do? What kind of problem?"

"I have friends here who tell me that your little telegram game may have led to a violation of federal law."

"I doubt that," Arthur said, not entirely sure of himself.

"That telegram got me back here on false pretenses. The military flight from Frankfurt had to have cost the government hundreds of dollars, if not more. You caused the military to spend taxpayer money on a false premise. A lawyer friend of mine says that could be wire fraud and felony misappropriation of government funds."

Arthur just stared. Was he getting a shakedown from his own son? He started to respond, but Mike cut him off.

"Imagine what that would do if it got out. Wealthy war department contractor defrauds the federal government for personal business. That would make quite a headline, and I know something about headlines. And think what it would do to your business. Your stock. And worst of all, your reputation."

Mike went for the kill.

"Think what that would do to mother. You'd be ruined. You'd have nothing to do but sit in this big old house, staring at each other. No parties, no club, no American Royal balls. No dinner with Harry and Bess when they take a break from Washington and come back to Independence. Nothing."

By the time Mike was finished, Arthur was furious at his son's insolence and at himself for letting his wife talk him into that bone-headed telegram idea. Under pressure from the public, Washington was sniffing around for anything that could show voters the government was cracking down on wasteful spending now that the war was over. Like any tycoon, Arthur had enemies who would make the most of what Mike was saying.

Searching for holes in Mike's theory, Arthur took wrong turn.

"Even if you're right, who's going to know?" Arthur asked.

"Dad, I'm a reporter. I can make sure somebody knows."

Now Arthur was ready to deck his older son. How dare he threaten his own father.

"You'd ruin your family and my business just to make a point?" Arthur raged. Doris was looking out the window at them, but Sam made sure she didn't intervene.

"I don't want to ruin this family or the lives of all those people working for you. And I think I know a way to turn this into a philanthropic exercise that might make you a hero."

Now Arthur was baffled. He seriously wondered whether his son was suffering from a delayed case of shell shock or some other combat-induced mental disorder.

"OK, son. What's on your mind. You obviously have some reason to bring up all this."

That's when Mike pulled out the wire copy he had picked up at the AP bureau. On it were a dozen names as well as contact information for a U.S.-based agency that helped Jews flee Germany before the war.

"Here's the deal, Dad. I need you to pull some strings and find as many of these kids as you can. They came from Germany before the war. They'd be teenagers now. This agency helped get them here. I bet they know where at least some of them are. I need to find these kids."

"Why? Is this some story you're working on? Have your people find them for you."

"No dad, this is personal. It's for Monica. And her father. These kids can help him out of a tough spot. But I need to find as many as possible.

"OK, so what happens if we do find some of them."

"You're going to pay for those kids to fly to Germany, just for a few days. Round trip. Plus a chaperone or two. You can say it's to let them see their homeland again. Or whatever you want to say. Just find them and help me get them to Frankfurt. I'll take care of the rest."

"This is nuts," Arthur said, walking away from Mike. "I'm not going to pay for some homecoming junket for a bunch of German Jews."

"I didn't say they were Jews. Why did you call them Jews?"

"The names are Jewish. And besides, I know what this agency did before the war. I helped them."

"You what?"

"They needed money, so a couple of times I wrote them a check. That's all. I read Hitler's book. I had an idea what was coming. So I helped to get a few of them out. Not that it did much good. My God, how any human being could do that, much less a whole nation. And now you're marrying one of them."

Mike's fist cocked, but Arthur climbed down right away.

"I'm sorry, that's not fair. Please forgive me. Your mother has me all riled about this Monica. I'm sure if you like her so much she must be nice. And I assume she comes from a good family."

Mike wouldn't take the bait and got back on the subject he wanted to pursue. At least he had the satisfaction of knowing his father could act with honor once in awhile. So he recited the story of the secret tutoring sessions in the Baumann basement, making a mental note of the coincidental collaboration of the two fathers to help those children.

"Monica's father is going through denazification, and the deck may be stacked against him. These kids can get him off the hook.

He's an old fashioned guy, but he's a good man. He's been through a lot. You gotta help."

Arthur liked the pleading tone he was hearing from his son far more than the threats that had started the conversation. He looked at the list, looked at his son, and then looked through the window at his wife, who had been trying to read lips while pretending to listen to Sam.

"I'll see what I can do. Are you staying at Sam's."

"Yeah. Call me as soon as you know something. I can put off my flight back. My boss will cover for me. But I don't have too much time. His hearing is scheduled for some time this month.

"O, there's one other thing. You better figure out how to pay the government for my transatlantic flight. Just tell them it was a misunderstanding or something like that. I'm sure they'll appreciate the refund."

Looking one more time through the window, Arthur nodded and made one more pact with his son.

"Let's not tell your mother about this. It'll just wind her up again."

"Yeah," Mike said. "We wouldn't want a relapse, would we?"

After a brusk goodbye for his mother, Mike left with Sam and stayed at his place that night. The next morning, Mike flew back to New York, clearing additional leave with MNS from there. He then waited for his father to work his magic, and he didn't have to wait long.

Through the rescue agency, the local office of Falwell Industries needed just two days to find six of the children in the New York area. Two were girls and would never get their parents' permission for such a trip. The families of the four boys at first balked. They were willing to have their sons, now ages 16 to 18, sign testimonial statements. But they did not want to subject the boys to the physical rigors of a transatlantic flight and the emotional rigors of a public forum dredging up issues and events they preferred to leave in the past.

Mike had anticipated the offers of written statements and said no. Max's file bulged with written testimonials, but they had not moved the tribunal to dismiss the case. Somebody had to counter

Bodo Fenslinger face to face. Otherwise, the smooth talking scoundrel might tip the scales against Max for a tribunal already criticized in some quarters for being too lenient in previous cases.

After further intense negotiations, the parents agreed to let their sons go back to Germany if properly escorted and supervised. They had never intended to expose their children to anything German ever again, and they forced Mike to promise they would be asked to testify only as a last resort. But they all agreed it was a fitting way to show their respect and appreciation for the honorable Herr Baumann.

In less than a week after hatching his improbable scheme, Mike was meeting the boys in the Hotel New Yorker's busy lobby. Michael Morgenstern, Arthur Borowski, David Salzmann and Adam Weiss each brought one bag, and two young men from the New York office's personnel department had joined them as chaperones. The boys had retained their German even though their families insisted on speaking English. They had brushed up in German classes, where easy A's pumped up their grade averages.

Mike's started relaxing when all the arrangements had been made for the flight to Germany on Sunday to give the boys the Sabbath at home. But his impatience re-ignited Sunday morning when a telegram from Monica via George reported that her father's hearing had been moved up. It would start Wednesday. He had less than 72 hours.

Pan Am tickets in hand, they left that evening for the 12-hour flight to Frankfurt. Since the boys still held valid German papers, they easily passed through the checkpoints. After claiming their bags, they were met by two of Mike's friends at the MNS Frankfurt bureau, who had somehow talked their motor pool into loaning them a small bus normally used for staff trips to major news events.

After a quick, smooth ride on the Frankfurt-Karlsruhe autobahn, the exhausted group rolled through the dark Karlsruhe streets, the boys pressing their noses against the windows, gawking at the shattered heart of what was once the center of their lives.

They were housed in a large, fully furnished and generously stocked apartment in the block next to Mike's. Monica had seen to that. Mike was learning more about his fiancee every day. Whenever he counted on her, she came through without complications or complaints,

She dropped by the apartment the next morning to say hello and make sure the boys had everything they needed. They greeted her as an old friend and reminisced for a few moments until Monica had to hurry off to work.

Then they got cleaned up and dressed, shared a simple breakfast that Mike had made sure was kosher, and waited.

Like most Germans called to duty, Lothar Hallmann hated tribunal work. A Social Democratic judge who had fled to Switzerland before the war, he agreed with the drive to purge German society of the vermin who had led, followed and profited from the Nazis. But most of the men he was judging had been low level functionaries or professionals who went along to get along.

He resented what he considered the hypocrisy of the OMGUS officials overseeing the German denazification effort that they had decided was too cumbersome and contentious to manage themselves. The Americans were expecting from Hallmann's and all tribunals the retribution demanded by public opinion back home. But individual officers were quietly delivering a conflicting message: most of these men are needed for the reconstruction effort, so clear the cases as quickly as possible so they can go to work.

Max stood in a no man's land between those two imperatives. He had played a notable role in Germanizing Strasbourg schools, but his profession was low on the priority list for Germany's recovery. So Hallmann and his two tribunal colleagues were ready to give Max Baumann's case unusually close scrutiny. While never saying so, they knew they could make an example of him to please their American watchdogs without depriving the German economy of a vital skill.

Schumacher knew this too, and that's why he was so relieved to hear that the boys were in town just in time for the hearing.

Friends had tipped him off to the cross currents tugging at the tribunal. He was sure his client was clean, but bitter courtroom experience had taught him that justice did not always prevail.

GOLDEN TIMES XVI

A cold drizzle was falling when the principals arrived for Max's hearing at a squat gray building that had once been a Luftwaffe barracks at the airfield near the Baumann home. It was poorly lit, poorly ventilated and sparsely furnished with rough tables for the tribunal and hearing participants and heavy wooden chairs for spectators. Witnesses were asked to wait in an adjoining room that was equally spartan and dreary. The boys were allowed to remain at the apartment. If needed, they were just a few minutes away by car.

Max and his lawyer sat at a table to one side of the tribunal's desk. Across from them, the tribunal's advocate, a euphemism for prosecutor, was seated next to a court reporter who would manage the official transcript. Another chair was empty. Behind them in the shadows sat an American observer. He was an officer, but Max and his lawyer knew nothing more about him. A few dozen chairs were arranged in rows of eight with an aisle dividing them. In those chairs sat Monica, Mike, Ingrid, Fritz and a few curious neighbors and former students. Conspicuously absent was Emma, who could not bear the thought of sitting through the ordeal, particularly if Max's personal behavior in Strasbourg entered the proceedings. She had insisted on staying home under the weak pretext that someone had to mind Elisabeth. Axel had no intention of attending, and that was fine with the family. Gisela joined the witnesses after her shift and would give Axel a full report later.

Just before the scheduled start time of 3 p.m., Bodo Fenslinger, dressed in a stereotypical full length black leather rain coat over a baggy gray suit, walked in and sat in the empty chair.

Hallmann and the two other tribunal members, all wearing three-piece suits and looking decidedly uncomfortable and unjudicial, walked in just as Fenslinger was sitting down, forcing him to pop up awkwardly as everyone rose. Before Hallmann could say a word, Max's lawyer took the offensive, challenging the snitch's presence.

"He is a central figure in this case," Hallmann explained. "We need him here for his insights as evidence is presented. Otherwise, we would have to call him into this room every few minutes. That would not be an efficient use of our time."

Schumacher gave up and sat down. His protest was on the record, and he knew further argument was pointless, especially when he caught a glimpse of the American officer in the background gently nodding his head in agreement. It was a sinister new element that worried Schumacher. But he didn't show it. He was on stage now, and he knew his role.

Hallmann opened by reciting Max's personal data and history, noting that he had served honorably as a decorated officer in the Bavarian Army during the first war and later developed a reputation as an able and respected educator.

He quoted pertinent passages from Max's questionnaires confirming his membership in the party and the party-run teachers federation. He noted for the record that Max had joined the party in 1937, believing the law left him no choice. His questionnaire addendum mentioned that Emma had urged him not to join. But with three children to feed, he had decided he had no alternative.

Hallmann countered that other than the late application date, there was no evidence that Herr Baumann had resisted joining the party, as some teachers and rectors had done as a matter of conscience.

The tribunal chairman then listed the main points of the allegation against Max – that in 1940 he had furthered the Nazi cause by imposing German standards on the Strasbourg school system.

Schumacher heard nothing new in all this. But Hallmann's stark, clinical opening remarks distilled the case to its bitter essence. It had unsettled Max, and at that moment he didn't like his chances.

The next phase belonged to the advocate, a chubby functionary with a suitably expansive name, Hans-Juergen von Tannenberg. He had wanted to make his own opening statement, but Hallmann had vetoed the idea to save time. So Tannenberg just thanked the chairman and swore in his first witness, a German-speaking French education official, Henri Meaux.

Guided by the advocate's questioning, Meaux explained how things changed in Strasbourg schools after Max Baumann. He described how Jewish children were barred, how texts slanted history, sociology, anthropology and other social sciences to match the party line. Teachers were told what to include or exclude from lectures on a broad array of subjects. Music classes changed repertoires. Art classes taught only classical methods. When Meaux finished, it was clear how thorough the Germanizing of the Strasbourg schools had been.

Schumacher took his turn with the witness, asking whether Meaux had known Max personally. He said they had never met, but he was familiar with Baumann's role in converting the schools.

Schumacher then asked Meaux to describe his understanding of Max's work there. Meaux said Baumann had concentrated on administration and organization, changing some job functions and titles, rearranging lines of authority and introducing some efficiencies in budgeting and financial operations.

"What is your assessment of the changes Herr Baumann instituted?"

"They were by and large effective. They did improve efficiency, as you would expect from a German."

Meaux meant it as a light-hearted aside, but it rankled everyone in the room. Schumacher moved on.

"Did Herr Baumann have anything to do with the content of texts or curriculum in the Strasbourg schools, or anything else directly imposing Nazi ideology?"

Pausing for a moment, Meaux answered, "No, not directly. That was done by others. But his changes led to those other changes. He created the structure..."

"Thank you, Monsieur Meaux," Schumacher said, cutting off the witness. "You may be excused."

Tannenberg nodded, so Meaux walked out of the hall. The advocate called his next witness, Bodo Fenslinger.

After admitting the key points of his own unsavory past, Fenslinger recited his allegations against Max, claiming he had heard accounts of the teacher praising the Nazi regime in classrooms. Fenslinger then alluded to the facts lined out by Hallmann concerning Max's work in Strasbourg. He added that he had heard numerous party colleagues praising the results of the school conversions there, and he had seen a letter of commendation prepared for Max.

Tannenberg had found a copy and placed it on the tribunal's table. Max had given his lawyer the original, so this was no surprise.

Then Tannenberg went for the kill. He asked Fenslinger if Herr Baumann had profited from his work for the regime in Strasbourg.

"Of course he did," Fenslinger said, half laughing. "He retained his position as rector because of that. And that's just one example. The others did not involve money or position, but I'm sure they were just as valuable to him."

Repeating his list of allegations for the record, Fenslinger alleged that Max's good work had kept Fritz out of combat, had ensured special treatment for Axel, had kept Monica in safe rural areas for the Labor Service, had shielded his home from French invaders and had protected his wife when she blurted something disloyal or defeatist in public (the bunker, Schumacher jotted in his notes).

"These are serious allegations," Tannenberg purred to his star witness. "Are you sure about these things?"

"I would not talk this way under oath if I was not confident they are true. They were common topics in party offices here in Karlsruhe. Everybody knew."

Tannenberg was satisfied and sat down.

Without waiting to be prompted, Schumacher charged the witness chair.

"Everybody knew about it," Schumacher parroted with dripping sarcasm. "If everybody knew, why can't this tribunal find anyone else who will say such things? Why are you the only one?"

"I guess some people are afraid. These hearings are not popular. I'm sure the tribunal feels the resentment, and testifying against someone with Herr Baumann's reputation is not a popular thing to do. Others want to put the past behind them and get on with life. I felt it was my duty to make these facts known."

"Facts." More sarcasm. "I wouldn't call any of this facts. It's gossip, hearsay. One man's word. Where is the proof? Do you have anything to verify what you are saying?"

Tannenberg stood up to defend the witness, but Hallmann motioned him to sit down.

"I wish I did. How can I? I can't get to the records concerning his family, nobody can. They're probably all destroyed. But it's pretty obvious, isn't it? I think the facts prove themselves."

"Herr Fenslinger, please stop calling these theories of yours facts. Monsieur Meaux just alluded to how efficient we Germans are. We are the world masters at record keeping. Just look at what the archives are telling us about the concentration camps. Those records weren't lost. They weren't destroyed. The Allies are still digging through all the paperwork from the Third Reich. That's one reason they handed this denazification business to us.

"And yet you come in here making slanderous accusations about a respected member of this community and claim that there is no way to verify what you say. This is the kind of behavior we just got rid of, Herr Fenslinger. We are now creating a nation of laws. It is not entirely ours yet. But it will be soon. And we will never tolerate behavior like yours. Ever."

Hallmann and Tannenberg rose in unison to stop Schumacher's diatribe. But he was finished with that point, if not with Fenslinger.

He walked over to his desk without looking at Max, and returned to Fenslinger holding a thin folder.

"You were a student when Herr Baumann was just beginning his teaching career, were you not?"

"Yes."

"Were you a good student?"

Tannenberg tried to interrupt. Again, Hallmann let the questioning continue.

"Average."

"Why?"

"I don't know. Some people are better suited for studies than others, I guess."

"Was Herr Baumann a fair teacher?"

Fenslinger stared at Max.

"He was very strict."

"Too strict?"

"Sometimes, yes. I thought so."

Schumacher pulled a piece of paper from the folder.

"You say you can't document the things that you have said about Herr Baumann. But I can certainly document some things about you."

Fenslinger's forehead sprouted sweat beads. Tannenberg looked at Hallmann for help but got none.

"These are some of the grades you earned under Herr Baumann. They are not good."

He gave the paper to Hallmann.

"Yes, I know." Fenslinger was getting irritated. "What does this have to do with anything?"

"Let me get to that. I'll ask the questions. Did your parents approve of these marks?"

"My mother died before I started school."

"I'm sorry. Did your father approve?"

"No, he did not." Fenslinger was fuming now.

"How did he react to your grades?"

"He would get angry. Sometimes very angry."

Schumacher opened the folder, pulled out another document and held it in front of witness's face.

"See, Herr Fenslinger, all kinds of documents survived the war." It had taken a diligent team of Max's admirers and former colleagues to find them.

"This one is a medical report from the university hospital here in Karlsruhe. It lists some pretty painful injuries. What caused them?"

"I don't remember. I guess I fell. Children hurt themselves all the time."

Another paper came out of the folder with a flourish.

"Well, Herr Fenslinger, here is a police report filed the same day as the medical report. It says you had to be rescued from a severe beating at the hands of your father. And all this is on the same day you received your grades from Herr Baumann. Isn't it obvious what happened?"

Fenslinger said nothing.

"Herr Fenslinger, did you ever finish your studies?"

Fenslinger assumed by now that Schumacher had a document for every question.

"No."

"Did you leave school?"

"Yes, when I got older."

"And did you leave your father's home?"

"Yes."

"How old were you?"

"16."

"And where did you go?"

"The Hitler Youth had a hostel in the Black Forest near Freiburg. I went to live there."

"And that's how you got started with the party?"

"Yes."

"So your failures in school caused you unbearable misery at home, where your father tried to raise you alone but could not cope. You had to blame someone for losing the only family you had, so the logical choice is the teacher who gave you the bad grades that turned your father against you. Isn't that what really happened?"

Before Fenslinger could answer, Schumacher grandly spun back toward his table and sat down, patting Max on the shoulder. Fenslinger and Tannenberg were jockeying for the floor, but the ex-Nazi prevailed.

"You are trying psychological nonsense to distract everyone from the real issue here," Fenslinger screamed, pointing at Max. "This sanctimonious classroom tyrant profited from serving the Nazis. That's all that matters."

Tannenberg took his turn.

"Herr Fenslinger is not on trial here. He will face judgment soon enough. I protest this personal attack on this witness. I demand an apology from Herr Schumacher and removal of the entire episode from the record."

Hallmann needed time. He had anticipated none of this. Rules of discovery in normal court cases did not always apply in denazification hearings. The tribunal chairman had seen surprises before, but nothing like this. His two colleagues flanking him were as ashen and confused as he was.

"This was completely unexpected. We need time to examine the documents presented by Herr Schumacher to consider the issues presented here today."

With a glance toward the American officer in the dark corner of the room, Hallmann called a recess. The hearing would resume at 9 a.m. the next morning.

Fenslinger leapt out of the witness chair and made a move toward the defense team. Mike made sure he never got there by stepping in his way and holding his ground. He had five inches and 20 pounds on the Nazi weasel, so it was no contest.

"Just walk away," Mike said. Fenslinger's eyes flitted around the room, looking for help. It wasn't there, so he hurled a German obscenity at Mike and stormed out of the hall.

"You have to tell me what that means some day," Mike said to Monica, who was now holding his hand and dragging him toward her father with Ingrid and Fritz right behind.

Max was drained and could say nothing. He gave his family a weak smile, shook Schumacher's hand and led the entourage out into the cool September night, already a prelude to the worst German winter in memory.

Mike rushed back to the apartment to tell the boys all about the hearing and to warn them they were not yet off the hook.

Monica walked home with her family and spent the night there. They had a quiet dinner while Monica and Ingrid took turns giving a full report. Emma just listened, dreading any reference to Strasbourg. When the girls finished, Emma got up to help clear the table, patting Max on the shoulder but not saying a word. Their secret was still safe, for at least one more day.

The next morning was again unseasonably clear and crisp. After a light breakfast, Max and his family, once more minus Emma, bundled up and took the 10 minute walk back to the hearing hall. Monica recognized Mike's jeep in the parking lot and hurried ahead of the group for a private hug and good morning kiss. They filed into the hall together, and within minutes all the principals were back in their places. Only Mike and the Baumann family occupied the spectator area this time. Apparently it was too early any other curiosity seekers to show up.

Fenslinger again took his place next to Tannenberg, and the mysterious American officer was again in the background. The tribunal entered as everyone rose, and then took a minute to let everyone settle down.

Hallmann placed a thick folder in front of him and looked at Max.

"We spent several hours last night and early today going over the issues raised yesterday. This is not an easy task. But we are trying to do what is right.

"We agree with the advocate that Herr Fenslinger is not the accused in his hearing. He is a witness and is not required to prove anything. That is the responsibility of the advocate and this tribunal. And as Herr Schumacher noted, all we have is the word of the witness under oath. Any witness who, while still awaiting denazification himself, commits perjury is an uncommon fool. We would hope Herr Fenslinger is no such fool.

"However, motivation can be a factor in presentation of evidence by any witness. Herr Schumacher did provide documentation that could be construed as providing a motive for vengeance by Herr Fenslinger. The documents offer facts, but the allegation they support is still just a theory. And they in no way have a direct bearing on Herr Baumann's case.

"If we disregard Herr Fenslinger's testimony as hearsay without ruling on what his motives may have been, we are still left with the issue of denazification for Herr Baumann. Did he gain profit or privilege from his activities as ordered by the regime in 1940? We have ample evidence of the effectiveness of his actions in Strasbourg, but we do not yet see any evidence that would raise doubts about his enthusiasm for the job or even for the NS regime itself."

That was Mike's cue. He knocked his chair over backward as he bolted out of the hearing room. Hallmann, momentarily distracted, was annoyed by what he considered yet another example of rude American behavior. Others stared at Mike as he disappeared but then turned back to Hallmann for what was now the obvious conclusion.

"If we are to clear Herr Baumann, we must have tangible evidence, not hearsay or tangential information. Does anyone here know of such evidence."

Schumacher rose.

"Herr Chairman, may I request a 10-minute break to consult with Herr Baumann?"

Nobody objected, so Hallmann led his colleagues into an anteroom for a cup of coffee. Everyone else stayed in their chairs. Fenslinger tried to lobby Tannenberg for some kind of legal or procedural counterattack, but the advocate knew the pathetic character next to him had no further role in the matter.

Tannenberg refused to even look at Fenslinger and stared across the room. He was puzzled by the activities at the table opposite his. There were none. Max glanced repeatedly at the hall's entrance, while his lawyer leaned back and closed his eyes. Tannenberg said to himself: Is that what Schumacher calls consultation?

After precisely 10 minutes, Hallmann led his two partners back to their table. Max was now staring uninterrupted at the door. Schumacher pretended to be sifting through some documents to prepare his next presentation. But he said nothing.

Hallmann endured the silence as long as he could, then addressed the defense table.

"Herr Schumacher, do you have something to present today?"

Schumacher stalled, recapping points already made by all sides and agreeing fully with the tribunal in its conclusions so far. Now he was glancing repeatedly at the door, and Hallmann was losing his patience.

"Excuse me, Herr Schumacher. This is all interesting, but it is getting us nowhere. Herr Tannenberg, do you have anything else to present here?"

"No, Herr Chairman. We think the facts are well established and will rely on the tribunal's wisdom."

Hallmann winced at the servile patronizing.

Just as he turned again to Schumacher, he heard two jeeps roar up to the front door and slide to a halt on the dewy pavement. Everyone turned to the entrance, and in walked Mike, followed by an American civilian and four teenaged boys. They wore blue blazers, white dress shirts, ties and gray slacks. They looked dressed for school.

As curious looks coursed across faces in all parts of the room, Schumacher smiled at the boys and motioned them to empty seats in the front of the spectator section. Max immediately recognized them, stood up and accepted their handshakes as each one reintroduced himself, bowed slightly to their former tutor, and sat down.

Mike sat next to Monica, who tried to look exasperated with him for making everyone late. But she was more relieved than anything. Mike just smiled and shrugged his shoulders.

Hallmann was baffled.

"Who are these young men and why are they here?"

Schumacher took the lead.

"Herr Chairman, you said you need, as you put it, tangible evidence of Herr Baumann's disapproval of, if not opposition to, national socialism. We had hoped to spare these young men this ordeal, but we have brought them all the way from the United States, and we believe they will provide that evidence."

"But these are boys," Fenslinger blurted. "What can they know?"

Tannenberg grabbed his arm, signaling his participation was over.

Schumacher ignored Fenslinger and recited the story of how Max Baumann had defied the 1935 race laws by secretly schooling these four and eight other Jewish children in his home until their families were able to secure safe passage out of Nazi Germany.

Then the boys were sworn in and recited their recollections of the devastation of being expelled from school because of their ethnicity. They also stated their gratitude and admiration for Herr Baumann's willingness to continue their education in defiance of the law.

They told about the lessons that mirrored those given to their former classmates, although often in abbreviated or condensed form. Lessons mostly dealt with basic subjects such as arithmetic, grammar, reading and writing. They kept their educational momentum going just enough so that when they reached America and entered special schools for Jewish refugees, they could resume at grade levels comparable to those they had left behind. All were good students, and the oldest had just earned a scholarship to study mathematics at Columbia University.

To preempt any more talk about hearsay, Schumacher had the boys show Hallmann and Tanneberg lesson books they had saved as souvenirs. Each had the teacher's scribblings noting errors or good work, and Max's handwriting could easily be verified.

Tannenberg said nothing. But Fenslinger was seeing the case evaporate, along with his hopes for leniency in his own case. He had counted on having Max Baumann's scalp on his belt, not only for his future but also to redress the injustice he felt the teacher had inflicted on him as a boy.

So without waiting to be asked, he jumped to his feet.

"This is completely unacceptable! Are you going to allow these silly theatrics to determine the outcome of this case? So what if he helped a few children in his basement for a little while. How does that compare the corruption of an entire city school system?"

The boys sat erect and pale on the front row of chairs, not sure who the screaming man was but afraid of him nonetheless.

"These boys obviously were brought here to distract the tribunal from its real purpose. It's clearly a desperate attempt to hijack this process.

"I don't know who arranged all this," he said, looking at Mike, "but the culprit should face charges for trying to obstruct the work of this tribunal."

He turned to the mysterious American in the background as if to solicit his support. But the officer, arms folded, just stared at him.

Hallmann had enough of Fenslinger's shouting, arm-waving and finger-pointing, so he tried to interrupt. Tannenberg was also tugging on his sleeve, but Fenslinger ignored them, turning instead toward the boys.

"These boys are just pawns in some game. Their families probably agreed to let them come all this way just so they could see the old homeland without having to pay for it. We don't really know who they are? How can we believe them? After all, they're J..."

He caught the rest of the damning word before it could slip out.

"Just boys."

Frightened by his narrow escape from the antisemitic slur, he flopped down into his chair, folding his arms and fixing a withering gaze on the four wide-eyed boys.

"That is quite enough," Hallmann said, disgusted and even ashamed by the tirade. "These witnesses are credible, they have information pertinent to this case and everything they said can be verified in time. But I don't think that will be necessary."

Max's supporters in the crowd smiled when they heard Hallmann's rebuff. Schumacher stood, thanked the chairman and waited for what he was sure would be a triumphal conclusion to the case.

It was his turn to be surprised.

"This is all very impressive," Hallmann said. "A bit theatrical, perhaps, but impressive. I think we now have tangible proof that Herr Baumann did take actions contrary to the spirit and letter of Nazi laws, endangering himself and his family to help students victimized by a racist totalitarian regime. For that he is to be commended.

"However, the matter of Strasbourg is still before us. I regret to say that Herr Fenslinger does make a point. This tribunal must decide whether Herr Baumann's efforts for these students in defiance of Nazism outweigh the effects of his efforts in Strasbourg on behalf of Nazism. We will now recess to consider our ruling."

Schumacher was stunned, as was Max and everyone else in the room, except Fenslinger, who sported an evil grin sensing he still had a chance for vindication. Monica stared at Mike, looking for help to understand why they weren't already walking out to celebrate Max's exoneration. Mike could only shrug as he rose and guided the boys to their jeeps. He sent them home but stayed to be with Monica. The day before he had been relieved to see that no news organization, not even MNS, was covering the hearing. Denazification for small fry wasn't news anymore. Mike wondered whether this case might be an exception, but he knew he was wasn't qualified to make that judgment.

Mike returned to his place next to Monica and looked to see how Max was doing. He was pale, slumped in his chair, looking down at nothing. His day of vindication had gone all wrong. He didn't know what to think, so he didn't try. He just sat there.

Monica chatted in nervous whispers with Fritz, Ingrid and Gisela, so Mike turned the other way and glanced at the advocate's table. Fenslinger was bending Tannenberg's ear in an intense whisper that at first startled the advocate, then made his jaw drop and then turned his face beet red. Mike heard something about "hotel" and "train" just before Tannenberg jumped out of his chair, grabbed Fenslinger by the lapels and through clinched teeth, said in a voice everyone could hear:

"You bastard. How dare you try to insert something like that into this hearing. What could that possible have to do with this case? That is the most outrageous, despicable thing I have ever heard. I suggest you leave at once, Herr Fenslinger, and never mention that disgusting piece of gossip to anyone ever again. If you do, I will hear about it, I can guarantee that. And I will personally insist that Herr Baumann is invited to testify at your hearing. He'll make a much better witness than you did. Goodbye, Herr Fenslinger."

A brusque shove started Fenslinger toward the door. He straighened his jacket, grabbed his storm trooper rain coat and walked out glaring at Max but saying nothing more. Max was startled by the outburst but was in no shape to guess its cause. Schumacher, however, guessed right. He nodded respectfully to Tannenberg, who rolled his eyes and shook his head in disbelief at the deplorable behavior of his former key witness.

It was the last time any of them saw Fenslinger. He never faced denazification. Before his hearing could be scheduled, he scraped together enough money to move to Argentina, where he felt instantly at home in the German community and later prospered as a Peronist lackey.

The tribunal took two hours before announcing a decision. Ingrid's nerves had given out and she had taken a walk with Fritz. They walked in almost on cue as the tribunal emerged from the anteroom and stood at their table.

Hallmann looked at a scrap of paper and then at Max.

"Herr Baumann?"

Max and his lawyer stood up.

"This tribunal has had a difficult time with your case," Hallmann said. Everyone was looking for a hint of what was coming, but Hallmann gave nothing away.

"It is a fact that you reorganized the Strasbourg school system in 1940 under orders from the NS regime. While you had no part in injecting Nazi ideology into those schools, your actions set the stage for those detestable principles. However, we can find no verifiable evidence that you or your family profited from your actions in Strasbourg.

"We are very impressed with your tutoring of the Jewish children after they were expelled under the race laws. The fact that four of them were willing to travel so far to help you is a testament to your stature as an educator and humanitarian. This was clearly a noble and brave act of defiance. It is a mitigating factor, but does not entirely exonerate you from the responsibility for what happened in Strasbourg.

"Therefore, we find that Max Baumann was a low-level functionary in the Nazi regime, in other words, a follower. We also are convinced he carries no lingering sympathy for or admiration of national socialism. We order him to pay a fine of 1,000 Reichsmarks, and he is cleared to resume his work as teacher and rector. This case is closed."

The ruling robbed Max and his family of the explosive joy of total victory. They weren't sure how to react, so they just looked to him for a cue. He made a small bow toward the tribunal as they left the room, shook hands with Schumacher, walked over to his family and hugged Monica first, then the others. There were no tears, no laughter.

Much later, Max would learn that he was just one of more than 880,000 Germans who faced tribunals in the American zone between 1946 and 1948. A half million were sanctioned, with more than 80 percent falling into the least serious category called followers.

Mike saw the shadowy American officer shake Hallmann's hand and walk out through a side door. Hallmann looked relieved and pleased, but Mike still couldn't read what that meant. He turned around and hugged Monica without saying anything.

They all shuffled out of the dark, cold barracks and walked back to the Baumann house in silence.

Emma saw the group walking down the street and met them on the driveway. She could not tell what happened from their demeanor.

"Well?" It came out louder and with more desperation than she had intended.

"It's good," Max said, hugging his wife. "It's over."

Emma heard the words, but they didn't match the mood. As they went inside and sat down in Ingrid's living room for coffee, Ingrid stayed at the side of her husband and sat down with him on the sofa, leaving the others to drag chairs in from the dining room.

"So, you can teach again?" Emma asked.

"Yes, I can go back to work."

Emma slapped his arm and smiled.

"But they fined me 1,000 Reichsmarks."

"We can pay that easily, now that our assets are released," Emma said.

Max kept talking.

"They called me a low-level functionary, a follower. That will be on my record for the rest of my life."

Emma looked around the room for some clarification but turned back to her husband.

"You weren't a low-level functionary. What kind of nonsense is that? Why would they say such a thing?"

"I guess my work in Strasbourg was too good."

The mention of that city froze Emma.

"Did anything else come out at the hearing?" Everyone saw her look, but only Max knew what she was asking.

"No. It almost did. But it did not."

The others babbled questions about what "it" was.

"Nothing," Max lied. "A minor tax problem a few years ago. I thought it might come up. But it didn't."

Emma's look of relief was far too intense for a minor tax problem. But they let it go.

A knock on the door preceded Schumacher's entrance into the room. Everyone stood and shook his hand in thanks, but he was in no triumphant mood.

"I can appeal the fine if you wish," Schumacher said, accepting a cup of coffee from Ingrid. "I think the ruling was unfounded. You proved everything they needed to know. We can try for full exoneration. It may take time."

Max just shook his head.

"I don't want any more of this. I can't put my family through it either. I want to start teaching. My daughter is getting married. We have a wedding to plan. She will be leaving us soon. I want to concentrate on that. People know me. The hearing confirmed I have a good reputation. They know what kind of a person I am."

"And even if they don't, we can't do anything about what they think."

Max looked at his wife, rubbed her cheek gently with the back of his hand, and smiled for the first time in two days.

"Since when do we care about what other people think? Right, Emma?"

Mike's jeep bounced gently on the rutted, muddy street that led into the village of Feldtal, just a few miles further into the countryside from the Baumann's neighborhood. This village had been the home to some of Max's students, most notably at this moment the Jewish emigrant, Adam Weiss, who had endured the trip back to Germany to help his former teacher.

Mike had tried to talk Adam out of this pilgrimage, arguing it could make them late or the flight home. But he knew Adam had plenty of time and only worried how the visit might affect the 17-year-old.

As the jeep stopped at the little village square with a simple round fountain in the middle, Adam pointed out some of the landmarks of his childhood to Mike. They both noted how pristine the village had remained, showing no scars of war.

Adam was at first somewhat energetic in his recital of his childhood memories, but the mood changed when they approached a side street and stood in front of a boarded-up shop. It had been his father's tailor shop, a prosperous business until the Nazis forced them out and gave it to a party hack. That man and his family had long ago fled Germany and justice, leaving the store an empty shell.

As Adam told of his family's last desperate days to get out of their homeland and the salvation they had received from the American Jewish organization, an elderly woman with an arthritic limp slowly approached the two men, starring intently at the younger one.

"Excuse me," she said, interrupting them. "Are you Adam Weiss?"

"Yes," the boy said, not recognizing the woman.

"O God, I can't believe it's you," she said, smiling and clapping her hands together. "I am Frau Saenger. I used to take care of you when your parents were working in the shop. Do you remember me?"

"Yes I do," Adam said, reaching out to shake her hand. "I'm sorry I didn't recognize you. It's been a long time."

"Yes it has," she said, ignoring Mike entirely. "But you are growing up to be a fine looking young man. How is your family?"

"They are well. We live in New York now. My father has his own clothing business. He is very successful."

Adam gathered his memories for a moment and then let them shape his next question.

"Frau Saenger, where are the other Jewish families who lived here? The Steinbergs? The Liebowitzes? And I know there were a few others, but I can't remember their names right now."

Frau Saenger's gracious demeanor faded, and then saddened.

"They are gone."

"Did they leave too, like we did?"

"No. They are just gone."

"You mean, to the camps?"

Frau Saenger could only nod. She was hoping the subject would end there. But Adam pressed on, with Mike silently watching from a few yards away.

"Didn't anyone try to save them? Hide them?"

"We all wish we could have. But there was no way. It was impossible."

Adam lost his deferential demeanor he reserved for his elders and bore down on the now fidgeting old woman.

"Impossible? Why? Jews all over Europe were saved by courageous people who took the risk. Look at the Dutch, the Danes."

"But they were in other countries. Here it was the law and we could do nothing against it."

"Did you know what would happen to them when they were taken away?"

Mike was tempted to step in but decided to let Adam pursue his line of questioning.

"We heard rumors. But we never thought anything as horrible as that would happen. We just thought it was Nazi craziness talking. How could we imagine they would do such terrible things."

Mike noticed the "they" and stifled an urge to shake his head.

"But you heard the rumors," Adam continued. "You had to have some idea. Some Germans did. Father Rupert Mayer, for example."

Mayer used his pulpit in Munich to preach against Naziism until he was exiled to a remote Bavarian monastery.

"But he had the Vatican protecting him," Frau Saenger shot back defensively. "We had nobody to protect us."

"The White Rose students didn't have anyone protecting them, but they tried," Adam said.

The small band of students – brave to some, foolhardy to others – tried to incite a revolt during the war with a pamphlet campaign that came to a tragic end at the University of Munich.

"And those students ended up being guillotined in a prison garage," she said, somewhat more defiantly this time."

Adam saw there was no point continuing the debate. He made a conciliatory closing comment and said goodbye to Frau Saenger. As he walked back to the jeep with Mike at his side, Mike waited for Adam to say something. He kept his head down in silence, except for one whispered final thought, more to himself than anyone.

"But they TRIED. At least they tried."

GOLDEN TIMES XVII

It took Max two weeks to find a job. The less than total victory in the denazification hearing ruled him out of a rector's position at the time, so he took a teaching job at a private business school. He liked the intimacy of the small institution, and in later years when the taint of denazification had evaporated, the school restored him to his prewar stature by naming him rector, a post he held until retirement.

Max had been surprised by his emotions on his last day in the canteen. People whom he had seen but never got to know, Americans and Germans, went out of their way to wish him well. Monica even dropped by for the only time they were ever seen together in the kitchen. When Max introduced the call center operator as his daughter, a few panicking colleagues wracked their brains trying to remember if they had ever said or done anything to offend the lovely young lady. They had no reason to worry. Monica never remembered that sort of thing anyway.

Monica was also in her final weeks at the call center, helping Avril to find a suitable replacement for her. The job was advertised at the city labor office, and this time a decent selection of candidates applied. He insisted on having Monica participate in the interviews, but she insisted on sparing applicants from the torture of Avril's mind games. After meeting a dozen or so hopefuls, they agreed on one young war widow who had traveled widely with her parents as a child and spoke four languages fluently. She was by no means as pretty as Monica, but her voice was superb, and her personality matched the requirements of the job.

For Monica, the real stress in her life involved the impending wedding and the move to America. She tried to hide it from Mike, but the prospect of total separation from everything and everyone she knew was intimidating. She worried about adjusting, fitting in with a new set of friends, and even how Washington would treat a German newcomer. She didn't realize that thousands of German women had blazed that trail before her, and most were thriving in a country proud to be a creation of and haven for immigrants and refugees.

Emma emerged from Max's denazification ordeal with more energy than the family had seen since the end of the war. The secret had been bottled up, Max was in school again, and now she could focus on her daughter's wedding.

Like mothers of the bride everywhere, she increasingly imposed her wishes on Monica, from the guest list and reception arrangements down to the flowers and refreshments. When they met with the pastor of their episcopal church, he barely said two words and Monica even less. Emma knew what she wanted and that was all he needed to know.

Ingrid knew what to expect and held herself in reserve for special tasks. Fritz was busy with his accounts and had no time or interest for what he saw as the frivolity of wedding planning. Gisela, who was still seeing Axel even as their relationship cooled, gave him regular updates relayed from Monica, but in her own sardonic style that could get Axel laughing, a rare break in his increasingly dour demeanor.

By the fall of 1946, Reichsmarks were good for almost nothing. So Emma had to hone her barter and bargaining skills to acquire some of the wedding necessities. She traded produce from her garden for flowers. Several bottles of liquor (including a few from Mike that bent the rules) worked for reception food and beverages. A few loaves of bread were exchanged for candles.

For the most important things, Emma had hoarded a few cartons of Lucky Strike cigarettes, the true currency of the occupation and more under-the-table gifts from the nonsmoking future son-in-law.

Armed with those treasures, Emma set off for town one Saturday with Monica to search for a wedding dress. Emma thought there was no way they could afford a new one, so they rode a street car to a stretch of shabby shacks on the south side of the train station where Karlsruhe's version of a grand bazaar had emerged from a barren lot over the past year. The offerings were dazzling and depressing. Meisen porcelain, silver, gold, Dutch and even Chinese ceramics, Czech crystal – the finest brands and best labels were on display.

Prices were posted in Reichsmarks, but everyone knew that was a sham to ward off police looking to stop black marketing. Haggling was constant and often ferocious. For buyers with the right commodities, treasures they could only dream of a few years ago were within their reach. Of course, all this booty came from somewhere – mostly from desperate sellers parting with family heirlooms for a fraction of their value to buy necessities they otherwise could not find or afford in normal shops.

Several of the booths fronted shacks that served as crude shops for stall operators, usually clothing merchants. A few displayed wedding dresses turned in by former brides with more pressing needs, and Emma stopped at every one, seeking an acceptable style that could be altered to fit her daughter. Monica tried a few on, changing in the shacks behind the stalls. But three hours of searching and haggling yielded nothing.

Ready to give up for the day, Emma and Monica headed for the street car line when they spotted a shack near the edge of the marketplace. It displayed a bolt of silk by the open door, and a sign scrawled on a board labeling the business as the workshop of a seamstress.

Emma and Monica walked in, and found a woman with bad posture and deeply furrowed face working in poor light on a baptism gown for an infant girl. Emma knew good work when she saw it, and this lady was an artist. She was sitting next to a crude sewing machine but left it idle, preferring the precision of hand stitching.

She introduced herself as Gertrude Hechinger. Emma got right to the point.

"My daughter is getting married. Can you make her wedding dress?"

The seamstress stopped sewing, looked at Monica closely for a moment, and then resumed her stitching.

"Yes, I think I have enough material for her. Her size is good."

Monica wasn't sure exactly what that meant but didn't care if she could get a new gown for her wedding. Emma asked for details on the design, what other materials would be used and so on, and she liked every response from the seamstress.

Without even looking at Monica, Emma was ready to close the deal.

"How much?" Emma finally asked.

"What do you have?"

Emma recited her cache of barter goods, but the seamstress was not impressed.

Emma took a mental inventory of everything at home, sorting out things that she could stand to lose for the sake of her daughter's wedding day. China, crystal, silver, just about anything of value came to mind, except for the Majolica figurine. That was off limits forever.

Emma started reciting her potential offerings, but the woman just shook her head and kept stitching the little gown.

Exasperated, Emma threw up her hands.

"Well, what do you want?"

"A room."

Emma and Monica stared at each other and then looked around them. Behind the seamstress was a cot covered by a rumpled down comforter that had seen better days. A crude shelf held some canned goods and basic kitchen utensils. A covered bucket by the bed was obviously her commode. A small wood-burning stove filled a corner, with a pipe bent at an angle to lead smoke out the back wall, if you could call the scrap planks loosely nailed together a wall. This was not just a shop. It was a dwelling.

The seamstress stopped sewing but did not look up.

"I have no home. My family is gone. My husband, our children. I came here to get away from the Russians, but I was not officially recognized as a displaced person. So I have no right to a camp or to assigned housing. Some of the others here helped me put this up last summer. One of them even found that silk bolt you saw when you came in and gave it to me. I don't know where he got it and I don't want to know. Now it's getting cold. I have to move but I have no place to go.

"If your daughter is getting married, maybe you'll have an empty room. Let me move in, and I'll make your daughter's gown. I'll add any other dresses you need, as long as the material lasts. That will be my rent. I will feed myself and keep the room clean. You won't have to do anything. Please, just give me a place to live."

Emma didn't tell the woman that Monica's room had been unoccupied for months. In fact, Emma had told the family not to mention it at all. Battling an acute housing shortage, the Americans were forcing anyone with extra room to accept displaced persons. Emma had rationalized that Monica still used the room occasionally, so she had always said the house was full. Soon she would lose even that spurious excuse, and she and Max had talked about what sort of people might be forced on them if the authorities learned the Baumann house was not fully occupied.

Monica was ready to take the woman's side in the discussion but knew better than to say anything. This was a matter for her mother and father to decide.

Emma saw some instant advantages. Some of the key wedding complications would be solved. Farther into the future, this woman could help with some of the household chores that involved sewing or even embroidery, something Emma had never enjoyed or mastered. She seemed honest, although Max might resist letting a stranger into their house. She looked to be in her 60s (she was a prematurely aged 53) and would not cause the kinds of trouble a younger person might bring into the house.

Even Emma, with her newfound assertiveness, could not make such a deal on her own. She said she would discuss the matter with her family that evening and return the next day with her answer.

Monica felt nothing but pity for the emaciated woman struggling to sew in the fading light. But she knew her mother had no choice but to hold a family council on the matter.

That night over a cold dinner of sausages, dark break, cucumber salad and beer, Emma explained the proposal to Max, Ingrid and Fritz. Monica had left them to spend the evening with Mike, but Emma told the family that Monica was strongly in favor of accepting the old woman's offer.

"It's easy for her," Ingrid said, holding Elisabeth in her lap. "She won't be here to live with this person. How do we know she is respectable and can be trusted in this house?"

"We don't for sure," Emma answered. "But the woman is all alone. What harm can she do? And she would solve several big problems for us?"

"She might also steal everything we have," Fritz said. "And we have a small child in the house."

It was Max's turn.

"This is a very serious commitment we are making just to get a wedding dress. I'm not sure it's worth the risk."

Emma was not about to give up.

"Monica and I like her. There is something about her. She has tragedy written in her face. We can help. Look at all the people who helped us while Max waited for denazification. Maybe it's now our turn to help someone."

Emma's force of will took over, and the others retreated, willing to take a chance, sight unseen. Max asked the woman's name and said he would call a police acquaintance to find out if anyone knew anything about her. But at the end of the evening, there was a consensus. Gertrude Hechinger could have Monica's room, at least for the winter.

Emma did not gloat, but she was obviously satisfied with the outcome in her favor. She called Monica at Mike's apartment to give her the news, and the next morning they returned to the shack behind the train station, where Gertrude was nearing completion of the baptismal gown.

"We have a deal," Emma said, skipping thc small talk. "Your room is on the third floor. Will the stairs be a problem for you?"

"No," Gertrude said with a relieved smile. "I can get around better than I look. I'll get some of the men here to help me move my things, and I will be there tomorrow. Or is that too soon?"

Emma said she would move what little of Monica's things remained, and the room would be ready. The relocation took place as planned, and the next day Monica was standing in her former room being measured for her gown. The two women spoke only when the measuring required communication, but Monica could see the relief in the old woman's face, and her gratitude in the quality and design of the gown. After the wedding, she insisted on having it carefully packed and shipped to America. It stayed with her the rest of her life.

Mike knew that as far as the wedding was concerned, he was little more than a prop. He did what he was told, agreed to whatever Emma and Monica decided for the wedding, and concentrated on the move to America.

The Associated Press had confirmed its offer of a general assignment reporting job in Washington, and he was due to start in early January. That would give him and Monica plenty of time to find an apartment and get settled.

Unlike Monica, Mike didn't have to worry about his replacement because the bureau was closing in early January. Other staffers drifted away and their slots were not filled. Manfred still toyed with his gadgets, but he was just waiting to turn the lights out before moving on to a technical job his brother had found for him at a local factory.

Also unlike Monica, who was leaving her home, Mike had few goodbyes to worry about. Friendships had never taken hold among the Americans Mike met because few stayed around for long. George was about the only real friend he had, and that was always tempered by their professional relationship. Mike knew that if a tough situation every arose, George would be boss first, friend second.

A few acquaintances of Mike volunteered to help with the wedding preparations, knowing that Monica's family would have a tough time finding essentials. One civilian in the finance office brought back a veil from a vacation in Sweden. Another delivered lace from Belgian for the gown. For Monica's shoes, Mike took a chance and ordered from the Sears Roebuck catalog. They were a bit loose but would work fine for a few hours.

Mike was constantly distracted by the demands of paperwork, German and American. Before approving Monica's marriage and move to America, OMGUS required a battery of documents, including a background check and financial statements. Max understood those requirements, but he groused when he had to submit to the same scrutiny. He thought denazification had scoured his background enough to satisfy any bureaucracy.

A week before before the wedding, Mike was in Monica's apartment helping her decide what to pack and what to leave. He was amazed at how one person in such cramped quarters could amass so much stuff. As he idly sorted through some jewelry and other trinkets on Monica's dresser, he felt a small pin prick. He sifted through the collection to find the cause, and froze when he found it. It was a round silver badge, about two inches in diameter. Stamped on the badge, in relief, was a swastika. Nothing else. No words, symbols or emblems.

Mike didn't touch it. He called Monica over to that side of the room and pointed to it with a revulsion usually reserved for a nasty discovery in the back of an icebox.

"What is this?"

"My Labor Service badge," Monica said with a shrug. She sensed trouble but hoped she could ignore the warning signs.

"Why would you keep something like this?"

"It's a memento from my time in the labor corps. It's the only thing I have left from that time of my life. It's just a badge."

"No, it's not just a badge. Not with that thing on it."

"I would never wear it. I don't even let it out of my jewelry box. It just happened to be there because I'm sorting things out. I keep it put away. It doesn't do any harm."

"Monica, you are keeping a symbol of Nazism as a keepsake. Your preserving the memory of the most evil regime in history. How can you even touch that thing, much less keep it like some souvenir from vacation?"

Monica was getting defensive and angry at Mike's sanctimonious tone. He, in turn, was angry at her lack of sensitivity about that icon.

They were having their first serious argument.

Gisela heard them from another room and decided it was a good time for a walk, even in a cold November rain.

Back and forth they went, Mike raging at the Nazi insignia in their midst, Monica hurt that here fiancé would take that attitude toward a small, harmless reminder of a pivotal time in her life. At her father's denazification hearing, Bodo Fenslinger had been wrong about the nature of her service like he was about everything else. She had not spent the war lounging in the pastoral tranquility of rural Germany. She and her comrades had endured duty with antiaircraft batteries, dodged strafing fighters and had stayed at their post in Vienna almost too long as the Russians stormed the Austrian capital. She had lost all contact with the other girls, so the little silver badge was her only link to those formative and sometimes frightening times.

Mike could only think of what might happen if at some awkward moment the silver embarrassment would slip out into public view. How would he explain his new German wife's attachment to a silver swastika badge?

It was clear to Mike that Monica was taking a stand and would not back down. He grew weary of the argument and ran out of points to make. Fearing the rhetoric could escalate into something causing real pain that could rub some shine off their relationship, he searched for a compromise.

She had to promise him the badge would be securely hidden where no one could see it or even find it. Monica saw a way out and grabbed it. She promised to always keep it in a safe place, and nobody would ever know she had it. She said she understood how Mike felt and thanked him for letting the issue pass.

There was no immediate make-up hug or kiss. The room stayed frosty until Mike left around dinner time. They separately saw the confrontation as a test. If its residue lingered, they might have to deal with a new, unsettling facet of their relationship.

But the next morning, Mike decided to walk Monica to work, just to test the water. She displayed no ill effects from the previous day's dust-up. He was all too ready to put it behind them as well. So they never mentioned the issue again. And they learned they could argue and let it go. It was a comforting revelation for both.

Their late October marriage actually covered two days. On Friday, they rounded up Gisela and George as witnesses and went to the town hall for the civil wedding, the one that made their marriage official in the eyes of the German and American governments. They toasted the day at a small restaurant across the street but had no time to waste.

Monica made a list for herself and one for Mike and they hurried off to finish preparations for the main event, the church wedding and celebration the next day. Mike did the heavy lifting thanks to his jeep. Monica relied on bicycle power to check in with the photographer, florist, baker and others with wedding assignments.

Their wedding day, the one they would recognize every anniversary, was a cool, bright day. Monica said a little prayer of thanks for no rain. She had her mother, sister and Gisela as seconds, with Gertrude available for any last-minute alterations.

As noted in the local newspaper's paid wedding announcement, the ceremony was set for 2 p.m. at St. Mark's Church, conveniently adjacent to the OMGUS complex. It was easy for anyone to find because of what it didn't have. It's spire had collapsed during an air raid and had not been replaced.

Mike could walk to the church from his apartment, so he spent the morning lounging around, drinking coffee, happily oblivious to the barely controlled chaos at the Baumann house. After fixing a small sandwich, Mike got ready. George, his best man, showed up on time, and they traded shop talk until it was time to walk to the church. A black Chevrolet loaned by a civilian friend of George was parked out front, ready to ferry the newlyweds around town later in the day.

At 1 p.m., the Chevy pulled away and returned a few minutes later with Monica and her parents. Thanks to the good weather, others were able to come by bicycle. As Mike and Monica separately preened and chatted in rooms behind the altar, pews started filling with friends and acquaintances, some civilian and some in uniform. Checking the crowd through a crack in the door, Mike noticed that the house was split – Germans on one side, Americans on the other. Too bad, he thought.

Promptly at 2, the organist played a majestic anthem but not the traditional wedding march. Monica wanted no Wagner in her wedding. Elisabeth toddled up the aisle first, spreading a few flower petals. Flowers dotted the church's interior but not to the extent Monica had hoped. The time of year and the florist's excessive barter demands saw to that.

Accompanied by her father, Monica in her splendid gown walked up the aisle, kissed her father on the cheek and joined a smartly uniformed Mike at the altar. The ceremony was generic and efficient. Mike sailed through his lines in German, and Monica fought tears only once, when the soprano from the state opera, whose services were a wedding gift from Axel, sang "Ave Maria," Monica's favorite. After 20 minutes, they turned and faced the congregation as Sgt. and Mrs. Michael Falwell.

Photographs by Gary Easterly, another gift, and hobnobbing with well wishers held them at the church longer than they had planned, but the tight part of the schedule was over so there was no rush. Mike helped his bride with her train as she slid into the Chevy's back seat and then got in for the short ride to the Baumann home.

There a rare collection of delicacies and beverages, some bartered, some from the PX, awaited the small group of family and friends who partied into the evening. Among them was Axel, who had agreed to a truce with his father in honor of the occasion. He sat with Gisela the entire evening, chatting briefly with everyone except his father. They never spoke. Monica noticed, and it was the only damper on what had otherwise been a glorious day. After a change of clothes, she rode with Mike one more time in the American sedan to an officer's apartment loaned to them for their wedding night.

Mike and Monica sat side by side on a sofa, munching snacks, sipping champagne, talking about the day past but thinking about the night ahead.

Gisela was the source of the climactic contribution for the newlyweds – an eye-popping negligee an American friend had carried back from leave in Paris. Monica left Mike on the sofa, went to the bedroom and changed.

She lit a candle, turned off the overhead light and called Mike. When he came through the door and saw her, his look was one that Monica would cherish forever.

"We don't need that, you know," he said, embracing his wife.

"I know, but I figured you had waited long enough," she said, whispering between increasingly intense kisses.

"Long enough for what?"

"That night you covered the explosion, the first time you saw me?"

"Yeah?"

"I was wearing something just like this. I borrowed it from Ingrid to see how it felt. So when we heard the explosion, I put my coat on over it and rushed outside."

"I'll be damned," Mike said, trading devilish smiles with his new wife as he guided her toward the bed. "Thank God I didn't know. I'd still be trying to write that story."

The next morning they stayed in bed as long as possible until forced to get ready for Sunday dinner at the Baumann home.

They pulled up in Mike's jeep, and Fritz was waiting at the front door.

"So, how was it?"

Monica rolled her eyes and Mike just smiled as they went inside for what was another festive gathering. Max and Emma seemed as relaxed as Mike had ever seen them. As Ingrid bounced Elisabeth in her lap, Fritz talked about how his work was piling up. Later, after the table was cleared, Gertrude took a break from her sewing and joined them from her upstairs room for coffee.

Talk turned to the journey to America, now just two weeks away, and Monica's parents turned more somber. They were having trouble coping with the thought of their daughter leaving and they didn't hide it well. Mike talked up the benefits of living and working in Washington, but it didn't help much.

The last days in Karlsruhe for Mr. and Mrs. Falwell were a hectic blur of farewells, packing, last-minute paperwork and errands. Shippers hauled away boxes and small items that would not travel with Mike and Monica on the Norwegian cruise ship North Cape when they sailed from Bremerhaven.

One last get-together at the house on Rosemarinstrasse, and the departure day had arrived. Another borrowed car collected the Falwells and their luggage at the officer's quarters where they had spent their last two nights in Karlsruhe.

They rode in silence to the train station two miles away. A porter helped them with their luggage, and they went straight to the platform, where the train to Bremen was already waiting. So was Monica's family. Gisela was watching Elisabeth after a long farewell tearfest with her best friend, and Axel had dropped by earlier in the week to wish them well, so the delegation comprised just her parents, sister and Fritz.

They had arrived well ahead of the scheduled departure, so awkward small talk filled the time. Monica saw a vendor selling fruit juice and decided she was thirsty. As she stood waiting for change, she saw a thin old man wearing a ragged raincoat and a yarmulke sitting on a bench next to the juice vendor. He was showing a heavy man in a thick wool winter coat several watches, and the dickering got loud and intense.

Monica was sipping her juice when the heavy, pig-faced man, obviously exasperated, turned and walked away from the watch seller without buying anything.

As he walked by Monica, he said two words, meant mostly for himself.

"Dirty Jew."

Monica almost choked on her juice. She reddened as the man stopped nearby to study the offerings of a newspaper stand.

She tossed away the juice and headed for the train. Mike saw her but didn't have a chance to ask what she was doing. She went to their compartment, pulled her small cosmetic case from the overhead rack, and reached into a concealed zippered pocket. Out came the silver badge that had set Mike off. She had taken a chance and kept it with her, confident nobody would find it.

Monica stepped out of the car back onto the platform and hurried toward the repulsive man still looking at newspapers. She stood next to him, pretending to study the magazines, and cupped the badge in her hand. Her thumb loosened the pin attached to the back, and very gently but quickly she pinned the swastika memento into the thick wool of his green winter coat. He felt her jostle him slightly, but she just smiled and he turned back to the newspapers.

The train was about to leave, so Monica gladly hurried her goodbyes to avoid more tears, rushed with Mike to their compartment, pulled down the window and leaned out to kiss her parents one more time.

As the train lurched and the four started the traditional hanky waving, Monica's glance was diverted to the awful fat man, now in a nervous, animated conversation with two policemen. Monica pointed the scene out to Mike and told him what had happened, and they both relished their last glimpse of Karlsruhe as the man was led away to explain why he should not face criminal charges.

Although Mike was happy to see the badge gone, he shook his head at the idea that any German could still feel comfortable saying something like that.

"I guess some people still have a lot to learn," Mike said, putting his arm around Monica.

"I hope it isn't more than some," Monica said before turning her full concentration on Karlsruhe as the train picked up speed for its run to Bremen and her journey to a new life.

Monica would thrive in America and returned often to see her family grow and prosper. In her homeland, Germany's greatest generation capitalized on currency reform, the Marshall Plan and honest hard work to forge an economic miracle that turned an international pariah into a political and economic model for Europe and the world.

Monica would often dwell on a final irony when she thought about that night at the end of the war when she and her father watched the ominous flashes on the horizon from her attic room.

No thanks to him and his gang, that disgusting little Josef Goebbels had finally gotten something right, even if his timing was off.

"The golden times stand before us."

Credits

Personal recollections and oral histories:

Ruth Nagel Iliff
Theodore Daniel Iliff
Max Nagel
Hedwig Bender Nagel
Hildegard Nagel Beck
Alfred Beck
Monika Raffelberg

Historical references and memoirs:

"The U.S. Army in the Occupation of Germany" by Earl Ziemke for the Center of Military History.

"Die Clique: A Journalists Life in Postwar Times" by Helene Rahms.

"Der Fragebogen" by Ernst von Salomon.

"Lebertran und Chewing Gum: Childhood in Germany 1945-1950" compiled by Juergen Kleindienst.

"Chronik" Series, 1945-1948. Chronik Verlag.

"Entering Germany 1944-1949" by Tony Vaccaro.

"Jahre unseres Lebens 1945-1949" by Dieter Franck.

Also thanks to Taylor Van Arsdale, Marla Young, Craig Deville, Ali Wolf, Rebekah Iliff and Antonia Scatton for their help and encouragement.